Get the Hell
Off the Bus!

Get the Hell Off the Bus!

Bus! The Warped, Wild, and Wicked Life of a Tour Leader!

CARL,
   TO THE MAN WHO MADE
THIS BOOK POSSIBLE. I
OWE YOU EVERYTHING AND
I HOPE FOR MANY MORE
FUTURE VOLUMES!
   EXPAT EXPLORE
      FOREVER!

William Michaelis

Library of Congress Control Number:		2022922762
ISBN:	Hardcover	978-1-6698-5799-0
	Softcover	978-1-6698-5798-3
	eBook	978-1-6698-5797-6

Print information available on the last page.

Rev. date: 12/29/2022

To order additional copies of this book, contact:
Xlibris
844-714-8691
www.Xlibris.com
Orders@Xlibris.com
849173

CONTENTS

Part 3: Did That Actually Just Happen?

Part 4: A Random Assortment of the Weird

Part 5: To Mother Russia, with Love

To all my passengers, with the hope of many
more adventures and stories to come!

Why Would ANYONE do this Job?

When you're growing up as a child, you dream of being many different things. At some point everyone is asked the inevitable question: "What do you want to be when you grow up?" The obvious answers for most little boys are obvious; race-car driver, fireman, train engineer, astronaut, dinosaur hunter (that one died a swift death). The one job I don't think any little boy or girl has ever claimed they want to do is that of Tour Leader.

It's a strange job. It's a unique job. And despite what it looks like, it's a tough job. But is it ever a lot of fun! It's a job for those of us who never truly grew up.

Think about it for just a moment. Take fifty strangers from varying countries, cultural backgrounds, ages, professions, religions, and countless other metrics; cram the whole lot of them on a tour bus in a strange place none of them have ever been before (Hey, it's not Des Moines, Iowa!) for anywhere from one week to one month, and put them under the direction and leadership of a lad who struggled to gain admittance to a second-rate Canadian community college as a young adult and see what happens. If this seems like a recipe for disaster, you're right.

Tour Leaders are very much a blessed group of people. We get to have fun for a living. We get to travel for a living. Staying in a different hotel every single night and dealing with fifty passengers all with differing needs, thoughts, views, and expectations might seem like a living hell for most people, but for a Tour Leader it's what we live for. You never know what will happen next! You wake up in the morning knowing that there's a decent chance that something unbelievable and shocking is just around the next corner. Is this the day that I'm going to walk in on a border guard who's decided that his primal urge to procreate is more important than stamping fifty foreigners' passports? Am I, at some point in the next couple of hours, going to witness my local tour guide attempt to kill a rival group's local tour guide? What are the odds that before the day is out the local mafia is going to steal my cash card and leave me penniless? Is it entirely in the realm of possibility that one of the passengers will do something so irretrievably stupid and insane that it will serve as a cautionary tale that I tell future generations? Believe it or not, the answer to each one of those questions is a resounding yes.

The life of a Tour Leader is full of some of the most shocking, crazy, and unbelievable stories that you'll ever hear. We get to experience it all; action, adventure, horror, elation, fright, bemusement, romance, you name it! With one exception, boredom. The life of a Tour Leader is many things, but it's never, ever boring. Not even for one minute!

So, sit back, relax, pour yourself a stiff drink if you need one (several stories require it) and take in some of the more memorable incidents that have come my way during my career as a Tour Leader. And, no doubt, as you work your way through this volume you'll ask yourself the inevitable question, "Why the f%&# would anybody ever want to be a Tour Leader?" I'll supply the answer right now:

BECAUSE IT BEATS THE HELL OUT OF AN OFFICE JOB!

Part 1

I Could Kill These People and Not Give a Flicker of Emotion About It!

Perhaps the most intriguing part of being a tour leader isn't the places you get to travel to, the things you see, or even the experiences that you have. I always found the passengers, who you get to meet and lead around to be the most compelling part of the job. Every tour presented a new, interesting, and diverse set of people all united together for the same goal; to have a once-in-a-lifetime holiday. Although, oftentimes it seemed that some passengers were far more interested in achieving a more different objective instead, TREADING ON MY LAST NERVE! I'm not merely talking about little bugaboos such as being five minutes late getting back to the coach, or deciding two minutes before a roast pork dinner that they've decided to be a lactose-intolerant vegan on this particular day. No-no; what follows are some of the most brutal passenger stories. Stories that could drive even the most patient tour leader to happily push certain passenger malcontents into an oncoming Paris Metro train!*

*Not that I ever actually did that. Forget I mentioned it, I've said too much already.

The Water in the Toilet isn't Warm!

It always seemed that the longer the tour, the more likely the odds are that you'd get a truly horrible passenger. Given that the longest itinerary I ran was twenty-six days, this could make for some challenging times if you got a rotten apple. There's no worse feeling than meeting a truly miserable piece of human flotsam, knowing that you'll be with them day-in and day-out for nearly a month. You know that it's going to be a constant strain to cater to their whims, deal with their constant moods, do it with a smile on your face, all the while being fully aware that the useless flesh-lump is only going to tip you five Euros at the end of the tour. Neil from Singapore instantly fit this bill.

Neil from Singapore was certainly sent from one of Hell's outer circles to make my life, and that of every hotelier he met, miserable. Nothing in his room could ever satisfy him. The man could have been staying in an executive suite in a Four Seasons and he'd still find an issue with it! Generally, his complaints were of such a ridiculous nature that if one didn't know better, you'd think he was just having a laugh. Below is just a small list of things in hotels that he complained about, and the response I would counter with:

"The room doesn't have an ice bucket" – No worries there, Neil; they don't have an ice machine either.

"The bedside table is almost broken" – That's fine; I'll make sure it almost gets fixed.

"The room doesn't have a city view" – Neil, the hotel is only two stories tall. None of the rooms have a city view.

"The television doesn't have any Asian channels" – Good reason for that Neil. There's no Asian channels because this hotel is actually situated in Europe.

It just went on and on, every hotel, for twenty-six days. The man must have, immediately upon entering a room, searched for something to whine about because he'd come back to the lobby to complain about things before I'd had a chance to get to my room. By the time we got to Switzerland, and after three weeks, I'd about had it with him. Luckily, we were staying at the hotel run by a very straight-laced Swiss-German hotelier named Ulrich, who will be covered in detail himself a bit later on. The one thing a Tour leader could be sure of was that Ulrich would not suffer this fool gladly.

One thing that really annoyed Ulrich was that he had to give all of our company's Tour Leaders a free beer upon arrival. Apparently, it was actually written into the contract. Ulrich did run a very relaxing hotel, and I always enjoyed my one freebie while the passengers were busy getting settled in. On this particular occasion, however, I knew full well that Neil would be down again imminently with God-only-knows-what to complain about. Within five minutes, and before I had even downed my beer, the Southeast-Asian Angel of Death came down the stairs, looking less than satisfied.

"Will, I need to talk to you. There's a problem with my room."

"Ah, Neil, yes. Right on time. What's the problem this time?"

"The water in the toilet isn't warm!"

I was quite surprised that he said this with a straight face. Certainly, I couldn't keep a straight face after hearing this. He actually meant this as a serious complaint. Now Neil was from Singapore and I had found over the previous three weeks that his English was very good, if not quite fluent. Clearly his English was not quite conveying what he actually meant. I assumed that what he meant to say was that there was no hot water coming out of the taps. This seemed like an easy one for me to fix.

"OK, Neil, look. This is alpine Switzerland, mate. The water is literally coming from a glacier. Let the hot water tap run for a minute, the hot water will come. It just takes a moment. No dramas!"

"No, Will, not the water from the tap. I mean the water in the toilet. The water in the toilet isn't hot. What are you going to do about it?"

At this point I wanted to say, "F%&$ all!" but I was a little too shocked that he meant the actual toilet water wasn't warm. I was more than a little curious about how he had ascertained this.

"Neil, I've got a few questions for you. First, *how* do you *know* the toilet water isn't warm? Second, *why* do you need the toilet water to be warm? In what other hotel has the toilet water been warm? Seriously, *how* do you *know* the toilet water isn't warm? Shall I go on?

"Well, all I'm saying is that it isn't warm." Clearly Neil expected a solution, and rather quickly.

"OK Neil, I'm gonna go over and speak to Ulrich about this. We're going to fix this problem for you. Wait right here."

Ulrich was going to love this guy! But I didn't want to miss the show that was to come. I went across the lobby to where Ulrich was and had a quick word.

"Ulrich! Thanks for the beer! Look here though; one of the guests has a problem with their room that they need you to fix." Ulrich is a clever guy and my acting isn't always so good, so I'm sure he could see that something was up that was beyond the ordinary.

"Yes, Will, what is the problem?" Ulrich replied, always in his slow and non-inflected Swiss-German drawl.

"OK, the man at the bar there has the problem. I'm going to have him come over and explain it to you himself. In the meantime, I'll be at the bar laughing."

I went back to the bar and directed Neil over to explain things to Ulrich, which he did in an increasingly animated manner. The looks on Ulrich's face were priceless; alternating from surprised to confused to bemused to shocked and any number of other expressions as well. I couldn't quite hear what exactly was being said, but that actually made things all the more enjoyable for me. After a few minutes of semi-heated discussion Neil stormed off back upstairs without saying anything to me. Ulrich though, still wanted a word with me.

"Will. This man. He is an...unusual man."

"Gee, Ulrich, do you really think so?" At this point I wasn't really able to drink my beer; I was laughing too much.

"Why does this man need the water in the toilet to be warm? Never has anyone complained."

"Ulrich, I don't know. He's complained about every hotel so don't feel too bad. By the way, did you find a way to fix the problem?"

"Yes. I said that I would bring him a kettle at dinner time. He can use that to make the water warm."

"Really Ulrich! That's brilliant! But I take it he didn't like that idea?"

"No, he seemed to be upset with that idea and he went away then."

"OK, Ulrich. That's fine. And thanks for the theatre; I enjoyed that! See you at dinner!"

I wish I could say that that was the worst incident we had with Neil, but sadly he actually caused himself a far worse bit of trouble the week before in Spain. One of the great sites in Barcelona is the Magic Fountain Show at the Palau Nacional. On certain nights it is illuminated in beautiful colors and the fountain sprays are set to music, not dissimilar to the Bellagio fountains in Las Vegas. It's a wonderful show, and it's free, and hence heaps of tourists are always there to watch them. I would always take passengers down there after dinner on our first night in the city. Unfortunately, Barcelona is one of the world's most notorious cities for pickpockets. I would often tell my passengers not to take their passports out in the city with them at all (I would tell them to do the same with their credit cards, and big banknotes). If you're likely to get pickpocketed there's no sense in letting them get too much from you. As for the whole "Don't you legally need to have your passport on you at all times?" argument, even in Spain the police need just cause to detain you, so unless you're committing a crime, the police aren't going to hassle you or ask you for your ID. Unfortunately, Neil decided it would be a clever idea to commit a crime.

It happened about ten minutes before we were all due to meet back up after the show at which time I would take back to the hotel anyone who wanted to go back. I was having a nice chat with a few of the passengers when one of them pointed out that Neil was having an incredibly involved conversation with two police officers. Of course, the passengers wanted to know if I, as the Tour Leader, was planning to go over to find out what was going on.

"No, I don't think so. It looks very much like a private sort of conversation." I've always found it prudent not to get involved in someone else's discussions with the police.

After a few more minutes of heated discourse, Neil was seen to be given some paperwork by the officers, handing over what was clearly a cash fine, and given what was a final dressing down before coming over to the group where he wanted a severe word with his Tour Leader. Sadly, that was me.

"Will, you owe me ninety-five Euros!"

"Neil, glad you could join us. I owe you what now?"

"I just got a fine from the police for not having ID, and it was thirty-five Euros. You're the one who said to leave my passport at the hotel, so it's your fault. You owe me ninety-five Euros."

"Neil, the police in Spain do not stop tourists on the street for a shakedown and demanding to see their ID. It's not the Franco regime anymore. If the police fined you for not having ID, then they must have stopped you for something else. Why did the police stop you?"

"Because I didn't have ID. I told you!" Neil was in a proper state at this point. He still wasn't getting ninety-five Euros from me.

"Neil, let me see the paperwork."

Handing over the paperwork it was immediately clear that there were in fact two separate fines. One for sixty Euros and one for thirty-five Euros.

"Neil, they made you pay two fines! What's the deal? One of them is for no ID, what was the other one for?"

"Nothing serious. I had to use the toilet, but I couldn't find one, so I peed in the fountain and that's when the police stopped me." Neil clearly didn't see that there was anything wrong with that.

"Ok, Neil. The police didn't stop you for not having ID. They stopped you because you were PEEING IN THE FOUNTAIN! The no ID fine is just an add-on fine."

"I didn't think that anyone would mind! And you said to leave our passports at the hotel."

"Neil, I told you to leave your passport at the hotel so that if you got pickpocketed then you wouldn't lose your passport. I also assumed that you were a law-abiding citizen who wouldn't get into trouble with the police. Let me ask you, Neil. You're from Singapore, do you go peeing wherever you want back at home?"

"No, if I did that in Singapore I'd end up in prison. I thought Spain wasn't so strict about that!"

"Neil, this is a proper country. You can't pee in the fountains and they could have arrested you. The fact that they didn't and only made you pay a fine for ninety-five Euros makes you the luckiest criminal in the history of Barcelona! I'm not paying your ID fine and from now on DON'T PEE IN THE FOUNTAINS OR ANYWHERE ELSE THAT ISN'T A PUBLIC TOILET!"

To say that Neil wasn't my biggest fan after these incidents is putting it mildly and the four Euro tip he gave me at the end of the tour was four Euros more than I thought I'd get from him. I've avoided going to Singapore ever since that tour just in case I happen to run into him. Suffice it to say, if I ever hear that the Singaporean government has caned one of its own citizens for being a truly annoying f%#&-wit, I'll have a strong suspicion about who it is they've done it to!

One-Thousand Euro Taxis and Idiots Who Hire Them

Of course, terrible passengers come in all shapes and forms. After some time, you get to know them all, and know them well. You can name the country and chances are that I've had a terrible passenger, at some point, from that country. Yet, there remains to this day the awful cliché of the ugly American. Naturally, they are out there, and in my case, I once had the most terrible two-for-one situation with a married American couple, Kendra and John.

Kendra and John, young retirees in their fifties, were native to the place that all terrible Americans seem to come from, Los Angeles! They were just in the process of moving back to the States after living in Zambia for two years. Given that they had taken on this amazing challenge, one would have reckoned that they'd be quite travel savvy. The truth of the matter, as several incidents would prove, was quite the opposite. A primary school drop-out would have had a better chance of successfully traveling in Europe than this pair of f%&#-wits!

The tour itself was plagued by terrible weather throughout. Two weeks in September in the Balkans and central Europe, starting and finishing in Munich. Ordinarily a lovely time of year, however, torrential rain followed us throughout. The group maintained good humor, however, and made the best of things. I had to tip my cap to them all after dealing with Kendra and John. The troubles started on day three in Croatia.

We were already dealing with the rain on this day, and lots of it! Unfortunately, on this particular day we were visiting the Plitvice Lakes National Park. A wonderful fairytale world full of gorgeous lakes and waterfalls. It's like something out of a fantasy novel. For the visitor it's a true treat, with boardwalks built over the lakes and around the waterfalls. Definitely a dream for an Instagrammer and a highlight of this particular tour. Generally, I'd give each passenger a map of the park, explain which trails they would have time to do, where the facilities were and where the bus would be parked, and how much time they had in the park. I always gave ample time, generally five or six hours, absolutely no rush. Due to the heavy rain of this day, most passengers weren't too keen on exploring a marine wonderland, but given that they'd never see any sort of place like this again, it wasn't too difficult to get them to muck on with things.

John happened to be a bit sick on this day. He had done a proper upchuck in a petrol station parking lot that morning and was making effective use of the supplied sick bags. Kendra was keen for him to go on a walk in the park though, and as I'm not a babysitter and not wanting a sick person hanging out on the bus for six hours, I was happy to see them go on their merry way. I would be punished for this.

The passengers enjoyed the park despite the rainy conditions. As they filtered back to the bus, they were quite pleased with the visit, but keen to get to a dry and cozy hotel a couple of hours drive away in Split. Things looked good as I counted everyone up, but the count produced only forty-three passengers. I was one short. Someone was missing. Not good in the middle of a waterlogged national park. I immediately reckoned that it had to be one of my single travelers, but they were all there and accounted for. No one seemed to know who it was that was missing. I eventually pulled out a passenger list and did it like a primary school teacher, doing a roll call and having everyone say here, one-by-one. Kendra and John's names weren't too far down the list. John turned out to be the missing person.

"Kendra," this was sure to be good, hopefully he was just out using the toilet at the café, "Where is John?" I asked.

"Oh, he's probably still out in the park, that's where I left him." She said this as though it was the most obvious thing in the world to have done.

"In the park still? Kendra, can you come outside for a moment." I really didn't fancy the rest of the passengers hearing how this conversation might go.

Once outside, I carried on, "Kendra, what do you mean you left John in the park?"

"Well, he's been a bit sick today, and when we were in the park he started throwing up again and he was complaining so much about it that I just left him out there to sort himself out."

"You did what now?" I was more than a little surprised that any wife would simply leave her sick husband to his own devices on a waterlogged boardwalk in a national park in a completely unfamiliar country.

"Well, it just got really annoying, so I left him there. I expected that he'd catch up and that he'd be here when we left."

Plitvice Lakes National Park is not a good place for mobile phone reception. In fact, there is none in the park proper. With no way to contact John, and after a quick discussion with my driver and the office in London it was decided; if John didn't appear by 4:30 we'd have to leave regardless in order not to go over my driver's legal work hours. By 4:30 John hadn't shown up.

Kendra decided to stay behind, so we off-loaded her luggage, made sure she had the hotel address, and went on our way. I was curious as to when we'd see them again. The bus service from the park to Split had ended for the day. It seemed likely she'd have to get a hotel room at the park itself. An hour and a half down the road, my phone rang. It turned out to be a representative from Trip Advisor of all people.

"Are you a Tour Leader missing an American passenger named John who's stuck in a place called Plitvice?"

"Yes I am."

"OK, well he and his wife called us, and they wanted us to call you to tell you that she found him and that they'll meet you in Split later tonight."

"Well, that's great, thank you so much for the message. We'll look forward to seeing them."

After hanging up it dawned on me. How, without bus service, were they going to get to Split to meet us up? I had any number of other questions, as did everyone on the bus. Another odd one being, why had they called Trip Advisor, instead of just calling me?

The tour was only staying in Split for one night. Not enough time to really explore and see the city, but with the continued rain, few passengers were keen to see Diocletian's Palace and dinner was at the hotel anyway. Finally, at nearly midnight Kendra and John arrived. I got them checked-in, but not before finding out what had happened.

After being ditched by Kendra, John made his way, eventually, to the parking lot. Unfortunately for John there were three problems. Number one, he was late by over an hour. Secondly, he was in the wrong parking lot. Third, he didn't realize that he was in the wrong parking lot. In time a national park worker got him sorted out, and brought him to the correct lot, where Kendra was still standing with their luggage and presumably waiting around for someone to show up and sell her some magic beans.

The most pressing question I had was obvious, "How did you two make it here in end?"

"Oh, there was a taxi at the hotel near the parking lot, so we got him to drive us here," said Kendra. Apparently, there is a travel god who protects morons.

And thus, I found out how much taxi ride costs to go from Plitvice Lakes to Split, Croatia. A journey of two-hundred and sixty kilometers and nearly three hours.

"Oh, it was a great deal Will, it was only three-hundred and fifty Euros, and he was ever so friendly"

For a three-hundred and fifty Euro fare I would have been a happy cab driver too!

"And why is it that you phoned Trip Advisor and had them phone me? Why not just ring me directly?" I asked.

"Oh, we booked this tour through Trip Advisor, it just seemed easier to have them call you!" Replied Kendra. It was a completely ridiculous thing to have done, but it was late and it wasn't a can of worms that I wanted to open.

"That's fine Kendra, but maybe next time you'll not want to abandon a violently ill person on a water-soaked footpath in a national park full of lakes and waterfalls and then have to get a taxi to drive you across an entire country in order to catch us up. Because that's a bit insane."

"Don't worry Will, I'm sure it won't happen again!"

One week later it happened again.

*   *   *

The events of the next week proceeded in an interesting manner. It was September 2015 and the big story in Europe at the time was the Syrian migrant crisis. Tens of thousands of refugees were moving, on foot, through the Balkans towards the European Union. As we were touring the same region my driver Milos and I had to really research which border crossings to use and reassure the passengers that things would be fine. Milos, the passengers, and I, all learned in this time that we had a special pair of nuts on our hands with Kendra and John.

We had arrived back in EU territory and toured Budapest, Bratislava, and Vienna. The time had come to head on to Prague. Ordinarily, there's little difficulty; but given the migrant situation we had been warned that the Czechs had reinstituted a temporary immigration check on their border with Austria. We announced this to the passengers in Vienna, making sure they'd have their passports in their hand luggage for the day's drive. I wasn't too concerned with things. Kendra and John changed that in a hurry.

Milos the driver knew the situation at the border. It was just a police officer who would come on the bus and simply check to make sure everyone had their passport, look at it quick, and carry on. Five minutes maximum. Ten minutes from the border I made the announcement on the microphone for the passengers to get ready.

"OK everyone, we're just coming to the Czech border in a few minutes, please have your passports and visas ready, there will be a quick check. Have your seatbelts done up too!"

Sitting back down in my front jump seat, it was only seconds later that Kendra came to the front for a chat.

"Oh Will, I just thought I'd let you know that John and I left our passports in the safe at the hotel in Vienna. Just in case the police ask about that. No problem I hope?"

Milos and I looked at each other in absolute shock. They only reckoned to mention this now? Milos's primary concern was the possibility of being arrested as it's illegal for a bus driver to transport individuals without a passport. There was really only one thing to respond with:

"Kendra, you did what now?"

"Yeah, John and I forgot, and we left the passports in the safe in the hotel in Vienna. But this won't be a problem, the police will understand, right?"

"Yes Kendra, the police will completely understand. They love stopping buses and finding people on board who have no passports."

"Great, no problem then!"

"That's right Kendra..." as I stood up to face her and to, frankly, let everyone on the bus hear me, "It's no problem......IT'S A VERY BIG PROBLEM! THEY'RE GOING TO DEMAND TO SEE YOUR PASSPORT AND WHEN YOU DON'T HAVE IT, THEY'LL DETAIN US FOR HOURS AND POSSIBLY ARREST MILOS AND ME!"

"Oh dear....what should we do?"

Given that we were only about two kilometers from the border, options were limited.

"OK Kendra, do you and Jim have a photocopy of your passports? For the love of god tell me that you do!"

"Yes, they're in my purse."

"OK. Here's what you're going to do (Kendra and John happened to be sitting in the very back row that day). You're going to go back and sit down. When the border guard gets to you, you give him the photocopies and YOU KEEP YOUR MOUTH SHUT, YOU SAY NOTHING, AND YOU ACT AS THOUGH EVERYTHING IN THE WORLD IS JUST PERFECT!"

"OK, we can do that." She then ambled back to her seat with me shouting at her the whole way back:

"NOT ONE WORD, NOT ONE BLOODY WORD! EVERYTHING IS JUST FINE AND DANDY AS FAR AS YOU'RE CONCERNED!" I yelled at them like Mussolini from a balcony. I had no confidence in their ability to get away with the ruse.

At this point we were just coming up to the border and sure enough the Czech police were there and they had that really angry and irritated look that border guards all around the world seem to have all the time. Being Czech, Milos did the talking, which was very little, and was just fine with me. The guard started his passport check, slowly working his way down the bus one person at a time....

The police officer worked with a casualness that gave nothing away. He spoke not a word; I doubt he spoke any English anyway. Every now and again he would open a passport and compare the photo to the person in the seat. Because his back was to me, I spent the whole time giving the evil eye to Kendra and John, along with the button your mouth mime, and the slit your throat and knife to the temple actions. It was really the quietest bus I'd ever been on. The passengers could quite clearly see that I was pissed off and meant business. Inevitably, the guard got to Kendra and John last, it was the moment of truth.

After what seemed like an hour, but in fact was probably only ten seconds, the border guard started his authoritative walk back to the front of the bus (checking the on-board toilet as he came, because if you are going to transport Syrian refugees, logically, you'd hide them in the toilet). Not knowing any Czech, I could only imagine what words he spoke to Milos as he stepped off the bus. As soon as he was gone, I could tell by the look on Milos's face that it was good news:

"OK, he says everything is good, we are welcome to Czechia!"

"Are you kidding me Milos?! We can go? He didn't care about Tweedle-Dee and Tweedle-Dum not having their passports?"

"Is OK. I not ask him anymore. You want to stay and ask?" Milos asked in his not-quite-fluent English.

"F*$% no! Let's get the hell outta here!"

Thus, we were out of jail! Everything was right with the world! Except for the fact that we were still transporting two illegals whose passports were now in a completely different country. Indeed Passport-Gate wasn't finished. It had only just begun.

*   *   *

Kendra and John couldn't quite grasp the seriousness of the bind that they were in. They seemed to think that a passport was something that you didn't need to keep a particularly close eye on or be able to produce at any given moment. It was my sad duty to shoot down every plan of retrieval that they came up with.

"Tomorrow, Will, we'll just take the train back to Vienna to get them," was John's first idea.

"No good, police on the train will do a passport check. You can't buy a ticket or board a train without it. Sorry," considering their intelligence level, it wasn't a terrible idea I thought as I responded.

Their next idea was to have DHL or FedEx ship the passports overnight from Vienna to Prague. I immediately saw the flaw there too.

"Sorry, won't work. Courier companies won't ship passports," again, not a terrible idea, but I'd had passengers try this gambit previously, and indeed courier companies don't ship passports. Apparently, there's a law in the EU prohibiting it.

Kendra and John were getting a bit desperate. It was also my sad duty to inform them that they wouldn't be allowed to board the bus to go to the next destination two days later, Munich, if they didn't have their passports. We would have to leave them in Prague.

Eventually they came up with a solution and put it into action all on their own. Taking inspiration from the Croatian taxi incident from the week before, they outlined their plan:

"Will, we've done it! We got the hotel in Vienna to contract a taxi driver to drive our passports to us tonight!" John was clearly pleased with his plan. I was a bit dubious.

"Really John, a taxi courier job from Vienna to here? That's a six-hour drive! When's he getting here and how much is it going to cost?"

Both good questions, I was guessing the cost would be about the same as the gross national product of a small west-African country, Guinea-Bissau perhaps.

"He'll be here at two AM, they said it was seven-hundred Euros," John said this as though that wasn't a lot of money.

"Great then John, hopefully that works out then," I was actually somewhat impressed with their unique, albeit awfully expensive solution. If you've got the money spend it! Sadly, though, John wasn't done explaining the particulars of his plan.

"Actually, it won't cost us anywhere near that. He's an Austrian, when he gets here, we thought we would just take our passports and haggle him down to just a couple hundred Euros. He'll just have to be happy with that because that's all the cash we have left. So, no problem!"

The fact that their actual plan was to stiff the taxi driver was shocking. Even more unbelievable was the fact that they thought that they would get away with it. Mind-blowing was the fact that they didn't see the obvious flaws in this plan. I thought I'd take a moment to point them out.

"John, don't you think that he's going to want the money first? The fact that he's doing this job on a C.O.D. basis is surprising, shocking even, but he's going to want the money first."

"But that's the genius of it Will! He's from Austria, this is Prague, he can't arrest us or anything! Besides, we're Americans!" John really didn't see the glaring problems in his plan at all.

"OK John, you say you're an American as though that has something to do with this. It doesn't. But you are right, a taxi driver from Vienna can't arrest you. But do you know who can arrest you? The Prague Police! And I think that they'll be more than happy to do that if you stiff a taxi driver out of five-hundred Euros!"

"I don't think so Will, you'll see, it'll be fine!" John responded with all the confidence in the world.

I decided I'd stay up to watch the show, as did a number of the other passengers, as John had informed everyone he saw about his foolproof plan. Staying up late in a hotel bar in Prague is nothing new for any group, quite a few of them were looking forward to it! It promised to be a good show! I also decided that in order to avoid a minor international incident that I would solve the inevitable fracas before it fully kicked off. A quick conversation with the hotel manager guaranteed that they had enough Euros on hand to pay the taxi fare and the hotel could make the equivalent charge to a credit card.

The driver arrived a good deal early, only shortly after one AM. Much like a Czech border guard, he looked like he was in a great mood! Sure enough, John and Kendra were waiting for him. Sure enough, the taxi driver wanted his money first.

The situation escalated fairly quickly. The second the taxi driver saw that they didn't have the money in hand he took out his phone to make an immediate call to the police. A proper screaming match and potential fight was about to develop. John decided that this was a suitable time to get me involved in the proceedings. He raced over to my table in the bar like a rat fleeing a sinking ship.

"Will, he won't give us our passports, and he says he's calling the police on us! We don't have his money!" For the first time these two idiots were finally seeing the flaws in their plan.

"Right John, and you want my help to do what?

"Can you pay the fare? We'll pay you back tomorrow!"

"John, you just said that you don't have any cash and now you want me to pay the taxi fare to a driver that just two minutes ago you were going to stiff. What happens when you try to stiff me?

"No, we won't do that, I promise!" John was clearly in a desperate state.

"You're lucky I'm in a good mood John, I think there's a way to sort this all out!" I responded.

The first thing was to calm the taxi driver down. Luckily, the manager was on hand to help with that while I dealt with the world's worst Americans.

"OK John, I've got bad news and good news for you. The bad news is that I'm not paying your taxi bill."

"Fine Will, what's the good news?" John was clearly now keen for a solution.

"The good news is that you're paying the taxi bill and not going to jail! Where are your credit cards?"

"In my wallet."

"Good, take one of them out, take it to the man at the reception where the taxi driver is and he'll charge your card and give the taxi driver cash. Problem solved, and once that's done, take a minute to THANK the taxi driver for saving your ass! He probably wants to get home to Vienna, you're lucky he doesn't throw your passports in the Vltava River!"

In short order, John's credit card got charged, the taxi driver got paid, and John and Kendra indeed thanked him; though I don't think the driver was too eager to listen to anything they had to say. It was a crisis averted and I returned to my beer with the other passengers who had stayed for the show.

Jeremy and Geraldine were a lovely retired Canadian couple that I had gotten on well with. It was near the end of a long and challenging tour. Geraldine in particular had certainly grown tired of John and Kendra's continued antics and didn't mind saying so. She also had a rapier wit and could always make me laugh. Her final comment to me that night was one I'll always remember.

"Good job sorting those two out Will, I don't know how you keep patience with people like that!"

"It's a challenge sometimes Geraldine, but part of the job as well."

"It makes me wonder though, they just spent two years living in Zambia, right?"

"Yes, they did. What difference does that make on anything?"

"Nothing Will. It's just, how they didn't get eaten by a pride of lions while they were there, I'll never figure out!"

We finished the tour the next day in Munich. For all our good work, Kendra and John were immensely generous tippers. They gave Milos one of John's used sweaters that was three sizes too small for him and I got a coupon good for 2-for-1 Whoopers at any participating Burger King in Hungary. Considering how well we got on, it was far more than I expected.

The Four Horsewomen
of the Apocalypse

Every tour has its own personality. It's an aspect of the job that I always enjoyed. Take fifty people from around the world, put them all together on a bus for a couple of weeks and see how things shake out. Will everyone keep their cool? Which people are going to become good friends? Which people will come to loath each other? One never quite knows what will end up happening. An important question for the Tour Leader and driver is which person or persons are going to cause problems? On one particular tour my driver Derek and I were cursed with a group of four friends that we came to call "The Four Horsewomen of the Apocalypse."

The Four Horsewomen hailed from Vietnam. All four of them were also the type of person that you know and understand almost immediately. They were always VERY well dressed; even their casual wear was designer brand. They tended to wear fancy hats. They were all in their mid-to-late fifties but looked much younger than that as they did tote around their makeup bags everywhere we went. They were all the same approximate height and weight, did their hair in the same style, indeed they did their absolute best to look as similar to each other as possible. Indeed, some of the passengers thought that they were identical quadruplets. They were certainly very upper-class, it made Derek and me wonder why it was they were on one of our tours, which were definitely marketed to the middle-class. Sadly, the upper-class designation also applied to their attitudes as they viewed Derek and me as serfs who were there to do their bidding at all times. They weren't best pleased to find out that they were responsible for bringing their own luggage to and from the bus every day and that the hotels we were staying at didn't do porter service. As the tour progressed it also became clear that they weren't listening to a single thing I said as they routinely asked questions that I had already answered on the microphone. For both Derek and me, our patience was being severely tested on a daily basis.

The big problem on this tour, and it goes to the personality of the tour, was that we had a lot of shoppers on board. It was a full bus of fifty passengers and the weight and quantity of luggage became a major issue. On our tours a passenger was allowed one large piece of luggage of up to twenty kilograms to put in the bus hold and a smaller day bag to bring into the cabin. Similar to what the airlines allow. The drivers and Tour Leaders could actually charge twenty British Pounds per bag for overweight or extra luggage. We never liked to, and instead of doing this, it's much better politics and manners to tell the entire bus that the luggage is becoming a problem and that anyone who's luggage is too heavy will need to move the excess weight into their day bag or simply ship some dead weight home. Passengers are generally good about the weight limits and will adjust accordingly.

Sadly, the weight and size of the luggage was really causing Derek and me problems, neither of us had ever seen anything like it. We were struggling to make it all fit in the hold. Loading the luggage in the morning was becoming a real-life game of Tetris. As we got halfway through the two-week tour and arrived in Venice, we had to make the unhappy announcement, no more new luggage for the hold! We were out of space!

The passengers took the news quite well, in fact many of them asked for advice from Derek and me on how to make further adjustments. Not surprisingly, the biggest culprits were the four Vietnamese women. By this point in the tour, I'd figured out that they didn't care for the sites, culture, food, or anything like that. The tour was simply a giant shopping excursion for them. Fair enough, that's what some people enjoy, but they took it to the max. I reckoned that they were spending several hundred Euros a day each on clothing, shoes, and accessories. The only thing they cared about was where the nearest Prada or Luis Vuitton store was located.

Still, as we arrived in Venice, the group's mood was upbeat and happy! It was late March, the weather was nice, and we had arrived in the city quite early in the day. The hotel actually had all the rooms ready for check-in and it was only noon! Things were looking up as we took the tram into Venice proper. I'd scheduled a great afternoon for the group. A quick lunch stop for pizza and gelato, a walk through the city, cross the Rialto Bridge, and finally to St. Mark's Square. During the afternoon I'd arranged for gondola and speedboat rides and a Venetian glass-blowing demonstration.

The Venetian glass outlet was always busy, but they specialized in big groups. The deal was quite simple; they'd do a quick ten-minute glass-blowing demonstration where the glassblower would make a small horse. The demonstration was entirely free of charge, but in return, afterwards they'd have the group take in the fifteen-minute sales pitch. A fair exchange, and great for Tour Leaders as we'd get a nice commission on any sales.

The visit to the glass outlet went ahead without anything noteworthy occurring. Some of the passengers purchased a few knickknacks and some of the women purchased a bit of jewelry. I never liked to make it obvious that I was making a commission, so I would always return later in the day to pick up my commission when I knew none of my group would still be there. It was always easiest to schedule the gondola rides right after the glass demonstration. While the passengers were on the gondolas, I'd duck back into the shop. On this occasion, there was a strange peculiarity as I walked into the showroom, the glass tiger was gone!

The first showcase in the main salesroom contained a truly gaudy, ornate, two-foot-long green glass tiger. I always took note of it because I couldn't imagine the type of person who would buy such a garish and ugly piece. I put the thought of the tiger out of my mind as I approached the sales manager to collect my commission.

"Buongiorno Luca! I have returned!" I exclaimed; the sales staff were always very friendly to the Tour Leaders.

"Si, Will, Buongiorno! You do very well today! Very, very well!" Luca looked exceptionally pleased. On a visit to the glassblowers, I usually expected a commission of anywhere from fifty to one-hundred Euros. Opening the envelope that day, there was nearly three-hundred Euros! Happy days indeed!

"Bloody hell Luca! That's the most I've ever made here! I can actually afford a coffee on the square! What did my people buy to get me a commission like this?" I was mildly curious.

"Si, Will, one of the ladies from Asia spent over two-thousand Euros!" Luca clearly meant one of the Vietnamese women, they were the only ones on the tour flashing that much cash.

"On what? A chandelier? One of those big red urns? A baptismal font?"

"No Will! She bought several items, but mostly it was her purchase of *la tigre*!" Luca pronounced tigre with the amazing inflection that Italians always use when they get excited.

"You mean the green one from the front case? One of my passengers spent that much money on the world's ugliest tiger? But it's hideous!" There was no mistaking the inflection in my voice.

"Si Will, the same one. You are correct, it is very ugly, we are pleased to have it gone! I work here for twenty years; it has been there all that time! I sell it to her for large discount as well, just to get rid of it!"

I was very happy for Luca, he never had to see the green tiger again. Better yet, I never had to see the green tiger again either! I thanked Luca again, said my goodbyes, and went to greet the passengers coming off the gondolas.

The Vietnamese women didn't do any of the optional activities in Venice, therefore, neither Derek nor I saw them until the next morning. We were in good spirits as we loaded the bus. It had been a particularly pleasant stay in Venice, and the weather looked amazing going forward, and most of the passengers had taken steps to lighten their luggage for us. Almost all of the luggage was loaded, but we were still waiting on the Vietnamese women, the hold was still going to be stuffed. Just as we were about to close it up and go to breakfast, the Vietnamese women finally arrived with their suitcases, and an extra box as well.

"Good morning, ladies. Just in time, we were about to close up and go for breakfast," Derek greeted them.

"Hello Derek, hello Will. Yes, we have our luggage, but we need to put this box in the luggage compartment as well," said the one with the box.

"Ladies, we went over this already, we do not have the space in the hold for ANY extra luggage, in fact we asked everyone to lighten their luggage so that we can fit it all in!" I wasn't too happy having to explain the situation again.

"But I was in the glass store and had to buy the most gorgeous tiger statue! I had to have it; it will go so nicely in my house!" Said the lady with the box.

"That's all well and good, but how much did you spend?" I already knew the answer, I just wanted to see what they'd say about it.

"Over two-thousand Euros! Oh, it's a stunning tiger! It's too bad it's all taped up and packaged, if not we'd show it to you!" Mercifully, they didn't, I, like Luca, was looking forward to never seeing it again.

"Ladies, for two-thousand Euros, the shop would have shipped it back to Vietnam! Free of charge! Why didn't you have them do that?"

"They offered to, but I was worried it might get mishandled and break in shipping. So, I decided just to bring it along with me," the glass tiger lady said. She was right to be worried about it being mishandled, I had half a mind to shatter the thing at that very moment. Derek looked like he was thinking the same thing.

It took Derek and I only a brief moment to discuss the situation. It was decided, for the first time in either of our careers, that we would charge for extra luggage.

The ladies didn't bat an eye at the luggage cost, but we made it clear to them that they only got this one. We would not allow any more luggage under any circumstances. Having paid the twenty Pounds and left their suitcases with Derek and me, the Four Horsewomen went off to breakfast. Derek still wasn't too happy with the extra box.

"So where do you suggest we store this moronic tiger?" Derek asked, not at all thrilled at the extra cargo.

"I reckon we place it under the front wheel. I'm not joking, I'll give them their twenty Pounds back provided you get to run over it with the bus! We'll record it and put it on YouTube, it'll be fun!"

In the end we stored it in the compartment that's usually reserved for the bus cleaning products. Modern buses actually have a number of semi-secret compartments. It was a good thing it was stored there as just the site of the box with the glass tiger was enough to make me want to chuck it off of a motorway overpass.

*   *   *

It took only one day to have the next run-in with the Four Horsewomen. The tour stayed in Italy and we visited Florence and overnighted in Tuscany. It was Easter weekend and the sites were busy. We were just leaving Pisa and taking the motorway in the direction of Milan. We were now heading for Switzerland for a two-night stay in Interlaken. We stopped at a roadside service center for lunch. As the passengers filed off, the Four Horsewomen approached me and they did not look happy.

"Will, we have a problem to talk with you about," said the lead horsewoman.

"And what would that be?" Who knew what the issue would be now?

"Why are we driving in the wrong direction?" She asked this as though we were actually going in the wrong direction. I was a bit mystified.

"We aren't going in the wrong direction. After Tuscany and Pisa, the next stop is Switzerland, this is the way to Switzerland," it was as simple as that.

"But we were looking forward to being in Rome for Easter Sunday. We were going to go to church in the Vatican! Our travel agent booked this tour so we could do that!" Said the horsewoman. Boy, were they going to be disappointed!

"Umm, ladies, I hate to be the bearer of bad news, but this tour doesn't go to Rome. Did you not read the itinerary?"

"Well, we booked it because the agent said it did! What are you going to do about it?" They honestly thought I'd be rearranging an entire tour just for them.

"I'm not going to do anything about it. This bus and everyone on it are going to Switzerland," the ladies were off their rockers if they thought otherwise!

"Well, what about our going to Rome for Easter?"

"Ladies, if you really want to be in Rome for Easter then we'll drop you off at the next rail station and you can take the train to Rome. That's it though because this bus is going to Switzerland, not Rome!" There was nothing more to say as far as I was concerned. I was actually now looking very forward to potentially ditching these women for a couple of days.

I wasn't to be that lucky. After a short chat, the Four Horsewomen decided to continue on, but not before letting me know that the entire Rome debacle, and the fact that I wasn't going to change the entire itinerary of the tour, was completely my fault. I couldn't have cared less.

The good thing for the remainder of the tour was that the Four Horsewomen didn't want to talk to me any further. This was no problem for me as I didn't want to talk to them either. The tour progressed on to Switzerland and then to Paris with nothing said between us, though we still had one dicey moment upon arriving in Interlaken. Our accommodation there was actually at a youth hostel, which I could tell when I made the announcement to the passengers that the Four Horsewomen were not at all happy with. The good thing about a youth hostel room in Switzerland is that it's still a better place to stay than any hotel room anywhere else in Europe. The only difference between a room at this hostel and a regular hotel room was that instead of two twin beds each room had two bunk beds. They were still sleeping two to a room, so everyone was happy. Bullet dodged!

The tour finished in London, as normal, and except for the Four Horsewomen, I was quite sad to see the tour conclude, it had been an excellent group! Looking over the reviews from the passengers, it was clear that they all enjoyed themselves and my performance was well rated. Except for the Four Horsewomen, all of whom gave me the following score on a scale of one to five:

Helpfulness: 1/5 **Attitude**: 1/5
Interaction with Driver: 1/5 **Accessibility**: 1/5
Historical Information: 1/5 **Cultural Information**: 1/5

Happy days there! The office was sure to ask what had happened there. I always took reviews from such miserable people as a badge of honor. Some people simply cannot be pleased and if they wanted to rate me so badly for NOT having taken them to Rome and ruined everyone else's tour, then so be it. The shocking and surprising thing to me was that they still tipped me a total of one-hundred Euros. Given how much they hated me, I was surprised they'd given me anything at all! I closed the door on the tour, finishing my administrative duties, and was ready to relax in London for a few days before starting the next tour.

My relaxation time started the next day. A few of the passengers from the tour were staying in London for an extra bit of time and my I was happy to show them around London. We were enjoying a mid-afternoon stroll along the Mall near Buckingham Palace when my phone rang, it was the driver Derek, who was desperate to ask a question:

"Will, did you go through all your tips from the tour?"

"Yeah, Derek, went through them all, did well, it was a good haul. Why?" It was a curious reason to call, I suspected an ulterior motive.

"OK, yeah it was a good tour, as good as I've ever had on tips actually. Just out of curiosity, did those Vietnamese women give you anything?"

"On top of all the grief? Oddly enough, yeah. They tipped one-hundred Euros, which is a hundred more than I thought I'd get!"

"Really? One hundred each?"

"No, total."

"Ohhhh….well that's interesting!" Said Derek. Now my curiosity was truly piqued.

"OK Derek, what's up? What'd they tip you?" I asked knowing full well that Derek was always a terrible liar and was completely incapable of not saying what was on his mind.

"Oh, a bit more than that."

"How much more?" I was completely taken in now, I had to know!

"You really want to know?"

"Out with it already Derek! What'd they tip you?"

"Six hundred Euros."

Keeping in mind that me and the passengers were walking along the Mall, one of the major roads in all of central London, the approach to Buckingham Palace, the road along which every British Royal dating back for centuries had ridden; there was only one thing to say:

"THOSE F$&@ING B%&*@#ES DID WHAT?!?!?!?" I felt badly for poor Derek, I shouted so loudly into the phone that I reckoned it was even odds that I had blown out his ear. After a few more choice words into the phone, Derek finally had a chance to respond.

"Sorry Will, I shouldn't have mentioned anything. See you in a few days then?" Derek and I were paired together again for the next tour.

"Dammit Derek! That's not fair! I should get half of that!" There wasn't a chance that Derek would let that happen, but a lad had to have a go.

"Not on your life mate! That's mine! You shouldn't have told them that we wouldn't take them to Rome!" It wasn't often Derek got to have one over on me, he was enjoying the conversation now, but was kind enough to make a small gesture of consolation before ending the call.

"I'll tell you what Will, they screwed you over on the tip in the end. What I'll do is I'll stock the onboard fridge with whatever beer you want for Thursday. Will that make you happy?"

"No, but if it's all I'm gonna get then I'll just have to get on with it. Guinness and Pilsner Urquell if you don't mind! And don't cheap out on me! Congrats on the tip and we'll see you on Thursday morning you cheap bastard!" Derek was a top lad and never had much in the way of lucky breaks, if anyone did deserve a six-hundred Euro tip, it was Derek.

The passengers who I'd been showing around London thought the whole thing to be hilarious, and in another bit of luck, didn't let me pay for anything the rest of the day. After a couple of Guinness's at the Westminster Weatherspoon's pub, I'd completely let the whole affair go. In fact, I was very much content and happy in the knowledge that there was one particularly garish green glass tiger that was at that moment likely on an airplane to Hanoi that I was never ever going to see again!

We all toasted to that!

What if He Vomits in the Dead Sea?

Despite the difficult passengers that a Tour Leader must deal with the, the truly terrible ones are actually quite rare. They do pop up every now and then, but you deal with them and get on as best you can. On exceedingly rare occasions though, a Tour Leader will be faced with a passenger that, for whatever reason, is so difficult that they must be removed from the tour. In all my time as a Tour Leader it has only happened once and it wasn't even because they were a nasty or terrible person.

It was on one of my tours through Israel and Jordan. The groups for these tours were always a good deal smaller than the ones I had in Europe. Usually twenty-five passengers as a maximum. A Tour Leader would get to know all the passengers much more quickly than was the norm on a European tour. The first day in Tel Aviv was simply a check-in and group meeting day with no official excursions or activities scheduled. Passengers would arrive to the hotel, meet me briefly, and then have the rest of the afternoon free to do as they pleased. We'd have a quick group meeting in the evening to go over the tour and get to know each other and that would be that. The tour would begin in earnest the following day.

For the Tour Leader, it was actually a bit boring on that first day, waiting for all the passengers to come and check in one-by-one. I'd usually have been in contact with all the passengers several days in advance, so I'd have a good idea when they'd arrive. It would take a bit of the stress out of the opening day, having already been in contact with most of them. On this particular tour in early May, I'd got quite lucky.

All the passengers had arrived and checked in with me quite early. All of them but one.

His name was Dhevi and he was from South Africa. According to my manifest he was a pensioner and traveling on his own. Nothing unusual in that. As the afternoon wore on, it started to annoy me a bit, having to hang around the hotel lobby waiting for one last passenger to check in. The beach was only two-hundred meters away and it was beckoning me! Still, I resigned myself to my duty. This Dhevi didn't have a phone number that he could be reached at and my earlier attempts to connect through social media had been unfruitful, all I could do was wait. While this was going on I was able to chat a bit with the other passengers, all of whom were very friendly and excited for the tour. My parents happened to be on their yearly tour on this occasion, and my uncle had joined us as well. As time crawled by, I noticed that there was a nervous and very reticent looking man skulking around in the lobby. He was a small and diminutive sort, he walked with a bit of a stooped posture. He actually looked a bit sickly to me. After a couple of hours, I started to wonder, could this be my missing passenger Dhevi whom I'd been waiting for? He was often looking over in my direction. After some time, I decided to approach the man and ask.

"Excuse me, sir, but are you Dhevi from South Africa?"

The man said nothing, instead, with a bit of a twitchy hand, he reached into his pocket and pulled out a South African passport and handed it to me. Looking at the ID page I could indeed see that this was the mythical Dhevi. I handed his passport back and introduced myself.

"OK, Dhevi, good to meet you! I'm Will, I'll be your Tour Leader. How are you sir?" I asked, pleased that my little tour menagerie was now complete.

The man still said nothing. He just stood there, no expression on his face. Nothing. It was like speaking to a blank wall. I gave him all the opening day information and material that he needed, but it was awkward. The man was absolutely mute. Or so I thought.

Once I was finished giving Dhevi the information he needed, he did speak. His words were uttered in such a low and hushed volume that I had to absolutely strain and lean right into him to hear them. All I could hear in a barely audible whisper were two words.

"Medicine. Missing."

If Dhevi was missing some medication, it might help to explain his unusual behavior. He at least had all of his paperwork, unorganized as it was, with him which I was able to look over. It became clear after a few minutes of looking things over that Dhevi's checked luggage had been lost in transit, and that was exactly where he had put his many medications. Dhevi himself had a lengthy list of ailments, none of them a pleasant sort of thing to have. The man needed a hospital, fast. I didn't have any confidence that Dhevi would be able to take care of himself and get to the hospital. I'd have to take him myself.

I informed the passengers that were around that the evening's meeting may not actually occur, but to be prepared for departure the next morning. Dhevi and I were off to the hospital in an attempt to set his medical ship right. If I'd known what was going to ensue over the next forty-eight hours, I'd have taken him to the airport instead.

The hospital was the first problem. They wanted to charge a massive upfront fee at the emergency room. We'd gone straight to the emergency ward because I couldn't find a general admissions area. Sometimes, it helps to play a complete fool, this was one of those times. Every hospital worker I spoke to got tired of us in short order. I mean, it was a marginally mute South African and a pain in the ass buffoon Canadian. No one wanted to bother with us for more than two minutes. Slowly but surely, over the course of about an hour, we were shuffled through numerous different administrators and nurses until we eventually found ourselves in a triage ward and speaking to the on-shift head doctor. Of all the people we dealt with he was the most accommodating, which wasn't saying much. I gave him the list of medicines that Dhevi needed.

"This is not so easy," the doctor said.

"Why's that?" I asked.

"These medicines all have English names to them. We're in Israel sir, I'll need to look up the Hebrew name for all of them. This will take a few moments, just wait while I take care of it."

There's not much for a Tour Leader to do in a triage ward, except watch while the nurses and doctors keep the various patients from going into septic shock. I was absolutely surprised that we had been allowed back there as it was clearly the part of the hospital that dealt with the most serious emergency cases. Luckily, the doctor was fairly quick about things and after fifteen minutes we had the new prescriptions that Dhevi needed. Now it was off to the nearest pharmacy, but not before we paid the hospital bill.

"Where do we go to pay the hospital fee?" I asked the doctor.

"Did they give you an admittance paper at any time when you got here?" The doctor asked.

"No, everyone shuffled us along until we ended up here," I answered.

"In that case, I'd shut up and just get the hell outta here before someone figures out you just got a freebie prescription!" Said the doctor, and with that we left just as fast as Dhevi could shuffle himself along.

The nearest pharmacy was just across the street, even though it was Shabbat, it was still, mercifully, open.

And out of stock! The pharmacist took one look at our prescriptions, laughed, and handed it back to us. The next closest pharmacy did the same. We finally struck pay dirt at the third pharmacy, they had what we needed. Sort of. The pharmacist had good news and bad news.

"Yes, this prescription is OK, but there is a problem. The first medication is fine, we can fill it. The second medication is simply not sold in Israel, no one will have it, I'm surprised the doctor didn't know. The third medication, the doctor has written the wrong dosage, it should be halved," said the pharmacist.

"So, what you're saying is we need to go back to the hospital and have them write a new prescription?" I asked forlornly.

"Yes," said the pharmacist.

It wasn't the pharmacist's fault, but I could have murdered him on the spot and not felt a flicker of emotion about it. We needed to go back to the hospital.

My plan of attack on the second visit was to simply walk into the emergency ward like I owned the place, but given his fragile condition, I left Dhevi in a waiting room whilst I invaded the emergency ward. I didn't need him slowing me down. Shockingly, it worked, no one said a word to me anywhere. I eventually made my way into the triage ward. The doctor from earlier in the evening was missing, but I saw that one of the junior doctors that I'd spoken to earlier was still around, I decided to ask him where the head doctor was.

"The head doctor? Oh, his shift ended thirty minutes ago. He's gone home. Is it something serious?" He asked.

"Not at all, we just need this prescription redone. Pharmacist says it needs to be halved," I pleaded with the junior doctor. Last thing I needed was a dramas about a cocked-up prescription.

For the first time all night, we caught a break. The junior doctor whipped out his prescription pad and rewrote it in a flash. Returning to find Dhevi sitting where I'd left him, we got out of there as quickly as Dhevi could shuffle himself along.

By now we'd been gone from the hotel for several hours and night had descended on Tel Aviv. The pharmacist worked quickly to fill the prescriptions, and we hailed a cab back to the hotel.

*   *   *

The next day I had hopes that Dhevi would be a bit more copus mentus. I found out immediately that this was not the case. Larry, Dhevi's American roommate, wanted a word with me.

"Will, I'm a patient and accommodating man, but if I need to share a room with that guy again, I'm going to kill him and anyone who tries to stop me!"

"Oh god, what happened?" I asked, Dhevi was quickly turning into a headache for everyone.

"The guy wouldn't go to sleep; he kept his light on all night. Now that I can live with. But then he woke me up at three AM to make him a cup of tea. While I did that, he took a piss in the corner of the room!" Larry's annoyance was evident. As were the bags under his eyes.

"Right Larry, no worries. I'll juggle the room assignments, don't fuss it," I said.

With four single males, my choices were limited. Someone had to share a room with Dhevi. My plan was to room my uncle with him, but then I thought better of it. My uncle was a good guy, why would I punish him by making him room with Dhevi? As the Tour Leader, I had a single room. It was a simple matter to give Dhevi my room and I would share a room with my uncle. Crisis averted!

It's a good thing I sorted that crisis out because Dhevi's next calamity arrived forthwith. The whole group had boarded the bus, ready to begin their Middle Eastern adventure, we weren't more than fifty meters away from the hotel when Dhevi vomited into a paper bag. At least he was prepared for it!

He vomited three more times in the next hour, never saying a word about what was wrong or how he was feeling, despite everyone's concern. It was impossible to determine what exactly was wrong with him. He improved to some degree over the course of the morning, but having to find extra puke bags was proving to be a chore that nobody wanted to be overly involved in. Luckily, Dhevi rallied himself a bit in the afternoon as we arrived at the Dead Sea.

"You're not actually going to let him float in there, are you?" Asked Larry.

"Well, I can't stop him. What's the worst that could happen? It's not like he can drown in there!" I replied.

"What if he vomits in the Dead Sea? It's pure salt, you're going to end up with a pickled bit of sick floating in here for the next ten thousand years! It's disgusting!" Said Larry.

"Larry, a bit of petrified vomit is the least of my concerns right now. I'm just hoping the guy doesn't keel over before we get to Eilat! And better he vomits in there than in the bus!"

Dhevi didn't keel over on the way to Eilat, Israel's southernmost town on the Gulf of Aqaba, but he did puke a couple more times, to everyone's chagrin. The bus was going to need a thorough hosing-down after we arrived. By this point my mind was made up. Dhevi needed to go.

I don't say that lightly. I'd never kicked a person off of a tour before, but this guy just couldn't hack it. I was having enough difficulties in keeping him together in Israel. Jordan would be an entirely different proposition. It was already well into spring in the Middle East.

Temperatures in Israel were hot, but still comfortable. Jordan would be roasting and we were heading there two days later. I really wasn't sure if Dhevi could survive that and medical facilities weren't necessarily going to be readily available either. Our time in Jordan also required the passengers to do a lot of walking, Dhevi needed the better part of an hour to shuffle from the lobby to his room. No, it was clear to me that for his own personal safety, I wouldn't allow him to go any further.

My decision was vindicated the very next day, a free day for the group in Eilat. No sooner had breakfast ended than Dhevi came to me. He didn't feel well, he needed to go the hospital.

I organized a taxi and took him to the nearest. Unlike the hospital in Tel Aviv, the one in Eilat wasn't at all busy and Dhevi was attended to straight away. The doctors were a bit bemused as Dhevi couldn't really tell them what it was that was wrong. I couldn't help them any as I didn't really know what was bothering him either. They decided to keep him for the rest of the day for observation. I went back to the hotel to see about how to get Dhevi back home in one piece.

The office in London was very supportive once it was explained to them how serious the situation was, "I can't take him into Jordan! The man's edging towards death here in Israel! We've gotta send him home! He vomited at least five times yesterday, and that's four times more than I'll allow!" The office managed to get hold of Dhevi's daughter, who phoned me. She wasn't surprised one bit at the turn of events.

"I thought when he said he was going on a tour to the Middle East that it would be far too much for him. He's not really well enough to even leave home anymore, as you've obviously seen" she said.

I had already felt bad for Dhevi, he wasn't a bad person, he was just an elderly gentleman who couldn't handle a very physically demanding tour, but now I felt really terrible for him. He was going to face a difficult journey home, alone.

Between his daughter and me, we organized every aspect of his departure. His daughter lived in Amsterdam, so we decided it was best just to have him fly there instead of South Africa. Dhevi needed a taxi transfer to the Eilat airport, a flight from Eilat to Tel Aviv, and then a flight to Amsterdam, direct if at all possible. Luckily, a direct

Tel Aviv-Amsterdam flight was available. In a further bit of luck, the manager at the hotel said that he would personally see to it that Dhevi was taken to the airport and that all the logistics there would be handled appropriately.

I went back to the hospital to check on Dhevi, the staff were pleased to hear that arrangements had been made for him to go home. They had done everything they could for him and were ready to discharge him. He'd be fine to get back to Amsterdam, so long as he packed his medications in his carry-on luggage this time.

I had a long talk with Dhevi back at the hotel. He seemed quite happy that he was leaving the tour and going to see his daughter. His soft, low voice was finally producing proper sentences. He was quite concerned about the fact that I wouldn't be around to help him to the airport the next day, but these concerns evaporated when I introduced him to the hotel manager who would be helping him out the next day. We'd even printed and highlighted the important items in his travel paperwork, so there'd be no confusion for him the next day.

The rest of the passengers were also happy to see Dhevi heading home. To have a passenger in such a bad way takes away from the enjoyment for everybody, and they, like me, had been genuinely concerned about Dhevi. We all felt a bit bad about everything that had happened, but we all knew it was for the best that he departed the tour. I knew that many of my colleagues had had to expel passengers from tours before for various reasons, often being very happy to do so. With Dhevi it wasn't like that at all. One felt as though it was someone who was extremely ill trying, unsuccessfully, to try one last great journey before time ran out.

The next evening, as the group enjoyed the Arab ambiance of the spectacular Wadi Rum, we raised out glasses to Dhevi, all of us hoping and wishing that better days would be ahead for the soft-spoken South African.

I'm a Tour Leader Not a Babysitter

One part of the job of being a Tour Leader that I never enjoyed was when families with children would be on the tour. I may be a people person, but I've never been too keen on dealing with kids. Teenagers can be OK; you can joke around a bit with them, but I dreaded any tour where there were going to be kids under the age of twelve on board. Our company actually had a lower age limit of around eight, but this would be routinely waived. After all, are you really going to refuse a booking for an entire family simply because one of the people is too young? No, you're not. There came a point when the crew assignments director wouldn't assign me a tour if there were children on it. Not because I didn't like them, but because the operations team learned very quickly that I wouldn't temper my language on the microphone to be more G-rated. A lot of the kids were learning a lot of fun four-letter words a bit earlier than their parents would have liked.

This No-Kids-On-Will's-Tours policy worked well until one point when we ran out of Tour Leaders during a busy phase of the summer season. I was meant to have a week off, but a couple of Tour Leaders quit on us and I was recalled to lead a week-long tour to Paris, Switzerland, the Rhine Valley, and Amsterdam. Looking at the passenger manifest, one could see that it was a full bus, as per usual. More alarming than that, though, as I looked at the passengers' ages was the fact that there was a five-year-old listed. I wasn't looking so forward to the tour now.

Departure day came and the family with the five-year-old was at the meeting point ready to go. It was a family group of five from India, but living in America: Mom and dad, aunt and uncle, and the five-year-old, Samar. Like most five-year-olds, little Samar did not seem to be so happy to have been woken up at five in the morning to get on a bus. At least he'd probably spend most of the morning sleeping.

It didn't take long to know what kind of people I was dealing with in this family of five. The four adults had very much an entitled attitude about things, not necessarily unpleasant, just entitled. They certainly had a bit of a belief that the driver and I were there to fulfill their every whim. If you've ever been on a bus tour you will have met this type; always wanting to be served first at dinner, always wanting to sit at the front of the bus, always wanting their room key before anyone else. You tend to have a person or group like this on every tour; these four were the "Me First" individuals for this tour.

Little Samar, on the other hand, was an absolute joy. The driver and I very quickly took a liking to him, as did the rest of the passengers. His parents and aunt and uncle might not have been very polite or considerate, but Samar was. He was always saying please and thank you, always asking quite fun questions, and never once complained about the food (which is more than can be said about the rest of his family). In time I started thinking that I might have to change my personal "No Kids" policy.

Everywhere we went, young Samar was eager to see and do everything. Going to the top of the Jungfraujoch in Switzerland, Samar got to see snow for the first time; great fun for a five-year-old. At service stops, we'd let him sit in the driver's seat and pretend to drive the bus. Samar also had no fear of public speaking. Every day we'd have him come to the front of the bus and I'd do an on-board talk show segment with him. He was turning into one of the highlights of the tour on his own!

Which is more than can be said of the rest of his family who were not the greatest passengers I'd ever had. With the driver and me getting along with Samar so well, they seemed at times to have the attitude that we were also running a baby-sitting service, which was definitely not the case.

We arrived at the Rhine Valley. The boat cruise was followed by hotel check-in, all of which went fine. The town of Boppard isn't a massively huge place and the only thing left to do was take the passengers for a wine tasting. As we settled in for a bit of wine-time I was very much at ease. The day was over from an administrative perspective. I had a lovely Riesling in hand; the passengers were all having a great time. Everything was on point. As I looked around and talked to the passengers, something seemed a bit off, but I couldn't quite put my finger on what it was.

Samar's parents were certainly enjoying their wine tasting, as were his aunt and uncle. It was then that it dawned on me: where was Samar? I joined his family for a quick chat.

"Hey guys, enjoying the wine?"

"Will, yes, the wine is fantastic! Best part of the day!" answered his father.

I didn't see any point in dancing around things. It needed to be asked, "And out of curiosity, where's Samar?"

"Samar? Oh, well, we didn't think a wine shop would be appropriate for him, so we told him to sit in the square and that we'd come and collect him when we're done." His father said it as though it was the most obvious thing in the world to have done.

"You did what now?"

"Yeah, he's in the square. We'll get him later. There's a fountain there. He'll be fine!"

Drowning the rest of my Riesling, I darted out of the wine shop. Now, the wine shop was located on the square, so it only took a few seconds to walk over to the fountain and see that little Samar, mercifully, was right where he was supposed to be. He also didn't look like he was having any fun. I'd never seen a five-year-old looking so down. It was at this point that I made two important determinations. One, poor Samar deserved far better than he was getting. Two, his parents and aunt and uncle would need to be punished. Luckily, I knew of a way to accomplish both!

"Samar, what are you doing here?"

"My mom and dad told me to stay here and wait for them to come and get me later," The poor kid was missing the spring in his step.

"Samar, you're not having any fun right now, are you?"

"No."

"Would you like to?" I had a mildly mischievous plan in mind now.

"Yes!" Samar was starting to look a bit more like the excited five-year-old that I was used to seeing.

"OK, you come with me. I have one boring stop to make, and then were going to do something fun!"

The boring stop was just a two-minute stop at the watch repair store where they were repairing a band for me. After that, I walked Samar straight over to a place I knew he'd love, a hot chocolate bar! It was a place I knew well, as it was owned by the same people who owned the wine store.

I sat Samar down and ordered two large hot chocolates. These things were absolutely laced in sugar, a heap of whipped cream, candy sprinkles, the lot! They looked like something that you see on the Food Network, and huge as well. A large was certainly enough for me, let alone a five-year-old.

Samar wasted no time in getting stuck in on his. It was gone within five minutes. I only had one thing to say to him.

"Samar, did you enjoy the hot chocolate?"

"Oh yeah! It was really good!"

"Would you like another?"

"Really? I can have another? Yes please!" Samar certainly had the spring back in his step now!

I hadn't touched my hot chocolate at all, so I switched his empty cup for my full one. It took Samar only another five minutes to down this one. With Samar now nicely loaded with enough sugar to make an elephant jittery, we went back to the wine store.

The wine tasting was nearly finished, and Samar's parents were pleased as punch that I'd gone to the square and looked after him. They wouldn't feel that way for long.

The passengers slowly but surely left the wine store, some after purchasing a good deal more. It must be said, Samar's parents and aunt and uncle seemed to be well-greased after the wine tasting. Not a problem, most of the passengers usually were. The Boppard wine tasting was well known for being generous with the samplings. After enjoying a couple of glasses with the staff and picking up a case of wine for the girls in the London office, it was back to the hotel for dinner.

The hotel dinner required no work on my part. It was always a very ample buffet with food for any type of dietary requirement. We always had a spot of karaoke after dessert as well, so I quickly lost track of what was going on with Samar. The evening proceeded with little incident (if you can call an off-key duet of "Don't Go Breaking My Heart" between me and a newly-single, seventy-five-year-old divorcee as not being an incident). The passengers and I eventually wrapped up our evening and headed off to bed.

While loading the bus the next morning, most of the passengers were in a proper good mood; some hangovers mixed in, but generally pleased with the free wine and karaoke from the night before. Eventually Samar and his parents rocked up. If any of the passengers had hangovers, it certainly looked as though Samar's parents could be counted amongst them.

"Good morning! And how are we today? Looks like you had a rough night! Still waking up?"

"Morning, Will," responded Samar's dad, "yes, a very difficult night. Samar just would not go to sleep. He stayed up well past midnight! Kept us up far later than we would have liked! He usually nods off quite early. Amazing how much energy kids have sometimes!"

I slightly snickered to myself with that final comment. I decided that it was a wise idea to keep my involvement in Samar's newfound, extra energy to myself.

"Well, that's a bad turn! I suppose he probably had too much ice cream at dessert?" I reckoned it was just as well to pin the blame on the hotel.

"That's probably it, but we're all still quite tired, so we hope to have a little nap again once the bus gets going after breakfast!" Samar's dad and mom certainly looked as though they'd be happy enough to skip breakfast entirely and head straight back to their rooms for an extra twenty minutes of sleep.

"I think that can be arranged. In the meantime, I'll see you at breakfast in a few minutes."

"OK, thanks, Will! Oh, and thanks again for looking after Samar yesterday during the wine tasting. We definitely owe you!"

"No-no! No problem at all! He's an absolute champ! I was pleased to help out!"

In reality, I wanted to say, "Hey, I'm the one who got Samar hopped-up on enough chocolate to last him until next Christmas! Next time remember, I'm not a bloody baby-sitter! Don't leave your kid all alone in a random square in a random town in a random country whilst you and your missus go and tie one on!"

Of course, as a Tour Leader, you can rarely say exactly what you want to the passengers. We do work on earning tips at the end of the tours. Too many parents do view an organized tour as a chance to take a holiday from parenting, leaving it all to the Tour Leader to do. Just don't be too surprised when your Tour Leader finds a cheeky way to get even!

How Do You Commit a Person to a Mental Asylum in Amsterdam?

Sometimes a terrible passenger or event isn't strictly on one's own bus but can, nevertheless, find a way of dragging you into its path of destruction anyway. This was the case on a Christmas Week tour during my first year as a Tour Leader. My Tour Leader colleague and friend, Alex, was running the exact same tour at the exact same time, so we were seeing each other several times every day. His bus had fifty passengers, mine had fifty passengers. Therefore, there was a degree of joint logistics that we had to work out, but nothing too serious. It was actually a nice little holiday itinerary encompassing Paris, Switzerland, the Rhine Valley, and Amsterdam. The tour presented no problems at all in Paris or Switzerland, where we celebrated Christmas. Going on up to the Rhine Valley, things continued to proceed smoothly and both Alex's group and mine stayed at the same hotel where we were able to have holiday karaoke and really enjoy ourselves. It was only when we were just on the road and an hour after leaving the Rhine Valley and heading for Amsterdam that things of a fecal nature hit the fan.

The problem wasn't on my bus. My driver, Grant, and I had no problems at all, but Alex's bus, travelling fifteen minutes behind ours, had a severe problem. A problem that, unbeknownst to me, had started at around three in morning, but was just now hitting its peak. Alex had to phone me up.

"Hey, Will, where are you at mate?"

"Alex, yeah, we're just coming up to Bedburger Land for morning services."

Bedburger Land, which I have to say, might be the best named service stop in all of Europe, was a German service stop approximately an hour south of the Dutch border. There was nothing special about the place, it had good toilets, an ample café, and all the services that a group of fifty tourists would need on a chilly, winter day. Our plan was to do just a quick fifteen-minute toilet stop and, hopefully, just get back on the road as Alex's group arrived.

"OK, fine. Look, we need a huge favor from you," said Alex, sounding more than a little flustered.

"And what would that be?" I asked, this seemed a bit curious.

"Don't leave before we get there! We've got a bit of a problem that we need to talk to you and Grant about. We've got a....situation." Things had gone from curious to very curious.

Luckily, we weren't in a rush as Alex's bus didn't get there for another twenty minutes after we were supposed to have left. As his group filtered into the service hall Alex and his driver, Derek, came straight over to Grant and me. Alex didn't wase any time with the niceties.

"You're not going to believe what's happening on our bus!"

Alex proceeded to outline what the previous seven hours had been like.

At three in the morning the hotel staff had awakened him to deal with one of his passengers, a twenty-something American woman who was in her room threatening to slit her wrists. Her concerned roommate had gotten the staff and Alex to the room to talk her down and it seemed to have been sorted out. After breakfast was over and they had gotten going the young woman lost the plot again and started acting out on the bus raving and screaming that she was going to tackle the driver and force the bus off the road. They stopped on the shoulder of the Autobahn (which is actually illegal) and tried to calm her down again only to have the woman lie in front of the bus and yell at them to run her over. Eventually they were able to calm her down again and continue to the service stop.

"We are at our wit's end, guys. We're not exactly sure what to do here. What do you think?" Alex was at a bit of a loss and I have to say, I did sympathize with him.

"And I don't want her on the bus anymore, not with her threat to tackle me and force it off the road," was Derek's view of things. He was right; this girl was clearly off her rocker.

"Well, I'd rather you didn't move her to our bus if that's what you're thinking," was Grant's view of the situation.

It took five minutes for the four of us to discuss the issue and determine a course of action. My one question was whether or not Alex and Derek had any rugby players on board.

"Yeah, we have a couple of guys from New Zealand; obviously they've played rugby. Why does it matter?" Alex didn't quite see what the point of my question was.

"Well, we're in the middle of nowhere Germany on the coldest day of the year so you can't just dump her here. You have to take her to Amsterdam. What you do, is you put her back on the bus, sit her in the very rear corner, and place the big kiwi rugby players next to her. If she moves or threatens to do anything, they knock her out and/or restrain her." It wasn't the best solution in the world, but it was all I could think of.

It was determined that Alex and Derek would do exactly that, and while we still had a moment together, we conducted the oddest Google search any of us ever did:

HOW DO YOU COMMIT A PERSON TO A MENTAL ASYLUM IN AMSTERDAM?

The search results were a bit muddled, so we decided we'd call Ruud, the man who owned and operated the cheese and clogs farm that we always stopped at. Ruud, who apparently knew something about such matters, told us not to worry about it. With nothing else to sort out at that moment, my and Grant's buses got going down the road to Amsterdam, leaving Alex and Derek to deal with their American Nightmare.

Both Alex and I were running slightly behind schedule, but it was nothing to be too worried about from a scheduling point of view. It dawned on me at this point that I hadn't actually seen the problem-passenger at any point. My and Alex's buses arrived at the cheese and clogs farm at nearly the same time. This wasn't the best of circumstances, but not the end of the world either. While one of the groups was in doing the cheese demonstration, the other would do the clogs demonstration and then we'd reverse things. Upon arrival, we had a very quick word with Ruud about the problematic American girl. Ruud, for his part, informed us that the first thing that had to happen was that a police psychiatrist/counsellor would have to declare the girl a public hazard and then they could take her on to a proper psychiatric facility.

This all sounded fine to Alex, the drivers, and me. We took time to get some coffee and cheese and talk things out a bit more. It was only at this time that I finally saw the infamous young woman who had caused all the problems. At this point she was standing in the gift shop in a completely catatonic state; a blank slate look on her face with what seemed like unblinking eyes. She certainly looked insane.

After a few minutes, the Amsterdam Police arrived and a number of officers came into the gift shop and proceeded to take the young American woman outside for a psychiatric evaluation. Alex and I left them to it. The passengers on my bus hadn't really been clued into what was going on. I didn't see the need to excite things any more than necessary. My passengers finished their turn in the clogs room and started their time in the gift shop. Once that was done, they made their way back on the bus so that we could go to the hotel. It was during this time that Alex came to me with an update.

"I just spoke with the office in London. They have a request for you that you and your bus don't leave here until the police have finished their business and taken her with them."

"No problem there," I replied. "How long do you reckon it'll be?" Hopefully, this would get done in short order.

"I don't think much longer. They've finished the evaluation and said that she definitely needs to go to a hospital."

As it turned out, the passenger had been on medication for a psychiatric condition, but over the course of the tour had decided that she didn't need her meds anymore. You'd actually be surprised how often this actually happens on a group tour; it wouldn't be the last time either of us dealt with a passenger who'd gone off their meds.

With nothing left for me to do except wait for the police to leave, and with all of my passengers having finished their shopping, there was no point in hanging around. I went outside and back to my bus.

Now, I'm not sure what exactly Ruud had said to the emergency services when he called them for us, but upon seeing the parking lot it looked to me as though half the Amsterdam police force was there; about a half dozen squad cars (with lights on), two paddy wagons, and even a SWAT truck!

Getting back on the bus, it only took a brief moment to explain to Grant that we'd need to hang around for a moment. With all the police activity the passengers certainly had questions.

"Will, what is with all the police vehicles here? What's going on?"

"The thing about the police presence is, well, you know Alex the Tour Leader on the other bus? Yeah, we're having one of his passengers committed to a mental asylum." I said this on the bus-board microphone.

The bus erupted in a mix of laughter and shocked awws, but mostly laughter. One of the passengers near the front then asked:

"Seriously, Will, what's with all the police?"

"I'm not joking. We are actually committing one of Alex's passengers to an asylum. We just have to wait around here until the police leave. As soon as they leave, we can go on to the hotel."

Now, I've always been known as a bit of a jokester Tour Leader who will say almost anything to get a laugh, but it was fairly clear to the passengers that I absolutely meant what I said on this occasion. I was soon backed up by one of my female passengers.

"Does this have anything to do with that creepy girl who was in the giftshop earlier? She was just standing there looking like she'd been possessed?"

"Yep, that's the girl. Let's just say, she needs to go away for a while and get some help," I responded. It seemed that a few of my passengers had clued into things.

Within a few minutes the police convoy had left, so my group was able to go on to the hotel and the incident of the homicidal American woman was put to rest. She was clearly also able to get her meds and a flight home without much difficult because two months later word came down that she was trying to sue Alex, me, and the tour company for having put her in an asylum. Luckily for all of us, we had documented everything we did and the Amsterdam police were more than happy to vouch for her mental state at that time. It would only be a few days later that this particular incident would look like a walk in the park with the horror show that was about to befall me!

Happy New Year, Now Get the Hell Off the Bus!

Immediately after the Christmas tour ended that year, we were right back on the road the very next day doing the exact same tour. The only difference was that this time it would be New Year's instead and Alex and I would trade drivers. This time I would be with Derek and Alex was paired with Grant. The weeklong jaunt looked promising and we didn't expect too many difficulties. Derek and I would be made to pay for this optimism.

The crisis hit in Paris and followed us throughout the tour all the way back to London. I got a bad feeling from the minute we checked into the hotel in Paris. It was in a suburb called Bobigny just outside the Peripherique, the large ring road that encircles Paris. Bobigny may sound like a pleasant sort of place, but is anything but. The area is home to many very desperate characters and isn't at all an area where tourists generally go. Upon check-in the entire group was given a demonstration in how to properly operate the lock on the door, which seemed a bit odd. During our two days in Paris, all went well, with little cause for concern. On the second evening, I looked over my belongings, and saw that everything was in order before I headed out into the city. None of my group was keen for cabaret, so I had scheduled an optional evening in Montmartre instead.

Coming back to the room, all still seemed in order and I retired for the evening. The next morning, during loading, things continued to seem fine until Derek went to retrieve the parking stub from his wallet. His wallet was noticeably thinner and his driver's license was missing. Derek freaked out!

"Will, we've got a huge problem! My driver's license, passport, and all my money is gone! Everything is gone! Credit cards, I've been robbed!"

I tried keeping Derek calm, certainly in front of the passengers who were just bringing their luggage to the bus. After a few minutes I had just brought Derek back to a workable emotional level and was about to give him some of my own cash out of my man purse when I realized…

"Oh s%$t! Derek all my money and my iPad is gone too!" It was just now that I had looked into my man purse for the first time that day to see that all my cash was gone too, along with a few other bits. Now the rolls had to reverse with Derek trying to calm me down.

Phone calls to London were quickly made and I had the unpleasant duty of informing all the passengers that their Tour Leader and driver had both been wiped out and that they themselves had to do a check of all their valuables.

I was expecting a full-blown theft job of every passenger. Surprisingly, none of them reported a single thing missing.

Derek and I, along with our office staff on the phone, quickly surmised what had happened. The hotel staff had broken into my and Derek's rooms and cleaned out our valuables while we had been out the previous evening!

Now, in these circumstances, whenever the Tour Leader or driver hit upon truly dire moments (and it does happen), the passengers are usually very sympathetic and keen to help. Our lot weren't.

"You know, Will, you still have a job to do. Just because you got robbed doesn't make it right for you to hold up the tour," was one very cutting comment from a young Australian woman who was far more concerned that we'd be departing late for Switzerland.

"OK, I never said that Derek and I weren't going to do our jobs, but we have an emergency. Everyone hold tight here at the hotel. We just have to duck over to the police station and file a report. As soon as we do, then we'll be back and head out!"

Derek and I expected to be at the police station for an extended period. We got there at 7:30 in the morning and caught the only break we were going to get all week. French police aren't generally too fussed over a Canadian and Brit who've been robbed. On this particular morning, however, a very friendly, English-speaking officer was on duty and upon hearing of our predicament gave us proper reassurance.

"Oui, that is not good. Very quickly, make a list of everything taken. I will write the report immediately and you will be away within an hour. Tres vite, c'est important! N'est-ce pas?"

While the report was prepared, we knew that we also had to get the ball rolling on replacement passports. I dumped out my valuables pack to see if anything was left. Out dropped, to my complete amazement, all of my credit and debit cards as well as my passport!

Well, at least I was still legal to travel. The officer in charge reckoned that the thieves had simply overlooked the credit cards. As for the passport, the officer had an interesting view on why that had been left behind.

"Oui, thieves in Europe do not want a filthy Canadian passport. It is useless and not valuable on the black market in Paris. Nobody wants to move to a country like that and nobody wants to pretend to be Canadian. Much better to pretend to be British or American! Much more valuable on the street!"

OK, so that was decided! It's useless to be a Canadian! Lucky for me; it meant I still had my passport and my credit cards as well!

Poor Derek was in the bigger bind on his documents. They were all gone. No passport and no driver's license. After chatting with both his bus office and my office about the situation, he came back looking quite rattled.

"They want us to just continue on to Switzerland," Derek didn't look pleased. "They say we don't have the time to wait around here for new papers from the British embassy or wait for a replacement driver to get here."

"They want you to drive the rest of today and maybe all the way back to London without a license or identification?" I was gob smacked at the idea.

"Yeah, I mean, what do we do if I get pulled over?" Derek asked, a very valid concern.

"It's OK, Derek, that can't happen," was my only response.

"What do you mean, it can't happen?"

"It can't happen because if it does happen, then we're completely f*#^ed! So, it won't." It was terrible reasoning, but it was all we had.

The officer helping us let us know that this was not an isolated incident. The hotel we had stayed at was well known for Tour Leaders and drivers getting robbed. This didn't make us feel any better.

Tour Leaders do carry around a lot of cash. All told, I reckoned I had been cleared out of about fifteen-thousand Euros. Happy New Year to me! It just happened to be New Year's Eve.

"Where can we party on New Year's Eve in Lucerne for twenty-seven Euros? That's all I have in my pocket!" was the question I put to Derek.

"Umm, maybe buy a six-pack and get smashed in your hotel room... by yourself? There is duty-free at the border!" was much of a response as Derek could muster.

The passengers had little time for our predicament in general. I was forced to have each of them cough up twenty Euros just to re-establish a tour cash-flow which I'd give back to them on the final day. Yes, the tips at the end of the tour looked not at all promising now. Derek and I just wanted to crawl in a hole and die. That's not to say all the passengers were against us, but enough of them were that it seemed like the whole bus was.

Derek and I were able to nurse things along and slowly get our wits back. I always found that when something terrible happens to a person on tour, whether it's being robbed, losing a passport, having a health emergency; whatever the predicament is, it takes three or four days to get over it and to let the emotions drain out and get back to square one. By the time Derek and I were able to get to that point, it would be the final day. We were certainly looking forward to seeing the back end of the tour and it wasn't even half over!

Everything for the next three days went by in a bit of a haze. The only thing I remember was the constant complaints and bad attitudes that Derek and I received from many of the passengers. As far as many of them were concerned, we were a completely incompetent pair of morons who were screwing up everything! Morale remained low amongst the road crew throughout. It may only have been a week-long tour, but it felt like a month.

The final day of the tour, driving back to London, was the only happy moment for Derek and me. Our tour from hell was coming to an end. Getting through British customs was actually a breeze for poor Derek, with no ID at all. The Brits weren't fussed at all once they read his police report. The British immigration officer was very good about things.

"So, your passport, driver's license, money, and credit cards were all stolen last week in France and you didn't have time to get replacements?" queried the officer.

"Yes sir, it happened in Paris, and as you can see, we had an itinerary to keep to," was the only defense Derek could offer.

"F*#^ing French! Always doing anything they can to ruin things for Her Majesty's citizens! Welcome back to Britain, lads!" It was the best thing I'd ever heard an immigration officer say.

Ordinarily, a Tour Leader gives a very upbeat and happy final speech to end a tour. Even if it's a tour that one didn't particularly enjoy, you still give the kind words. This one was different. The tips were terrible, and during the ferry ride back to Britain a quick look at the tour review forms confirmed a deep hatred of the passengers for Derek and me. Based on the reviews, you would have thought that we were the cause of every terrible event in the history of mankind. One review after another completely roasted us. Good reviews were few and far between and the more we looked at them the angrier and more depressed we got.

So, therefore, upon arriving back at Greenwich, my goodbye speech was short and sweet.

"Thank you very much for a miserable New Year's! Please ensure you take all your belongings with you and have a Happy New Year and GET THE HELL OFF THE BUS! Everyone! Do it! Now!" Looking at Derek, I could see that he entirely agreed. We basically threw the luggage out of the hold and bolted out of there as fast as we could. We didn't feel like final hugs; not that we would have received any.

Upon completion of any tour, the Tour Leader will go into the office for a debrief as to how it went. Usually, you'd wait until you were preparing for your next tour which could be a week or two later. I was in the office the very next morning.

Now, anyone who knows me in real life can tell you, I swear. I swear quite a bit. During that tour's debrief I used enough four-letter words to fill most people's lifetime allotment. It was thirty minutes of pure, unadulterated anger and frustration that vented out of me. I felt sorry for our deputy operations manager having to listen to it and for the HR manager who was taking the notes. After the most florid and brutal rant of my life, there was only one thing for the deputy operations manager to say.

"So, Will, should we just call a mulligan on this tour and burn these reviews then?"

"Yes, yes, for the love of God yes! And despite it only being ten in the morning I'm off to the pub where I shall get unforgivably drunk! If anyone needs me, I'll be there for the next three days."

The operations team was forgiving in the end. Three thousand Euros of the stolen money was actually company money, as well as the phone and iPad. They pulled every financial string possible to lessen the loss, but I still had to pay them back a good deal of money.

It was at the end of January that I was recalled to the office and told that I'd be taking over two twelve-day tours during February and March. I was surprised at this turn of events. Both tours were allocated to another Alex already. I was told very quickly why a change was being made.

"Will, remember how bad you felt that you were robbed of a lot of money, had a terrible tour at New Year's, and thought that you had the worst luck in the world?" asked the operations manager.

"Yes, I can hardly forget. It just happened a few weeks ago! I still have flashbacks!"

"Well, you're going to stop whining about that now because Alex has mouth cancer and that's why you're doing the February and March tours and he isn't. He's going to be out of commission for…a while anyway," said the operations manager.

News like that really put things in perspective. You can feel sorry for yourself all you want, but there's always someone in a worse situation than you. Poor Alex was a good friend and I felt a right heel in complaining about my lot after that. Luckily, Alex, after a brief period in hospital and surgery, was back to full health. The two tours I took over for him were full of great passengers and the driver for both was my favorite driver, Ron. By the end of the two tours, I was definitely not complaining about my bad bit of luck; not one bit.

The Tour from Hell taught me some very good lessons, both in how to be a Tour Leader as well as about life in general. No matter how terrible things seem, no matter how low you get, the sun will shine again, and things will get better. Still, every now and then you do get a rough group of passengers who all you want to do with is get on a microphone and tell them to, "GET THE HELL OFF THE BUS!

Part 2

Can I Have this Person on Every Tour? I'll Pay for it!

Of course, not every difficult passenger is a terrible sort of person that you end up loathing and hoping that they'll end up being kidnapped by the Italian Mafia. Some of them are actually really sweet people who, whilst difficult, you really come to like and even enjoy their crazy antics.

They may not be the sort of people that you remain lifelong friends with. Sometimes a tour ends and you never hear from them again. Sometimes, you continue to talk to them on a regular basis, even years later. The thing that makes tour leading such an interesting and fun job are the great and fascinating people that you get to know. They come from all corners of the world and make just as big an impact on a Tour Leader as a Tour Leader makes on them.

The people and stories in the following section made such a huge and positive impact on me, that I've remembered them all fondly well after the events described. They certainly made their respective tours ones that won't soon be forgotten!

Just What in the Hell Kind
of Lettuce is This?

He was the craziest, the most hilarious, and certainly the most unique passenger I ever dealt with. He was completely out of his depth in Europe, but I sense that he was probably out of his depth back at home as well. He could say and do the most insane things, yet get away with it and leave you wanting more. Disaster seemed to follow the man around like iron to a magnet, but strangely enough, you came to look forward to it when it happened. His name was Skeeter. He was from West Virginia.

His name might have been Skeeter on the manifest and written that way in his passport but he made it very clear, very quickly that it wasn't actually his name. His preferred name and what he liked to be called was KFC; that's what his friends called him.

"KFC? Why do they call you that? Are you from Kentucky?"

"No, they call me KFC because I have three cats at home."

I wanted to point out the obvious errors with that particular statement, but I also didn't want to go down the rabbit hole and find out any more about his personal life back home in whatever West Virginian hick backwater he came from. KFC, as we all would come to call him, was good for at least one crazy moment every day, sometimes more. KFC had never left Appalachia country in his entire life and wanted to do one proper look at the non-American world at some point before he died. Naturally, every word he said was spoken in one of the thickest Appalachian drawls you'll ever hear in your life, with many an unexpected bit of local slang thrown in. And for those of you wanting to paint a mental image, KFC looked exactly like what a stereotypical, uneducated, blue-collar American looks like; baseball cap, sneakers, cargo shorts, and his potbelly sticking out of a NASCAR t-shirt that was probably two sizes too small for him. Yep, he had hayseed American written all over him. I quickly abandoned any illusions of KFC blending in with the locals whilst on tour. He also often spoke of his wife back home and how much he loved her and missed her, which begged an obvious question:

"KFC, why didn't she come on this tour with you? Is she afraid to leave home?" Seemed there had to be a reason that he had come on his own. Without adult supervision I wasn't sure how the Americans had let him out of the country.

"No, she didn't want to come; she said that she needed a holiday from me. So, I left her at home to take care of the cats and to look after Doug."

"And who is Doug?" I was finding out more about KFC than I ever wanted.

"Doug? He's the squirrel who lives in the birdhouse."

These types of conversation were entirely normal. Amazingly, my driver Ron and I came to absolutely love KFC. Everything he said was an adventure! Over twenty-six days he became a beloved figure on the bus. He was utterly amazed at some truly simple things, like European pay toilets. After about two weeks on the road, he had to tell Ron and me his thoughts on the operation of the bus.

"You boys are doing one hell of a job! I think it's a HELL OF A JOB! And you don't get lost or anything!"

"Thanks, KFC. Ron and I really appreciate that."

"And this giant bus, that's some amazing tech-nol-o-gee (KFC often spaced out the syllables of words when he got excited). We don't have anything like it in the U-S-of-A!"

I was a bit surprised at that. America has buses that are more-or-less the same as the one we were driving him around in.

"Really, KFC, you haven't seen buses like this back home?"

"Not like this. These ones are fancy, not like American ones. We haven't stopped to fill this bus up with gas even once. It must be a bus that runs on some of that new space technology like they use in space. Why, I think that's just the cat's meow!" Besides the syllable thing, KFC also found that anything interesting or amazing was "the cat's meow." He certainly had a thing about cats.

Ron and I had to glance at each other and stifle a chuckle. Did KFC really think we didn't fuel up the bus? Did he really think we were driving a bus that ran on fusion power or pixie dust of some sort? Ron decided to handle this one.

"KFC, we put fuel in this bus every couple of days. It takes diesel. All the buses take diesel here."

"But we haven't pulled over even once to do that. That's just amazing, simply amazing how the bus can do that then all on its own!"

I had to stop the madness. "KFC, the bus doesn't fill itself! Ron goes and fills up the bus after he drops us off in different places. Ron fills up the bus while you're off taking pictures!"

Poor KFC looked almost like a kid who had just been told that Santa Claus isn't real. I almost felt bad that we had ruined his belief that the bus didn't need to be filled with fuel and ran on some kind of technology that's ordinarily reserved for Star Trek.

"Oh, well that's just too bad then, so it's just like an A-mer-i-can bus?"

"Yep, KFC, it's just like an American bus."

"Well, that's a bit more disappointing then. I thought it was a Eur-o-pean bus!"

I couldn't keep up with this particular conversation anymore, but it kept Ron and me chuckling for the remainder of the day.

*   *   *

Berlin was a major stop for KFC. First, he was quite shocked to find that it was not actually a part of Holland. Second, we were able to determine that whatever historical education KFC had accrued in his life, the system had clearly failed him. This became evident during the course of the city walking tour. The local guide was naturally discussing some of the city's unfortunate Nazi history. A stop at where Hitler's bunker had been, the memorial to the murdered Jews of Europe, and the old Luftwaffe Ministry were all included. At one point, walking between spots, KFC had a few thoughts he wanted to share with me.

"Will, this city is just the cat's meow. Some crazy stuff was going on here!"

"KFC, well, yeah, lots of history here. Absolutely, some crazy stuff, as you say." It was generally a fairly easy task to impress KFC, but nothing prepared me for where the conversation was about to go.

"And this guy Hitler. He sounds like a pretty bad guy!"

If it were possible for my chin to hit the ground it would have. The fact that KFC, up to that morning, didn't really know about one of the worst mass murderers in human history came as a bit of a shock. It took a moment to collect myself and respond.

"Yeah, KFC, he was really quite a bad guy! Not a nice man at all. That's true." One of the great understatements ever, really.

"But he ain't around no more, right?" KFC asked, another jaw-drop moment.

"NO, KFC! He's been gone for some time. We got rid of him. It was called World War Two!"

"Oh, was that what that was all about? Well, that's just the cat's meow then, don't you think?"

"Yes, KFC, it's the cat's meow! Look, you might not want to ask any more questions about it or say anything about it to any of the people who live here. I think they might still feel a bit bad about it. Probably best just to talk about your cats or anything else really. Bit of a sore subject still. I'm not sure the locals want to talk about it."

"That's OK, Will. I can't understand anything anyone here says anyway. Their ac-cent is really hard to figure out!"

"That's because they're speaking German, KFC."

"Oh, so that's not English then?"

"NO! It's a whole different language!"

I didn't think it was possible for a person to not know who Hitler was and not be able to figure out that German is a different language to English. Somehow KFC had and he'd managed all that before lunch.

*   *   *

KFC decided to save his best work for Italy. The country never saw him coming! He left quite a trail in his wake though! It was certainly the country he was most excited about visiting. Mostly because he had seen an actual television program about it before he came. As such, KFC reckoned that it made him a bit of an expert on the place. For myself, Ron, and the other passengers, it simply put a special twist on the insanity.

It's amazing what KFC could get away with. On this particular tour, some passengers would only book the first or second half of the tour, so we always had a slight passenger turnover in Rome. This time around we had two young women, one from New Zealand and one from Australia, who were leaving us in the Eternal City. Ron and I had gotten along quite well with them and it was decided that on their final night in Rome we would take them out for dinner at our favorite Italian restaurant, Joseph's. Just ahead of leaving the hotel, we ran into KFC, who after telling us about his day, wanted to know what was going on.

"KFC, we're just about to go on to dinner," I told him.

"That's just great, Will. You going to go and get a slice of pizza from that truck outside?" The hotel was located in an area of Rome that had its share of unique take-away joints, or in this case, a truck.

"No, KFC. Ron and I are taking the girls out to a proper sit-down restaurant, a steak house actually." I should have realized that offering any extra info was an error. Too late this time.

"Well, that sounds like the cat's meow! I'll come with you!"

And thus, what Ron and I thought was going to be a nice double-date turned into babysitting KFC at a restaurant where wearing cargo shorts and a sweat-stained t-shirt with a picture of a Donald Duck on it wasn't going to be looked upon kindly by the wait staff.

Reading the menu was the most difficult part. Joseph's was not a tourist restaurant. A couple of the staff spoke reasonable English, but everything was in Italian, including the menus. Ordinarily this isn't a problem for English speakers. After all, pizza and spaghetti translate directly into....well, pizza and spaghetti. Yet this was all too much for KFC, who, after a good deal of difficulty decided that he just wanted a Roman house salad. Apparently, he'd already stopped by the pizza truck earlier in the afternoon. The staff was quickly growing impatient with this ill-dressed and immensely ignorant American. It got worse when the food arrived, which was not quite to KFC's lofty standards.

"Will, now, just what in the hell kind of lettuce is this? I ain't ever seen no lettuce that looks like this. Is this some kind of fancy It-al-yan lettuce?" KFC asked, more like yelled, as he held up a piece of regular, ordinary arugula between his index finger and thumb; inspecting it as though it was a fine gem.

"KFC, it's just a bit of arugula. I'm sure you've had it before at home. It's fine; just eat your salad. It's OK."

Not a chance; he kept on with his salad inspection.

"And what is this white stuff in this salad? Is this some kind of vegetable?"

"No, KFC, that's a bit of goat cheese. It's fine. It's just like feta cheese."

"Well, I don't like that at all. Do they have any American cheese? And don't they have any ranch dressing like in the U-S-of-A?" shouted KFC, who, at this point, would have done much better at an actual KFC.

The finer points of Italian dining were clearly lost on KFC. Ron found the whole thing hilarious, whilst the girls were clearly as embarrassed as two twenty-five-year-olds can get who are out to dinner with someone old enough to be their grandfather. Meanwhile, the wait staff was clearly on the verge of tossing the whole lot of us out. I was at my wit's end as well.

"KFC, do you want something else instead of lettuce? Maybe just a small pizza or spaghetti instead? Because I don't think the staff appreciates your picking apart the salad."

"Well, if you can just get me spaghetti and meatballs instead, I think that would be the cat's meow!"

"OK, fine KFC, but you have to calm down and just eat your spaghetti then and try not to say anything to the waitress."

Thus, KFC's meal got sorted out and a potential international incident avoided. KFC's adventure at Joseph's was not quite at an end. He had a key topic that he wanted to discuss before the tiramisu arrived. At least by this point he had happily eaten his pasta, which, as you can guess, had been the cat's meow in KFC's eyes.

"Will, this It-al-y is one hell of a place! Just one hell of a place!"

"Yes, KFC, it's a very interesting place. Ron and I enjoy coming here. I'm glad you've enjoyed it."

"Will, there was this show on the tel-e-vision back at home and they were talking about It-al-y, just before I left home. You should have seen this show!"

"I'm sure it was a very good show, KFC," God only knew what he'd seen on this program that he was about to go on about.

"And can you believe it, Will! There's this town in It-al-y that's got this tower. And this tower it just leans over like that." He used his arm to illustrate the lean as though we had no idea what he was talking about, "and it don't fall over or nothin'! You ever heard of anything like that?"

Given that it is one of the most famous tourist sites in the world, it's safe to say that, yes, we had heard of this tower. But KFC wasn't quite done.

"And even more than that, you know what the craziest thing about this tower is?"

"What's that, KFC?" I was half expecting him to say that aliens had built it or that a family of werewolves lived at the top of it.

"This tower is in a town called piss-a (and he pronounced it just like that)! Can you believe that? Have you ever heard of this tower?"

"YES KFC! We've all heard about this tower! Everyone knows about this tower!" KFC remained undeterred in his talk about the Leaning Tower of Piss-a.

"Do you think if there's time and if we drive near it that we can go see it?"

"Yes, KFC, we'll go see it. Tomorrow! Tomorrow we'll go see it!"

"You're sure? We won't have to go too far out of the way?"

"KFC, it's in the itinerary; it's always been in the itinerary. It's the most famous tower in Europe. Of course we're gonna see it!"

"So, you already know about it then!"

"For the love of God, yes, KFC. Ron and I know all about it, we've been there many times!"

"Well, that's just the cat's meow then!"

And with that, dinner was over. Ron, the girls, and I would have liked to have been upset with KFC over the entire dinner affair. Yet, Ron stated it best later at the hotel bar as the four of us had a nightcap:

"That guy is gold, seriously. We need to have him on every single tour and take him to every restaurant in Europe! That was about the funniest thing I've ever seen in my life!"

KFC was far from finished.

*   *   *

The French Riviera at Nice was our next port of call after Italy, quite possibly my favorite spot on any tour. The French Riviera has anything you could want for a relaxing day: heaps of sunshine, pleasant Mediterranean weather, amazing food, bikini-clad women from northern-Europe. All-in-all, an excellent place to stay for two nights. The hotel was only a hundred meters from the beach and after two weeks traversing Europe, most of the passengers were very keen on getting some time in on the beach and in the surf.

We would always arrive late in the afternoon. I would show the passengers all the highlights of Nice by walking them into town along the Promenade des Anglais, a pleasant jaunt on the road right along the beach. It would take about thirty minutes to get into the town center, but no one ever minded that. The most important fact that I would impart on the passengers was the fact that nude sunbathing is, in fact, not only legal in the French Riviera but actually quite common. This would usually help and suffice enough as a warning for the more reticent and demure passengers. Poor KFC must not have been listening that night.

The great thing for the Tour Leader in the French Riviera was that the free day was an actual free day. We would do an evening trip up to Monaco, but that wasn't until well into the afternoon. The morning and early afternoon were completely one's own. After going to the nearby supermarket to load up on cheap champagne and caviar for the trip up to Monaco that evening, I was keen to change into flip-flops and swimmers and head over to the beach where Ron would hopefully be waiting for me with several minimally clad northern-European women, possibly Swedes. Unfortunately, KFC was just arriving back at that moment, and he had news for me!

"Will! Will! Good thing I found you!" As per usual, KFC was sporting his well-known "I-can't-possibly-be-mistaken-for-anything-but-a-blue-state-American" look.

"KFC, you're looking well. Have you been enjoying the Riviera?" I couldn't imagine him fitting in with the jet-set Riviera crowd, but KFC always did have a way of figuring out his own form of fun.

"Will, this is one hell of a place! One hell of a place! I been walkin' 'round and you wouldn't believe it if I told you!" Clearly KFC had seen something good!

"What's that KFC? What did you find?"

"I was walkin' down on the beach and there was some ladies on that beach and would you believe it? Some of them didn't have any clothes on! And I saw their boobies and everything!" I couldn't really tell if he was pissed off or pleased.

"Is that a fact, KFC? You saw their boobies?" At this point I was just hoping I wouldn't have to have a birds-and-the-bees chat with KFC.

"Yeah, and you know what I think, Will?"

"What's that, KFC?"

"I think some of them ladies should put their shirts back on! Some of their boobies weren't so nice!"

"Well, sometimes, KFC, the girls on the beach don't look like the girls that you see in the magazines."

"And that's also why I kept my shirt on at the beach. I think that those girls would have thought that I was too fat and that I should keep my shirt on!"

"That's probably a good idea KFC, good thinking!" I know I was pleased that he was keeping a shirt on. "And are you going to go back to the beach?"

"No, there were too many naked people. I'm going to stay here where everyone has their clothes on!"

With that KFC went on his way and within five minutes I came to find out for myself that for once, KFC was right. Most of the people at the beach that day should have put their shirts back on. They don't always look like they do in the magazines!

Twenty-six days across Europe with KFC in tow provided more entertainment than the actual scenery and activities. KFC may not have known the difference between Switzerland and Sweden, he may have been surprised and shocked to learn what a bidet did, but at least he wasn't peeing in public fountains or plotting how to rip off taxi drivers! To go into detail about everything the man said and did would take a full book in itself. KFC was by far the craziest and most entertaining passenger I ever had on tour, but he was full value for it. I almost cried when the tour arrived back in London and we had to bid goodbye to the man, but it was time for his adventure to end and for him to back to the "Good old U-S-of-A."

Why Do You Have Cheese in Your Underpants?

The good thing about KFC was that he always simply said what was on his mind. He may not have been the smartest of cookies, but he was always happy with things and approached everything with an almost childlike naiveté. That's why everyone loved him and why everyone was always willing to overlook and forgive him for his moments of madness.

Then you have passengers who you become convinced are just completely mad and should be under a professional's care. They are so unfathomably out of their element and so completely insane that it keeps a Tour Leader awake at night with concern. People about whom you honestly wonder how it is that they've stumbled their way not just onto a tour, but how they've managed to stumble through life as well. Saul and Nina were two of those people.

In introducing Saul and Nina one thing must be made clear; they were very nice people who I think were just insane on some level. They were never rude or obnoxious. They never complained about the food or the hotels or the long bus days. They were simply crazy people who, as a Tour Leader, I always tried to keep an eye out for because they were the type of people who would probably get lost in their own home, let alone in the giant adventureland that is Europe.

Saul and Nina were a retired couple from Los Angeles. Saul had been a high-level engineer of some type. He possessed a number of patents, all for inventions that, once explained to me, made even less sense than they had when he first mentioned them. Saul was clearly one of those people who was an absolute genius when it came to a very narrow and specific area of human knowledge, and a complete washout outside of that area. He definitely had the look of a retired engineer, most days wearing a button-down office shirt, glasses, and trousers. He looked like a guy who worked at NASA mission control in the 1960s.

Nina was originally from Guatemala and had been a happy housewife her whole life. She was quiet, but friendly, and loved three things: Saul, her son Fred, and Jesus. She wasn't a Bible-thumper. She was simply just a deeply religious person; very sweet and innocent and I continually felt bad for both of them for the constant misfortunes that they generally brought upon themselves.

It was definitely Saul who we had to keep the biggest eye on. Over the course of eighteen days, he drove us completely crazy. My Dutch driver, Johan, learned very quickly that he didn't quite know how to use the onboard toilet correctly. The onboard toilet is really only to be used in an emergency. Toilet stops are frequent on tour and much like an airplane toilet, the onboard toilet is not the most convenient. Saul would make a regular routine in using it, and using it often. Even if we were shortly coming up to a service stop. Johan and I didn't like that one bit. Just like an RV, once the toilet tank is full, you can't use the toilet until the tank gets emptied, and that's not the easiest thing to do in Europe. Places to drop a toilet tank are rare in certain countries, especially for a fifty-passenger bus. One morning, just as the passengers were finishing breakfast, I was reminding everyone to use the facilities before we left for the day. I reminded Saul as well, whose response was truly baffling:

"I don't want to use the toilet here at the hotel. I'll save it for the bus!" Saul said. First of all, that was probably not what I wanted to hear immediately after eating. Secondly, no one in their right minds would choose to use the onboard toilet if they had a proper one available.

"No you won't, Saul! Use the one here at the hotel! In fact, the toilet on the bus is full! It's out of service because too many people have used it!" I informed him. In fact, it wasn't full at all; we were simply tired of Saul using it all the time.

Saul had slowly but surely been frustrating everyone, but it was on the day that we were going from Avignon to Barcelona that he did something truly baffling.

The hotel we used in Avignon had one very strange characteristic; passengers sometimes didn't believe me when I explained it. The breakfast room at the hotel would actually employ a security guard whose sole job was to make sure each breakfast patron took only one croissant. It was very much enforced as well. You were free to take as much of everything else as you wanted, but if you tried for a second croissant you ran the risk of being put in the stockade. This croissant rule would be the catalyst for the strangest moment I ever had on tour thanks to Saul.

I never was much of a breakfast guy. My preference was always to hang out at the bus with the driver and help with the luggage. It was a straightforward process. Passengers had a fifteen-minute window to bring their luggage to be loaded and a further thirty minutes for breakfast and then we'd be off. I knew something was up that morning when one of the passengers, a New Zealander, spoke to me about Saul during loading.

"Will, have you seen Saul this morning?"

"No, not yet."

"Well, you need to talk to him about his clothes."

"What's wrong with his clothes?" I asked. The passenger thought for a moment before responding.

"You'll know it when you see it!"

This filled me with a good bit of both dread and curiosity. A few minutes later I saw why. Saul had gotten himself a bit mixed up when getting dressed that morning. He had put his shirt on first, then hiked up his tighty-whitey underwear, and then, for some unfathomable reason, decided to low-ride his shorts that day. His underwear was in clear view. The problem for me was that I couldn't just say something to him about it. A discussion like that needs to be handled with a bit of tact. I simply didn't have a chance to speak with him about it at the hotel. There were always other passengers around. I had to wait until the first stop of the day to have a word with him about it.

Luckily, the first stop of the day was the Pont du Gard, quite possibly the best-preserved Roman aqueduct anywhere in Europe. It's only a short drive out of Avignon and I would always give the passengers a full hour there for photos and, on a nice warm day as this was, a chance to go swimming in the Gardon River.

Arriving at the Pont du Gard, it took only a few minutes to give the passengers the history of the aqueduct, point out where the toilets were, and what time they needed to be back at the bus. The group quickly dispersed to get their photos and have a wander. It was also time for me to have a swim, but first, I had to have the unpleasant chat with Saul about his underwear. He was busy by himself taking photos as I caught up with him.

"Saul, are you enjoying the aqueduct?"

"Yes Will, very much. I used to work with aqueducts. This is very exciting!" He was genuinely happy with this stop.

"That's great Saul. Listen, I have to talk with you about your pants." There was absolutely no point in dancing around the issue.

"My pants? What about my pants? What's wrong with them?" Saul was honestly unaware of the issue.

"Saul, your underwear is sticking quite clearly out of your pants. You've gotta fix it, mate. You're making everyone uncomfortable."

"Oh, right. Can you help me?" Amazingly, Saul was finding a way of making the situation even more uncomfortable.

"No, Saul, this is one of those do-it-yourself situations. Look, it's very easy; just untuck your shirt and then hike up your shorts a bit. Easy-as!" I couldn't imagine why anyone would need help to fix this problem.

It was at this moment that Saul's wife, Nina, entered the fray and thought she could help the situation.

"I told you at the hotel, Saul, that your pants were all wrong. Let me help!" Nina was keen to help Saul and was working at helping him untuck his shirt, but oddly, he became very defensive and started swatting her away.

"Get off me, Nina. I can do it myself, but I have to get them out first!"

What happened next, I wouldn't have believed had I not been there to see it with my own eyes. Saul reached into his underwear, started feeling around and then pulled out three of those triangular foil-wrapped cheese wedges. We had now crossed from the slightly uncomfortable to the insanely bizarre. After collecting myself I had to address this new and very strange turn of events.

"OK, wait a minute, Saul! Just wait a bloody minute! Why do you have cheese in your underpants?"

I wasn't sure I wanted to hear the explanation, but how could you not? This was going to be good. Horrifying as well, I was guessing! Saul was quick to explain.

"Well, you said that there was a guard in the breakfast room and after breakfast I thought that I might like some more cheese later. So, I took some extra ones and hid them in my underwear." Saul said this as though it was the most obvious thing in the world to do! Of course, hide food in your underwear. Why wouldn't you hide food there?

"Saul, that is disgusting!" I said before continuing on with my remonstration, "I'm going to go swimming now and try to forget that I ever saw you do that! And un-tuck your shirt and pull up your pants before you come back to the bus! And throw that cheese in the bin and don't dare try to bring it back on the bus with you! And no more taking food out of the breakfast rooms! Bloody hell, it's turning into one of those days already!" With my tirade over, I went off for my swim.

Johan didn't quite believe me at first when I got back to the bus and told him about Saul's underwear/cheese incident. I didn't blame him as I could hardly believe it myself. Johan though, was coming to the realization that we had a special case in the form of Saul and the underwear/cheese incident wasn't to be his last bit of craziness.

* * *

The tour that Saul and Nina were on was a very relaxed one to run for the Tour Leader. There were only twenty-two passengers in total so everyone got to know each other quite well and it was a nice group to lead for eighteen days. We all learned early on that Saul and Nina, Saul

in particular, were a unique pair. Everyone did well to keep an eye on
them as they were apt to get lost or lose track of time. It was a proper
babysitting job. Amazingly, we never once lost them to such a degree
that we had to leave them behind. Nina did get proper lost in Siena,
Italy; but through sheer dumb luck, accidentally made her way back to
the bus. Ordinarily we do leave passengers behind; our itineraries left
little time to sit around, and most passengers are capable enough to
catch a bus or train to the next destination. With Saul and Nina, I had
little confidence that they would be able to figure that out, so always
keeping an extra eye out for them became second nature for everyone.

Saul proved to be completely lacking in social mores. Early in
any tour we would do an introductions activity on the bus. I always
kept it simple. Give us your name, where you're from, what you're
most looking forward to seeing/doing on the tour, a quick interesting
fact about yourself, and what your favorite movie or song is. From
time to time, I'd mix it up with something different, but that was the
gist of the introductions. For the most part, the responses were fairly
predictable. People often would be looking most forward to seeing Italy
or Switzerland. Seeing the Eiffel Tower or going on a Venetian gondola
ride were popular responses as well. In terms of interesting personal
facts, most people liked to talk about their kids or grandkids or what
line of work they were in. Once in a while someone would have a really
amazing personal fact such as they'd climbed Kilimanjaro or slept with
Mick Jagger. On this occasion, Saul decided to let the entire bus in on
his interesting fact:

"My interesting fact is that when Nina and I were in the taxi to go
to the airport to fly here for the tour, I peed my pants!" He said this as
through it was the most obvious thing in the world to say to a group of
strangers that you didn't know and that you'd be spending nearly three
weeks with. As the Tour Leader it's difficult to respond to something
like that.

"OK, thanks, Saul! That's Saul from Los Angeles." I figured it best
to completely ignore that elephant in the room.

Early on in the tour we celebrated one of the passenger's birthday. It
was actually our youngest passenger, a young boy named Matteo from

the Philippines, who was turning eight during our visit to Rome. Of course, between his parents and myself, we put together a little bit of a bus birthday party for him. We tracked down a cake and a few little gifts and Matteo was well pleased with all the attention and everyone enjoyed seeing him celebrate his special day. It just so happened that Saul was turning sixty-five a few days later and in the wake of Matteo's birthday, he had a few questions.

"Will, that was a very nice party that we had for that young man," he said. I don't think Saul ever did learn any of the other passengers' names.

"Yes, it was Saul, it's always nice to see the kids enjoy things and to get a bit of attention." I had a feeling about where the conversation was going, but I wasn't going to push things.

"Did you know, Will, that on Friday it's going to be my birthday?" Saul said this as though we were due to celebrate Christmas, the Fourth of July, and Thanksgiving all at once.

"Yes Saul! I did know that! And you're turning sixty-five. You'll be a senior citizen!"

"Do you think that maybe we can have a party with cake and presents and birthday hats for my birthday, too?" Saul was really angling for his party to be as big or bigger than Matteo's. Bringing Saul back down to Earth was going to hurt him a bit.

"OK, Saul. Matteo's eight years old. He's still a little kid. Little kids get to have birthday parties because they're ... little kids. You're an adult, Saul. You're going to get a birthday card and probably a magnet or a keychain or maybe a souvenir shot glass with a picture of a Swiss cow on it. And then we'll sing "Happy Birthday". That'll be it." I almost felt bad having to say it to him, but as it turned out, there was no problem at all.

"Really? I might get a keychain for my birthday?" Saul was excited again!

"Yeah, Saul, we can get you a keychain! Would that be OK for your birthday?"

"Oh yes! I like keychains! Oh, and Nina will be so happy when I tell her!"

"OK, Saul, maybe you should go and tell her right now!"

So Saul got to celebrate his sixty-fifth birthday in Switzerland and got both a keychain and a magnet and looked to be just as happy as Matteo had been a few days earlier. At least Saul was easy to impress!

*   *   *

It was on the drive from Switzerland up to the Rhine Valley in Germany that Saul found a way to break Johan, the driver. Johan was an immensely likeable driver. He knew his job well. The passengers liked him and he and I worked well together as a team. Johan, though, was a very quiet and reserved guy. He didn't make a habit of hanging out or engaging with the group so much; only when he really had to. Johan, over the course of the tour, grew increasingly agitated with the things Saul said and did. I would notice that every time I was speaking to Johan. If Saul came by, Johan would leave. The dam was ready to break.

Leaving Switzerland to go to Germany we would actually re-enter France. This was done to avoid the German tax office where we would have to pay an extra fee when we exited Switzerland. Whereas if you crossed into France and then into Germany, you'd avoid this fee altogether. It's not exactly the most compelling drive in the world once one is out of Switzerland. It's basically just forest and one toilet stop all the way to the Rhine Valley. On this day I can remember very well that Saul was sitting about two-thirds of the way down the bus. I was sitting in the very first row in the Tour Leader seats. An American woman, Claire, was directly behind me with her college-aged daughter, Joanna. Directly across from me at the front was a lovely young Canadian couple, Fern and David. Behind them was a retired Kiwi couple, a tough former police officer named Frank and his wife, Diane.

I was on the microphone for a short spell. I can't remember exactly what it was that I was talking about. Likely some very innocuous and not very memorable information. The Rhine River in that area does act as the German/French border and the area near Strasbourg does have a historical appeal. At some point, however, I had finished whatever it was I was talking about and I did the standard thing; I asked if anyone had any questions. I didn't expect that there would be, but cue Saul at this point, he had a question.

"Yeah, Will, I have a quick question."

"Fair enough, Saul, shoot!"

"Yes, I'm just wondering, what's the scenery like here in France?" Again, he asked this as though it were the most obvious thing in the world to ask.

Even though he was fairly close to the back of the bus, Saul's voice carried. I know his voice carried and that Johan heard him because the bus swerved a bit. Clearly Johan was shocked at what he'd heard.

I had a tough time keeping myself composed as well. I actually had to turn off the mike and duck my head down to keep Saul from seeing me laugh. I took just a few seconds to sort myself before ducking back up. The problem now was that I could see the reactions of the nearby passengers.

-Joanna, the college-aged American girl was giving me a giant smirk that said, "Answer the question! And please answer it in the most ruthless way possible!"

-Joanna's mother, Claire, was clearly whispering to Joanna to behave herself.

-Fern, the young Canadian wife was holding her left palm to her forehead and muttering, "What the f%$#!"

-Both David, the Canadian husband, and Diane, the Kiwi wife, were sitting quietly and looking straight ahead but shaking their heads in disbelief.

-Frank, the Kiwi husband, had turned around in his aisle seat and was glaring at Saul and said, loud enough for almost everyone to hear, "He can't possibly be serious!"

Unfortunately, Saul WAS serious. He was sitting there eager for an actual answer to this shocking question. I had to double-check to make sure I'd heard it right.

"Um, Saul, I didn't quite hear you, maybe. Did you just ask what the scenery is like here?"

"Yes, what is the scenery like?"

"OK, Saul. If you'll refer to your window, the one directly beside you, you'll see that there's a lot of rocks, trees, and hills." I really thought this would put an end to it, but Saul had his hand up again. Somehow, he had a follow-up question.

"Yeah, Will, is the scenery going to continue?"

I could see the looks of every person on the bus at this point and to describe their facial expressions as shocked is putting it mildly.

"Yes, Saul, the scenery is going to continue. Later on, there will even be a river! OK, no more questions!" I certainly couldn't take it anymore. Luckily, the passengers had all changed their view of things from shocked to amused.

The toilet stop came in short order. The passengers only needed a quick fifteen minutes. With only twenty-two passengers there was plenty of time to get a quick coffee and croissant as we headed on into Germany. It was a lovely, sunny day and Johan and I were having a chat with some of our Filipino passengers before reboarding. I could see from a distance that Saul was making a beeline straight for us and he looked a bit perturbed.

"Will, I need to talk to you!" Saul was coming straight to the point.

"Saul, what can I do for you?"

"You said that the scenery was going to continue and that there'd be a lot of rocks, trees, and hills!"

"Yes, Saul, that's generally what scenery is. What's the problem?"

"Well. then what is that?" Saul pointed to the adjacent football pitch as though it was an alien spacecraft from Mars. It was also at this point that Johan and the Filipinos went back to the bus, abandoning me to my fate with Saul.

"Saul, that's a soccer field. That's where people go to play soccer." It was impossible to put the answer more delicately than that. Still, it wasn't good enough for Saul.

"Oh, so that's not part of the scenery then?"

"Saul, do you want it to be part of the scenery or do you not want it to be part of the scenery?"

"Well, it looks like part of the scenery. It's green just like the scenery."

"Fine, Saul, it's part of the scenery then! Get on the bus now. Time to go!" I was dreading the very thought of Saul asking another question. How complicated could scenery possibly be?

We continued on our drive into Germany. We were not so far from the Rhine Valley now. The Rhine Valley was always a fun stop, especially for the Tour Leader and driver. We usually stayed in a riverside hotel in a town called Boppard which was right beside the boat dock. We would stop and spend time in St. Goar, another town about twenty kilometers upriver. Once the passengers had had a chance to buy cuckoo clocks, beer steins, get their pictures, and a quick bite; I'd put them all on the river boat. It was a general tendency that the Tour Leader wouldn't go on the boat with the passengers. We Tour Leaders usually preferred to go to the hotel with the driver. We'd get there about an hour before the boat would and organize the keys and check ourselves in. I also usually had time enough to go talk to the folks at the wine store and get a wine tasting organized and stop at the Euro Shop, a sort of European-style dollar store. On this day, I was looking forward to this short bit of time away from the passengers. At least, I was until Johan needed to have a talk with me not too far from the Rhine Valley.

"Will, can you come down to the jump-seat. I need to talk to you," Johan whispered to me as I was doing some paperwork.

"Yeah. Sure, Johan." I could tell immediately that he didn't really want the passengers to hear us. Clearly, he had something particularly important to discuss, but I couldn't imagine what it could be.

"Look, Will, when we get to St. Goar, I need you to go on the river cruise with the passengers." Johan asked with more than just a hint of desperation.

"Johan, I don't want to go on the cruise. I just want to go to the hotel, sort out the keys, get checked in, go see about the wine tasting, and chill out for a few moments. No, Johan, I'm not going on the boat cruise." It was as simple as that as far as I was concerned.

"OK, Will, you HAVE to go on the boat cruise with them. Call it a personal favor, but you HAVE to. I need you to go on that boat." Johan was undeterred; he needed this one.

"Fine, Johan, I'll go on the cruise as a favor, but you have to tell me why. Why is my going on the boat cruise of such vital importance?"

"OK, Will, I'll tell you, but you can't tell anyone. You keep this a secret." Now I was looking forward to things. What fantastic secret did Johan have to impart to me? Johan continued:

"I need you to go on the boat so that I can have thirty minutes to myself, so that I can be all alone…so that I can cry." That was it, nothing else. I was taken aback.

"So, you can go cry, Johan? What's the deal?" I was mildly curious.

"That man, that crazy American man, is driving me crazy and I can't take it anymore! It's only one more day after today that I need to see or hear him, but I can't do it! Everything he says is crazy and I can't do it anymore. So, I need some time to be alone and cry and I need it as soon as possible!"

Johan was clearly in a bad way, and you always want your driver at the top of his game. Since it was a spectacular day, going on the Rhine cruise wasn't going to be the end of the world. Johan was a good guy, so I'd do him this favor, but not without getting one in return.

"OK, Johan, I'll go on the boat cruise. But, after you're done being a Johnny Weeping Willow, can you take care of my keys for me and sort out the check-in?"

"Yeah, no problem, and take five Euros out of my money box and get yourself a beer on the boat, too. Thanks for that, Will. You have no idea how much I need this."

"That's fine, Johan. You go and enjoy your cry!"

"Oh, and one more thing, Will," said Johan. I knew that couldn't have been the end of it.

"What's that?" I asked.

"You keep that nut away from me at all costs. You do whatever you need to, but I don't want to hear or see him again." Johan meant business.

"I can't guarantee anything, Johan, but I'll do my best! And I'm taking ten Euros and having two beers."

We arrived very shortly after in St. Goar. The passengers enjoyed their time there and were very pleasantly surprised to find me joining them on the boat.

"Why did you change your mind, Will?" asked one of the passengers.

"Oh, it's such a lovely day on the river. I'd be a fool not to be on the boat today!"

The cruise was fantastic. Being on the Rhine River with a fine German beer and a slice of Schwartzwalder Kirsch Torte (Black Forest Cherry/Chocolate Cake) is not the worst fate a Tour Leader can face. The time flew by and soon enough we were at Boppard where Johan was waiting at the dock with a full basket of keys.

I made sure to be the first person off the boat and ran straight to Johan so that I could have a quick word with him before the passengers arrived. Sure enough, his eyes had a slight redness and puffiness to them.

"Did you have a nice cry then?" I asked him.

"Oh God, Will, it was better than sex!" Johan was back to normal.

"Glad you're feeling better, mate!"

"Much better, and all the keys are there and the room numbers and who's staying where. And I got all of your luggage moved to your room already, so you don't have to worry about that. Thanks again!" I definitely had a much happier driver, for sure!

"No worries, Johan. Thanks for the check-in."

"Oh, and Will, don't forget: keep that crazy man away from me!"

We got the passengers' luggage offloaded and into their rooms in good time. Saul wasn't quite done with his particular brand of craziness that day. Later on, at the wine tasting, I caught him trying to pour a fine glass of Rhine Riesling back into the bottle.

"Saul, what in god's name are you doing?" Marcus, the wine shop owner, would lose his temper in a hurry if he saw this.

"I didn't like that glass and I didn't want it to go to waste, so I thought it would be a good idea to pour it back in the bottle."

"Put the glass and bottle down, Saul. We don't need your potentially backwashed wine contaminating the rest of a perfectly good bottle! I

said this from a bit of a selfish perspective. I had designs on finishing
that bottle off on my own.

"Well, what do I do with the glass?"

"Just leave it. Marcus will clean it up later!" I certainly wasn't going
to drink his used glass of wine.

By this point, we were near the end of the tour. The only destination
left was Amsterdam and a final drive back to London to finish the
eighteen-day tour. Johan would finish his tour in Amsterdam and
we would use a shuttle driver to do the final drive back to the United
Kingdom. I wish I could say that Saul and Nina's tour finished on a
high note. Unfortunately they never made it back to England with the
rest of the group. On the final day, during breakfast at the hotel, well-
dressed thieves walked into the breakfast room and snatched a number
of purses and handbags. Passengers had been warned about this. Tour
Leaders would always tell the passengers to leave all their belongings
in their rooms and not to bring them into the public areas of the hotel.
Nina, sadly, did not heed this warning. Her purse with all her money,
credit cards, and worst of all, her passport, were all taken in the blink
of an eye. Even worse luck, we were due to leave in just five minutes.

With no passport it was impossible for Nina to return to the UK
with the group. Saul, ever loyal, stayed behind as well. I took as much
extra time as I could to outline to them what they needed to do to
get sorted out. A police report would be needed, then a visit to the
American consulate, and calls to their credit card companies. Luckily,
the hotel staff were well known to me and promised that they would
help where they could.

I felt really rotten for this final twist that Saul and Nina would have
to face. No one deserved that. I never did find out if it all worked out
for them, though, I'm sure they managed in the end. The rest of the
passengers also felt quite badly for them as well. The only silver lining
for us was that we didn't need to worry about a final day of baby-sitting
Saul and Nina, but to see them have to leave the tour in such horrible
circumstances did sting.

It was only as we entered France on the way to the cross-Channel
ferry port at Calais that the mood lightened a bit. Frank, the ever-tough

police office from New Zealand, raised his hand with a question as I was describing the customs process for going back to the UK:

"Yeah, Will, I was just curious, and seeing as how were just about to leave France I have a final question to ask you."

"What's that, Frank?"

"What's the scenery like here in France?"

Barry! You Talk Barry!

Of all the thousands of passengers that a Tour Leader meets over the course of a career, there's always that special passenger or passengers that melt your heart and are impossible to forget for all the right reasons. Ironically, the couple that I remember most and who I absolutely adored, I couldn't even converse with! Duc and Lien, over a two-week period, came to be the most cherished of individuals and the most unforgettable pair I ever met on tour!

It wasn't often that we would get Vietnamese people on tour. We would get plenty of Filipinos and Malaysians, but people from these countries speak English, so we'd always have heaps of them. Every so often, a Vietnamese person or group would be booked on, but a Tour Leader could be fairly confident that they would be highly educated, speak English, and be able to mix in with the group. Duc and Lien were none of these.

Duc and Lien were at the meeting point in London on day one, ready to start a twelve-day tour. What struck me on first impression was how short they were. Neither of them was any taller than about five foot, two inches. They patiently waited as I checked in all the other passengers and the luggage was loaded. Once this was finished, I walked over to the two of them. They had a young man in his twenties with them. He was the first one to speak and introduce himself.

"Hello! You're Will the Tour Leader?" he asked in perfect English.

"Yes, yes, I am. And who would you all be?"

"Will, my name is Barry, and these are my parents; my father, Duc and my mother, Lien." Barry's parents were beaming great big smiles and both shook my hand straight away with a great deal of enthusiasm. I liked them immediately! Barry continued.

"Will, I've come down with my parents this morning to help them get checked onto the tour and to speak with you about them and the unique situation that you'll be facing." Barry spoke these words with a little bit of trepidation. Tour Leaders are used to dealing with odd situations, but I could tell that this one would be a bit quite a bit different.

Barry took a moment, speaking to his parents in Vietnamese and then returned to chatting with me. As it turned out, Barry was living and going to university in London. His parents had never left Vietnam until this trip, spoke not a single word of English, or any other language for that matter. Since Barry was busy with his studies and his parents were visiting for several weeks, he thought it was best to book them on a European tour. I had one very obvious question.

"Was there not a Vietnamese speaking tour they could book on?"

"They aren't running at this time of year and your company has the lowest priced tours. You have to understand, Will; they worked their whole lives to send me to school in London. They've never seen anything outside of their village, they've never even been to Ho Chi Minh City!" Barry spoke so tenderly about his parents that I couldn't help but feel for them. I made it my mission to put on a good show for them for the next twelve days.

Since his parents didn't speak anything except Vietnamese, which I certainly didn't, I took the next twenty minutes with Barry to go over how I would be able to help his parents out any way I could. Barry made it remarkably simple in the end.

"Will, my parents are the loveliest people in the world. They will never complain about anything and they won't cause you a problem. They'll eat what you tell them to eat and they'll do what you tell them to do. They just don't understand English. I'll give you my phone number here in London. If anything happens, feel free to call me any time, day or night!" With that, there was nothing left for Barry to do. He said his goodbyes to his parents and we were left to it.

Duc and Lien continued to smile the biggest smiles and immediately had me take a photo of them with the driver. I had them come on board and they found a spot to sit and we were off to Paris!

My first comment to the entire group wasn't "Hello, my name is Will," or to introduce the tour. On this tour I led off with:

"Does anyone on this bus speak any degree of Vietnamese whatsoever?"

Crickets. Not a single other person spoke a single word of Vietnamese. I'd be all on my own in trying to communicate with Duc and Lien. Just them, I and Google translate, which we came to find was almost completely useless. The algorithms hadn't been perfected quite yet.

That first day was a learning curve. The biggest issue was how to communicate to Duc and Lien at what time they had to be back at the bus and where they needed to be. This was solved with a simple notepad. I would write down at what time they needed to be back and then I'd point at the place they would need to be. Simplicity is often best and this system worked for the whole two weeks. They were never ever late or in the wrong place. Not even once. If only all the English-speaking passengers could have been that good!

Barry was right about one thing; his parents were happy about everything! Even really boring things were of interest to them. Getting to Paris and checking into the hotel, you could see how excited they were to be in France and what adventures they would have. I had a few spare moments after check-in, so I went to their room, just to ensure that everything was fine for them. I reckoned that even rural Vietnamese people would know what OK meant and I wasn't wrong. When they opened the door and saw me there making the OK sign with my index finger and thumb, they insisted that I join them for a quick in-room tea. I was really learning to like this couple.

The group met shortly after and boarded the bus for a tour of the city, after which time we went on to dinner in Montmartre. Every stop we made, they were keen to immediately come to me to know at what time to be back and then join the group for photos. The word "photo" was one English word that they learned very quickly. It wasn't just me that was learning to love this couple; the entire bus took a liking to them and were happy to help them out and keep an eye on them. No one wanted to lose this adorable Vietnamese couple! Their enthusiasm was infectious! The fact that the entire coach had taken a liking to Duc and Lien took a great deal of stress off my shoulders as we now had forty-five sets of eyes keeping an eye on them instead of just one. Even on that first night at dinner, Duc and Lien fit in brilliantly! They sat and conversed in Vietnamese with everyone as though it made no difference at all! They were just happy to be there and to be accepted. They weren't just being accepted; they were becoming the most popular people on the tour!

The first night in Paris on any tour is a long one and we arrived back in the hotel at just after eleven. It never mattered how tired I was; I always had a night-cap at the hotel bar and anyone who wanted to join me was welcome to do so. I'd only just sat down to my beer and a chat with two of the Filipino passengers when there was a tap on my shoulder. It was Duc and Lien, both standing there smiling. Lien was holding a phone out to me and said only one thing:

"Barry! You talk Barry!" At least Google translate got this one more-or-less correct.

So, a nightly tradition was born. Every single night of the tour, once we were back at the hotel and done for the day, I would have a long chat with Barry about what would be happening the next day and any issues that his parents needed to know about. It worked exceedingly well. Barry made it clear that I was to sign his parents up for every optional excursion and to collect money from them in the same way that I was informing them of where to be and at what time. It worked a treat every time. Every evening whilst I spoke with Barry, Duc and Lien would always wait patiently, never in a rush. I never once saw them not smiling!

That's not to say that Duc and Lien weren't smart. They were exceedingly intelligent people. They were able to pick up on subtle cues as the tour went. Whenever I came down the bus to collect money, they always knew what was going on and had cash ready to go. It was on the second night in Paris speaking to Barry that I had a question for him.

"Barry, we go to Switzerland tomorrow. During the drive, each passenger comes to the front and speaks on the microphone about who they are, where they're from, stuff like that. How should we do this for your parents?"

Between the four of us we figured out a plan. Duc and Lien would come to the microphone and both would speak in Vietnamese. It didn't matter at all what they actually said. Once they were finished speaking, I would then tell the bus about Duc and Lien in English.

The next day the stage was set and the big moment came as the bus ambled along the French motorway. Duc and Lien listened intently to everyone else, even without understanding a word. When it was their turn, they came up, clearly excited to have a turn to speak on the microphone. For two minutes they spoke entirely in Vietnamese before thrusting the microphone back into my hands.

"Hello! I am Duc and this is my wife, Lien. We are from Vietnam and we run a fruit shop. We love our son, Barry, who lives in London, and we've never been to Europe before! We are excited to see the mountains in Switzerland and we hope to be fluent in English by the end of the tour and we hope that you will all be our friends and come visit us in Vietnam!" Duc and Lien sat smiling the whole time and grinned even more broadly as they walked back to their seats to a huge applause!

Duc and Lien never did anything particularly noteworthy or funny or memorable at any point. There never was a crazy situation that they got themselves into or a strange moment that needed to be sorted out. They were simply a super happy couple who were enthusiastic about everything. They just couldn't communicate verbally with anyone else. It didn't stop them from having an amazing time. Everywhere we went they wanted their photo taken. Not just of themselves either; they wanted their photo taken with everyone in the tour! It became a regular feature of every photo stop that all of the other passengers as well as the driver and I would be included in their photos. This little couple from Vietnam did more to create a cohesive tour group than any other passengers I ever saw!

One day on the drive, during a quiet moment on the bus, Lien came to the front of the bus. She had a giant bag of candy with her. This had been arranged the previous evening during the Barry talk. It was a bag of Vietnamese candy that they wanted to share with the whole group. Lien took immense pride in showing everyone how to carefully unwrap it, as each wrapper had a Vietnamese proverb written on it, not unlike a Chinese fortune cookie. It was agreed by everyone later that the candy was actually inedible and rather awful tasting, but we all got it down anyway so as not to hurt Duc and Lien's feelings. We all appreciated the gestures

Many Tour Leaders might have gotten annoyed at having to take time in the evenings to have someone in London translate all the necessary information into a different language for two passengers. I, however, came to really enjoy the conversations with Barry and having Lien search the lobby for me, holding out her mobile phone and saying "Barry! You talk Barry!" I had to ask Barry, near the end of the tour, the question that I had worried about the whole time.

"Barry, you obviously speak with your parents every day for a considerable time about things. Are they actually having a good time? They seem to be, but they can't speak English. Are they just putting on a brave face? They haven't been too frustrated about the language barrier, I hope!"

"Will, I can tell you honestly; they are having the most brilliant and amazing time of things! They are so happy that you, the driver, and all the other passengers have done everything you can to make them feel comfortable and included! All they talk about is how upsetting it will be to get back to London and not see their new friends! They really have had the most fantastic trip!"

It really pleased me to know that we had all had a massive impact on Duc and Lien. When we did arrive back in London and were saying our goodbyes, Duc and Lien gave everybody, myself included, a huge hug and we all said goodbye to them as the closest of friends. When they said goodbye to me, they included a beautiful handwritten card. It took several months for me to find a Vietnamese person to read it to me. It was an incredibly special and heartfelt message thanking me for all I had done to help them throughout the tour and best wishes for all possible happiness and success in the future. Barry was there to pick them up as well. I think he thought that it would be a short and simple process, but between all the goodbyes and tears, it took nearly twenty minutes for him to finally pry his parents away and get them on the train. I'm sure that Duc and Lien continue to run their fruit shop in Vietnam and I hope they're doing so with smiles on their faces as wide as the ones that they had every single second of their tour through Europe with me.

Will, That's Captain's Orders!

Every tour contains a number of passengers that make a long-lasting impact on the Tour Leader. Whilst most people on a tour will be quickly forgotten and not remembered for anything at all memorable, you do get the passengers who make a very deep and lasting impact. Then, every once in a great while, you get a passenger who is so utterly unforgettable, that rarely a day goes by that you don't think of that passenger.

Captain Ned was one of those passengers.

He didn't start that way. At the beginning of the two-week tour, during check-in at Greenwich, he seemed to be a run-of-the-mill British pensioner. He was a large, well-built individual, but he carried himself with a certain air of authority. He had just turned eighty, but had the look of a man fifteen years younger. He was on tour with his best mate, a man named Danny, who was the exact opposite of Ned. Ned was a talker and always gabbing on about something or other. Danny was very quiet and soft-spoken and whilst Ned was well above six feet in height, Danny was barely five and a half feet tall and was rail thin. They made for quite the odd couple physically. The one thing they had very much in common, though, was they both enjoyed a good time!

I knew we had a couple of lads right from day one. One thing I would make abundantly clear in my first day remarks was the need for the passengers to be on time. The bus leaves at the appointed hour! If you're not there, my assumption as a Tour Leader is that you've found something better to do and we'll just leave. Captain Ned wanted a quick chat with me about that policy.

"Will, about your "I'll Leave You Behind Policy," if ever Danny and I are late to meet the group back up, don't ever fuss it! You get on with things. Danny and I will catch you up at the next destination! If we're ever late it's probably because we've found a bar with some women in it and we're there for the duration!"

"Gee, Ned, sounds like fun. If you're ever going to be late like that, can you please phone me and tell me which bar you're at?" I had to ask as Captain Ned's excursions seemed like far more fun than the scheduled ones.

"No problem, Will. You'd be a welcome guest! And while we're at it, please, call me CAPTAIN Ned!"

It was during introductions on day two that we found out how it was that Captain Ned came to be a Captain. As it turned out, he had been a cruise ship captain for one of the major cruise lines for thirty-five years. He had sailed the world many times over in that capacity. He had also sailed the world many times entirely on his own. Over the course of the tour, he came to tell me and the entire bus stories of such action and adventure that my own paled in comparison. He had actual pirate stories! Ordinarily at group meals I would try to sit with different people every time, get to know everybody; I soon noticed on this tour that I was trying to sit with Captain Ned every chance I got!

It was a great tour overall in terms of passengers. It was the most chilled-out group of passengers I ever had. We had a major problem on day one entering France. My driver Derek (yes, the same driver that seems to appear in all the disaster stories) was ticketed for a major violation by the French police. There was a fault in the tachymeter reading in the bus. The driver from the day before had not put their card into the onboard driver log system, so there were three-hundred kilometers of unregistered driving on the meter as a result, a major violation. This wasn't Derek's fault, but since he was the driver in the moment, the French police ticketed him and we ended up delayed by nearly four hours. This often makes for some very cranky passengers, but this group, all fifty of them, took things very much in stride and never complained once! We were fortunate, Derek and I, to have a considerate and happy bunch of passengers. The passengers all busied themselves by finding the most fun way to kill time at the French roadside service center that the police had consigned us to wait at. For most of the passengers, it was listening to the first of Captain Ned's many amazing adventures!

"Oh, being stuck here for a few hours isn't so bad! Why, I remember one time when I was sailing through the Straits of Malacca…" Captain Ned managed to kill off the four hours by narrating, in full detail, the many times he'd been delayed by over-zealous harbormasters, angry port police, high-strung pirates, and cranky dock workers. Captain Ned quickly became the most beloved and popular passenger and it was just day one! Yes, indeed, Captain Ned became captain of the passengers.

The next day, on the drive to the Rhein Valley, during his introduction, Captain Ned spoke briefly of more adventures and his work as a cruise ship captain. Apparently, cruise ship captains don't actually have much to do with sailing the ship. This confused me. Captain Ned was happy to clear up the issue.

"Bollocks to that, Will! Sailing the ship is the job of the First Officer! It's the job of the Captain to entertain the first-class bigwigs, drink the finest alcohol, sample the finest food, and put the moves on the attractive women!"

"Really, Captain Ned? And how would one go about getting this sort of work….?" I asked, as it seemed like a good career for me.

"I don't know, Will. Seems like you've got a remarkably similar sort of gig going on right here! And without the seasickness and vomiting pensioners!" (This happened well before I ever met a certain man named Dhevi)

To me, Captain Ned became deputy Tour Leader. One of the unwritten roles of a Tour Leader is that you must also provide a good deal of entertainment. For me, this was never a problem; talking on a microphone, making jokes, telling stories, are all things I enjoy doing. Captain Ned reveled in doing these things. I quickly determined that I didn't need to provide the onboard entertainment on the tour. If things got a bit boring and we needed a bit of energy all I had to do was pick up the microphone and say:

"Captain Ned, this is Will. Could you please come to the front of the bus for a minute?"

It wouldn't take long before Captain Ned would be up at the front, "Yes, Will. What did you need?"

"About an hour of storytelling from you. The passengers are starting to nod off a bit. Gotta get the energy back up!"

"No problem, Will! What do you want this time? Action? Adventure? Comedy? Romance?"

"I don't know, Captain Ned. You decide! Surprise us!" It never mattered what story he told; it was engrossing every time!

Captain Ned, in addition to pirate stories, had ones about becoming a Buddhist monk, trekking the Amazon, getting involved in civil wars, partying with celebrities. You name it, he had it! Passengers would get cranky if Captain Ned went too long without being on the microphone!

Paris was the final stop on the tour. We always sold passengers on a cabaret show for the second night. Captain Ned came to me on arrival day in Paris with a question.

"Will, has anybody signed up for that cabaret show yet?

"Not as yet, Captain Ned. Would you like to?"

"God no, Will, it sounds awful! Well, the nudity bit's alright, but other than that, well, never mind. I just need you to not take any bookings for it. I've got a much better idea for tomorrow night," Captain Ned said. He clearly had something up his sleeve.

Captain Ned's plan was simple. He had me book out an entire restaurant in the Nineteenth Arrondissement near the hotel for the evening. He wanted to take everyone out for the final night of the tour!

"You know, Captain Ned, this won't be cheap. Between dinner and what is likely to be a lot of alcohol, we're looking at possibly a, well, awfully expensive night anyway!" I said. I figured Captain Ned should know that the cruise line wasn't going to be picking up the tab on this one. This would be all on him!

"Yes, Will, I know that! I'm eighty years old, I have the world's biggest pile of money and I want to get rid of a bunch of it! The only way I can do that is to take this entire group for dinner and it's only going to work properly if I have you and Danny sitting on either side of me while I hold court! And make sure those cute Australian girls are sitting across from us as well! I'll give you a seating chart later!"

"OK, Captain Ned, just thought it was a good idea to remind you that dinner and drinks for fifty people…" I started to say, but Captain Ned cut me off.

"Will, that's Captain's orders! I won't have any dissention in the ranks! We're all going out for dinner, we're all going to have the greatest night of our lives, and I'll be paying for every cent of it!" You couldn't accuse Captain Ned of not having a very thorough plan in mind!

And thus, on the final night of the tour, Captain Ned indeed held court and was the master emcee of one of the great nights that I and everyone privileged enough to be there ever had! Every single passenger on the tour came out (save for two cranky Australian pensioners who must have been allergic to fun). The final bill came to nearly eight-thousand Euros, which Captain Ned put onto his platinum card without a second thought!

Captain Ned kept surprising me right to the end the next day on the drive back to London. Arriving at Calais and boarding the DFDS ferry back to the United Kingdom, he came to me and Derek as everyone was filing up to the passenger area of the ship.

"OK, boys. Let me guess; you two are heading to the lorry driver's lounge, aren't you?"

"Well, Captain Ned, that's what we usually do. Not much else to do on a two-hour DFDS ride back to Dover," I responded. Usually, we sat there doing out end of tour administration work and counting our tip money while eating the world's worst free buffet meal.

"No, boys, that's no good at all! Stuff the driver's lounge. You're coming with me and Danny!"

"And where, pray tell, are we going?" Derek asked.

"Up to the bridge. I know the captain of this ferry and he's invited us up to the captain's lounge. The liquor on offer will be of the highest quality!"

Sure enough, within two minutes of speaking to guest services, the captain of the ferry was on hand and greeting Captain Ned! We were led immediately up to the bridge where passengers certainly aren't meant to be and given a full tour of the place. They even let me sound the horn as we left Calais!

It turned out that Captain Ned wasn't lying. He and Captain Dave were old friends from their days in the Royal Navy. Apparently, all the captains of all the large ships know each other, it's a very tight fraternity. For the duration of the crossing, we were treated like royalty. Not that we went anywhere. The bridge was where all the action was and we spent the whole time listening to Captain Ned and Captain Dave trade old war stories (in some cases they were actual war stories). It was the first and only ever DFDS ferry ride that I was unhappy to see end.

It was an extremely sad end to that tour. The group had been brilliant, but it was Captain Ned who made that tour into what it was. His personality, love of life, and desire to share that outlook with everybody he met made it such an enjoyable time for everybody on board. I put a recommendation into my tour report that read as follows:

"Suggest that for the future benefit of group and passenger cohesiveness, give a free paid place on any tour of his choosing to Captain Ned. One can give him the title of "Entertainment Liaison" for administrative purposes, but continue to employ the moniker "Captain Ned" for practical purposes."

James the Giant Peach

Florence always seemed to be a city in which things happened on tour. We never stayed there long, but there was always action for my groups when we were there.

It was a city in which I always told my groups to be highly vigilant of themselves and their belongings. Italy and Spain were always the two biggest pickpocketing countries in Europe and Rome, Barcelona, and Florence were generally the three cities in which a person was most likely to be pickpocketed. With Florence being such a beautiful city, passengers were often taken in by the majesty of the place and would become a bit lax in watching over their personal belongings. As we would drive into the city, I would take great pains to tell my passengers over and over to take care of themselves in a security sense; don't take any valuables with you if you don't need them and keep a constant eye attuned for strangers trying to mix in with our group during the walking tour. This went for myself as well. I spent most of my time on the walking tour looking out for potential thieves and pickpockets who might have an eye out for our goodies.

Amazingly, I very rarely had pickpocket problems in Florence, so I like to think that the passengers took heed of my warnings there. One visit, though, did find one of my passengers in a spot of trouble and his solution to the issue was the most brilliant and memorable that I ever heard!

The passenger in question was a real peach of a fellow! Literally! His name was James and he was and still is the largest person I've ever had on a tour. He was a huge lad in his late twenties from Malaysia. He tipped the scales at nearly five-hundred pounds. He's the only passenger I've ever had who needed two seats on the bus, preferably near the door. He was not a tall man, just a shade over six feet tall, and he actually carried his weight well. He didn't really have any mobility issues; he was just a big, huge guy. He was also an absolutely wonderful, friendly, and happy chap. With his rosy complexion and his enormous size, he soon took the nickname of "James the Giant Peach," which he adored! In many ways he became the mascot for the tour. Everybody loved the big guy, me included! He was joined on the tour by his parents and two sisters, who were all of a size that fit within the statistical norm.

Our visit to Florence was one where we had abundant free time after the walking tour. Many passengers pre-arranged tickets to the Galleria dell'Accademia to see Michelangelo's David, or to the Uffizi Gallery, or any of the other wonderful sites in the city. Many of our passengers from Malaysia and the Philippines preferred to spend their time shopping in the various markets. Florence is a great city for leather goods and jewelry, so it was very normal to point out the best markets and shops for passengers who were so inclined. It was clear that James and his family were keen for the markets, the leather markets in particular. I bid them adieu for the afternoon and joined our local guide for a quick aperitif and a bit of lunch.

My favorite thing to do in Florence is to find a nice local café and to let the world pass me by at a leisurely pace and let the hours flow by, live the Florentine *dolce vita*. I was very much doing this and enjoying a quiet afternoon when my emergency phone rang. It was James and the news was not good!

"Will, it's James. Me and my family, we have had a problem with a pickpocket!" For a man who had just had an incident with a pickpocket, he seemed rather sedate about it.

"Oh no! James, that's not good! What happened?" It looked like my quiet afternoon was about to be shattered.

"Well, we're at a police station now." Again, James sounded quite calm about things.

"Oh no! James, who got pickpocketed? Was it your mom or one of your sisters?"

"No, it was me! She tried getting me!"

"Oh no! James! Do you need me to come to the police station? Which station are you at?" I had to ask if he needed help. Passengers often need a bit of Tour Leader assistance when dealing with the police.

"No, it's OK. We don't need any help. The pickpocket didn't get anything. When she put her hand in my pocket, I grabbed it, then I picked her up and shook her! Then the police came and arrested her and asked me to come to the station just to give a statement. We're done here now. I just thought I should tell you!" James, in fact, seemed really quite pleased with the events that had transpired. I certainly was; I could stay at the café!

"OK, James! If you say so; that's great! Good for you! I'll look forward to seeing you later! Well done!" The crisis was averted, but the action and excitement were just getting started!

By the time the group met up and walked back to the bus, it was well known that James the Giant Peach had thwarted a pickpocket! He was feted and celebrated as a hero in the group, and deservedly so! It was clear that there'd be a lot of questions about what he'd done once we got going down the road. Like a game of telephone, James's heroics were quickly taking on a life of their own. By the time everyone was back on the bus, some passengers could be forgiven if they were under the impression that James had single-handedly prevented a terrorist attack! As soon as I'd counted everyone and made a few quick announcements, it was time to have James come to the front of the bus and describe to everyone what had actually happened.

"OK, James. We all understand that you had a bit of an adventure in Florence. We're all very keen to have you tell us what happened!" With that, I handed the microphone over to the man of the moment.

James took the microphone and with a great deal of zeal, began to relate his heroic tale.

"We were in the leather market and mom, Tina, and Mary were looking at the handbags and I was keeping an eye out for pickpockets like you told us to, Will. Then, suddenly, I felt a hand reaching into one of my back pockets. So, I turned around and grabbed the pickpocket by the neck!"

"Really, James? How did that go?" I asked. I was expecting him to continue with the story, but James took it as an invitation to use me as a prop and he grabbed me by the neck!

"Just like this, Will," as he put one of his massive hands around the back of my neck and tried lifting me in the air. Now, I didn't know how big the pickpocket was that he nabbed, but I'm guessing that I was a good bit bigger than that. I felt my airway constrict just a bit and rasped at James.

"OK, James. You can ease up a bit there. No need to choke the Tour Leader!"

"Sorry, Will. Just wanted to show everyone what I did!"

"Right, James, no worries! Was it a girl pickpocket then? And how did the police get involved? Go on with the story!" We were all keen to hear how James's adventure played out.

"Well, it was a girl pickpocket and she was really small, maybe not even an adult! And when I grabbed her by the neck, I lifted her up and shouted, "I've got one! I've got one! I've caught a pickpocket!" and there was a big commotion!" James was really relishing his narrative now!

"And that's when the police came?" I asked James.

"Yes, there were police nearby and they came over and grabbed the woman out of my hands and they forced her onto the ground and handcuffed her! Then one of the policemen asked me what had happened and I told him that she was trying to rob me and that I had caught her with her hand in my back pocket."

"And you ended up going to the police station? Were the police upset with you at all?"

"No, they said right away that I had done a good job and that if I came to the police station with them and filled out a report for them then they'd be able to keep the pickpocket in jail for a longer period of time. So, we went and did that and all the police officers thought I was a real hero! They kept offering me snacks and patting me on the back and shaking my hand!"

"Well, that's brilliant, James! You are a hero; there's no doubt about that! You kept a close eye on things and didn't get taken! Did the pickpocket say anything at all when you grabbed her?"

"No, but she made a loud honking noise when I grabbed her neck! Then, I think she swore at me in Italian when the police put the handcuffs on her! I don't think she liked me too much!" James was very pleased with himself, as rightly he should have been.

"Probably not, James, but that's not for you to worry about. Did anything else happen that you want to tell us?" I felt like a late-night talk show host wrapping up a celebrity interview.

"Well, just that it's not a good idea to keep a wallet in your back pocket. I think it's too easy for a pickpocket to get it and you're right. It's important to keep your eyes open and to be aware of things all the time. They're very fast, these pickpockets!"

"That's right James! But not this time. This time you were the one who was too quick for them! Excellent job and I reckon that when we get to the hotel, we're going to make sure that you get your room key first! And maybe a drink at the bar! It's just rewards for today's hero!" With that, the whole bus gave a very generous round of applause and James ambled back to his seats, beaming with pride.

I've thought about James the Giant Peach many times since then. He was such a loveable fellow and a great bit of fun. The thought that sticks with me the most is the image of him in the Florence leather market, holding up a pickpocket by the neck shouting, "I've got one! I've got one! I've caught a pickpocket!"

The Frogman

One aspect of being a Tour Leader that I found to be most fascinating was seeing how first-time travelers to Europe would react to certain cultural differences. It happened all the time and it was an important part of the job to explain to passengers why these differences existed and, in some cases, to foresee potential problems before they arose.

The most obvious cultural difference that we Tour Leaders would have to deal with, especially for North American and Australian passengers, was the size issue. By this, I mean the hotels. European hotels have smaller everything in comparison to their North American and Australian counterparts. The rooms are smaller, the elevators are smaller, the bathrooms are smaller. Everything is smaller. The most alarming issue though, were the beds. Hotel rooms in the Anglosphere often come with two large double beds or two queen beds; this is the norm. However, this is not at all the way it is in Europe. In fact, having two double or two queen beds is almost unheard of. As such, you'd have to prepare passengers for the reality of the bed situation. There may be one double or queen-sized bed in the room, but it's more often the case that there will be two single or twin beds instead. In certain circumstances, in order to create a double bed, hotels will push two single beds together, put double bed sheeting across them, and call it a double bed. You could easily enough turn it into two single beds again just by pushing the beds apart. This would all have to be explained to the passengers.

Two distinct groups of passengers would have issues with the potential bed situations. Some married couples wouldn't like the idea of sleeping in separate beds and the single people who were sharing a room wouldn't like the idea of sharing a made-up double bed, even if they could push them apart. A good Tour Leader would account for all of this with the hotels, and generally, everyone would be satisfied in the end.

In terms of the couples, married or otherwise, it could create an additional odd situation. It happened on a number of occasions, but it's the first time that it occurred that I remember most fondly. We had two lovely Australian families as part of the group. The Drakes and the Leightons. The families were friends back in Sydney and were almost mirror images of each other. Mom and dad in both families were in their late forties or early fifties and both families had three teenage children ranging in age from thirteen to seventeen. We all got along well immediately and developed an instant rapport. We happened to be loading the luggage on departure morning from Paris when Mr. Drake, Rupert, brought his and his wife's luggage to me for loading. I could see that Mrs. Drake, Sheila, was walking with a noticeable limp that morning.

"Hello Rupert, Sheila, all well? You and the kids enjoy Paris then?" I asked as I took the luggage and helped my driver, Nigel, load it.

"Morning Will, yes, a very good time of it mate! Looking forward to getting on to Switzerland," replied Rupert.

"Hello, Will. Right dear, I'm just going to go on to breakfast straight away dear, I'll see you in there,' said Sheila as she walked off back into the hotel.

"Gee Rupert, I see Sheila has a bit of a limp there, did she have a bad fall in the city yesterday? I hope she's alright," I asked, as passenger care is always an important consideration.

"Not in town actually, it happened here at the hotel. There was an… incident, I guess is the best way of describing it," replied Rupert. The way he said incident led me to believe that there was more to the story. I intended to find out what.

"So, what was this incident? Anything I need to talk to the hotel management about before we leave?"

"No, it was our…Listen Will, Nigel, can you I tell you guys what happened without you saying anything to the kids?" Replied Rupert. Nigel, didn't have any luggage to load at that moment and was standing beside me, readying his first cigarette of the morning.

"Yeah Rupert, no problem. Unless it's a really good story and I write a book one day!" Nigel remained silent and lit his cigarette. I could see he was keen for a good story too.

"OK, well, it's like this. Last night Sheila and I decided that since this is Paris and it's the city of love, we should probably have…marital relations. You know…." Rupert said a bit reticently, I could tell this was going to be a good one!

"Well, yeah, as you do I suppose," I replied. There was really nothing surprising so far. What was surprising in the grand scheme was the number of couples who were more than happy to keep me informed as to the quantity and quality of their on-tour sexcapades.

"Well, we were going at it and having a fun time of it, when all of a sudden the bed separated entirely and Sheila fell through, landed on the floor and bruised her butt!" Rupert was more than a bit embarrassed about it. Nigel and I stood there nodding at him, not at all shocked at the revelation.

"Nothing worrisome there at all Rupert," I said very matter-of-factly, "You just ended up doing *The Frogman* I bet, that's all!"

"There's a name for it?" Rupert was now the one whose turn it was to be surprised.

"Yeah," I continued, "It's called *The Frogman*," Nigel stood there nodding in agreement at everything I was saying.

"Why's it called *The Frogman*? What kind of a sex game is this?" Rupert was now quite invested in finding out this crucial new bit of information.

"Oh, it's no game! Not at all! OK, Rupert, I'm going to ask you a question, I don't mean to pry, but it's pertinent. You guys were doing missionary position, weren't you?"

"Well, yeah, we were. How did you know?" Rupert asked.

"Ah, Rupert, you and the missus are over forty, that's how over-40s do it!" Nigel piped in. Rupert nodded a bit sheepishly at this before I explained this mysterious Frogman.

"OK," I went on, "The bed was two singles that had been pushed together, but at this hotel you don't know that because they put a thick pad on it so you don't feel the crack. You and the missus get going, you're in a rhythm when suddenly, the beds fly apart, Sheila falls through, but because of the way a guy is positioned in missionary style, your arms and legs stayed on the beds and you didn't fall through, but you were hovering directly over Sheila, right?"

"Yeah, Will, that's exactly right! But why is it called *The Frogman?*" Asked Rupert. Nigel took the lead at this point to clarify the final point of confusion.

"Because, from Sheila's perspective your forearms and lower legs are holding you up, one on each bed as you're hovering over the split, so you look like a frog with suction cup pads that's climbing up a wall! You're a frogman!" Nigel elaborated.

"Oh, good, I suppose you lads are right. You've had this happen?"

"Had it happen!? Who do you think named it?" I countered.

"Of course!" Replied Nigel, before I added, "You don't think Tour Leaders and drivers spend all our time in our rooms revising and getting ready for the next day! We like to have our fun too!" Nigel stood nodding in complete agreement.

"Well, no, I wouldn't have thought so. Nor should you! Look, just do me and Sheila one favor. Please don't say anything to any of the kids or to Tom and Nancy about this. It's a bit embarrassing and we don't want our kids thinking that we still....do that," Rupert implored us.

"Yeah, no worries, Rupert. Just, come up with a good lie, after all, they're smart kids, they will figure things out. Tell them she slipped in the shower or something," I cautioned Rupert.

"Yeah, a slip in the shower will do! We'll go with that. It's nothing serious, she'll be right in a day or two. It's not like it's a far drop, is it?" Countered Rupert.

"No, not so far, but it gets you by surprise, that's for sure!" Said Nigel.

With that Rupert went off to breakfast. Nothing more was ever said about it, except for later in the day when Sheila came to me during a quiet moment at a service stop and said, "*The Frogman*, huh? That's genius, that's exactly what he looked like!"

I'm glad that Rupert and Sheila were able to have a laugh about it later on. It should be noted that I hadn't named it *The Frogman* at all, but I reckoned I'd take the credit for it on this occasion. The name had been given to me by a driver after I had told him a story of my double bed splitting apart into two singles whilst engaged in a moment of passion. That driver, likewise, had had the same thing happen to him at one time. No doubt continuing an ancient on-tour tradition of embarrassment and sore butts!

"It's Your Body Rejecting the Engagement!"

It doesn't happen too often on tour, or even in life in general, but once in a while one runs into a coincidence that doesn't seem possible. The timing of events can be so perfect that circumstances don't seem real. That was the case when it came to two passengers on tour, Timothy and Caroline.

Timothy and Caroline were a lovely young couple from Australia, both in their late twenties. I got on with them straight away. They were always keen for whatever the activity was and were never fussed about anything. They enjoyed having a laugh as well. We had quite a few young people on that tour, a two-week jaunt through western Europe, so taking everyone out in the evening in each city was standard procedure for me. Timothy and Caroline could always be trusted to be in the heart of the action. They both had a natural charisma about them.

Switzerland was the penultimate stop on that tour. It had been a brilliant tour up to that point. No real dramas to speak of. The weather had been good considering it was early spring and the passengers had been quite easy-going. A Tour Leader's dream! I had already taken the group up the Jungfrau that day and had just come back to the hotel from a late supper and was just enjoying a beer in the hotel lobby when Caroline, in a very excitable state, came running up to me all a-flutter.

"Will, Will, look, look at what Timothy gave me!" shrieked Caroline as she waved her hand in front of my face. A hand that was now sporting a shiny, new ring.

"Timothy just proposed to me! We're getting married!" Caroline's enthusiasm was apparent; any girl's would be.

"Well, well, Caroline, that is fantastic! Congratulations for sure! Brilliant stuff!" I had seen proposals on tour before, but Caroline's joy was by far the most pronounced of all the happy reactions I'd seen.

Timothy was quickly on hand as well, and between them, me, and all the other passengers in the lobby and bar area of the hotel, there was a good deal of hugs, handshakes, and congratulations being exchanged. It was a proper happy moment. Once all the congratulations had been offered, Timothy and Caroline retired to their room, no doubt to celebrate privately.

In a moment of inspiration, I had a quick word with the barman and asked if he had a bottle of bubbly on hand, which he did. For the shockingly low price of only twenty-five Francs I arranged to have the bottle and two glasses delivered to Timothy and Caroline's room, which the barman duly arranged. Duty done, I decided to retire for the evening and headed up to my room.

I had only just come out of the shower about fifteen minutes later to see my emergency phone ringing. Hopefully, it would just be a passenger ringing to ask some banal question. It was Caroline on the line.

"Hey, Will, it's Caroline here," she said with some urgency in her voice. I was a bit surprised that she'd be ringing me at that moment. I expected that she and Timothy had other things that they'd prefer to be doing, but whatever. I fully expected that she was simply ringing to thank me for the bubbly.

"Caroline! No need to call over things. The bubbly is my gift to you two! Enjoy it!" I responded.

"Oh, yeah, thanks, Will, but that's not why I'm calling. It's Timothy. I think he's dying!" It was only just then that I could hear an almighty scream in the background.

"Good god, Caroline! I can hear him over the line! What's wrong with him?" I asked. The situation was clearly an actual and very real emergency.

"I don't know! Can you come up and help me?"

"Of course! I'll be there in two minutes!"

Arriving at their room, I saw Caroline was in a state and Timothy was curled up in the fetal position howling like a banshee. Whatever was wrong was seriously wrong.

"Caroline, what the bloody hell happened?" I asked.

"Well, we were just having a bit of champagne when Timothy came over all flush and started sweating and convulsing and then he started screaming like this!" Caroline informed me. At this point I had to ask Timothy a rhetorical question.

"Tim, buddy, do you want me to ring for an ambulance?"

"FOR THE LOVE OF GOD, YES!" screamed Timothy.

The hospital in Interlaken was only a three-minute car ride away. It was just as well to grab a taxi in front of the hotel. Within five minutes the three of us were at the hospital and immediately being attended to. Luckily, there were no other patients in the emergency room on this night. If you're going to need to go to hospital whilst on holiday, Switzerland is probably the best country to be in.

Timothy was taken straight in to see a doctor, leaving Caroline and me in the waiting room to speculate as to what was wrong with the poor bugger.

"He said it was in his side, this pain? Just above the hip?" I said to Caroline.

"Yeah, what is that?" asked Caroline.

"I'm not sure. I don't know anything about doctoring. But, isn't that about where the appendix is? A ruptured appendix can be quite painful like that, so I've heard." Doctor Will isn't exactly a dependable authority on anything medical. I was only guessing and speculating.

"I don't know," responded Caroline, "but, you reckon he'll be OK?" asked Caroline, with an understandable level of fear and concern in her voice.

"He's in a Swiss hospital with a Swiss doctor looking at him and we got him here straight away; I'm sure he'll be fine. We'll just have to wait and see," I tried reassuring Caroline.

"What a way to spend my engagement night! Seeing my fiancé in the emergency room!" said Caroline. It was a statement that needed no response from me.

Over the next hour time passed at a snail's pace as we made calls to my company office in London, to Timothy and Caroline's families in Australia, and to their insurance company as well. Then, we waited. After about an hour the doctor finally made an appearance. He had a diagnosis already.

"Yes, we have done a full scan on your boyfriend, Mr. Timothy. He is now resting comfortably and you can go and see him," said the doctor.

"Well, what's wrong with him?" asked Caroline.

"It's nothing so serious. He has a couple of large kidney stones that must be passed. It will be quite painful for him," responded the doctor.

Caroline then went in to see Timothy on her own while the I waited on my own. After a few moments she returned.

"Timothy wants to see you, Will. He just wants to thank you for taking care of him and getting us down here."

As I entered his room, I could see Timothy was in a much better way. A bit drugged up and confined to a bed, but looking in much better spirits.

"Will, thanks for helping us out tonight! What a disaster to deal with! I hope we haven't been too much of a bother!" Timothy said. He was sounding better, too; no more banshee screams! He looked and sounded well enough for me to have a bit of fun with him.

"Timothy, I don't know what it is that they told you is wrong. They said it's kidney stones, but I don't think that's it at all!" I exclaimed to Timothy.

"What? You don't think it's kidney stones? What is it then? That's what the doctor said it was!"

"Don't you see what's happening, Timothy! You proposed to Caroline, you put that ring on her finger and she said yes. Fifteen minutes later you're collapsed in excruciating pain like you've never had before! That's not kidney stones! That's just your body rejecting the engagement! It all adds up! You're meant to stay single! Stay with me on the dark side!"

Timothy had a quick but tired laugh at this. His spirits were in much better standing. I actually felt a bit bad having made my little joke, but luckily, Timothy was all smiles.

"Dammit, she's worth it, Will. I'll take my risks!" responded Timothy.

With Timothy in a stable condition there was no reason for me to stick around the hospital anymore. Caroline decided to stick around as Timothy was to be kept overnight. The next morning Caroline was back at the hotel for breakfast. The group was leaving for Paris and she was there to say goodbye to us.

Instead of waiting for the kidney stones to pass, the doctor decided it was much better to remove them surgically. It was an easy day procedure, and with any luck, Timothy and Caroline would catch us up in Paris the next day.

Most of the group were in tears upon hearing of Timothy's situation, even though he would be OK. He and Caroline were sorely missed for the rest of the day. I was just hoping that we hadn't seen the last of them.

The next afternoon in Paris, I had my answer. Timothy had been discharged and he and Caroline were on the train to Paris, due to arrive at the hotel at around midnight. They wouldn't be seeing any of Paris, but that was the last thing they were concerned about by that point.

Timothy and Caroline took a taxi from Gare de Lyon train station to the hotel. It was clear that Timothy was still feeling the effects of his ordeal, but would be fine, with a gnarly scar as a souvenir of his visit to a Swiss hospital.

The next morning Timothy was like a new man, feeling much better, no doubt happy to be back where he belonged. Attention shifted from concern over his health to the unbelievable coincidence that had occurred. The odds of proposing to one's girlfriend only to be struck down by a severe medical ailment which requires surgery just fifteen minutes later are shockingly small. One would probably get better odds on Elvis being found alive. Luckily for Timothy and Caroline it was a case of all's well that ends well and a happy ending after a difficult ordeal.

Part 3

Did That Actually Just Happen?

Besides the passengers and the adventures that they get into, there are general moments of craziness that a Tour Leader must face which sometimes have nothing to do with the passengers. It's no exaggeration to say that much of the time, the real action takes place behind the scenes. While the passengers are off snapping photos of the next cathedral, happily enjoying an optional excursion, or even zonked out on the bus, the Tour Leader is often embroiled in an adventure of his or her own.

So, whether it's an overly passionate Croatian border guard, an incompetent squad of French police officers, or a very bored Polish waitress, a Tour Leader never quite knows when the next shocking turn of events will produce a memorable story that may or may not be appropriate for public consumption.

How Dare They Do This to an Australian! And a Canadian!

Unpleasant experiences and the inevitable work that one has to do to make things right are part of being a Tour Leader. If you can't handle the stress of such situations then you won't last in the job very long. You have to be prepared to use any resources at your command to fix the problem and be humble in what assistance you'll accept.

For some odd reason France was always a country where robberies would occur for my groups. It's strange how every Tour Leader has a boogie country or city. France was mine, which is a shame because I quite like France, the people, the culture, the language, the food; I am a Francophile. Sadly, the French don't always seem to reciprocate.

During the summer of 2014 I was spending quite a bit of time in France. By the time August rolled around, I had developed a real affinity for the different spots in France that our tours went to. One spot that we would go to in the south of France was a city called Arles. Arles is quite famous for having one of Europe's best preserved Roman coliseums (not nearly as big as its more well-known Roman cousin, but in far better condition) as well as being the place where Vincent van Gogh produced some of his greatest artworks, and chopped his ear off! We would generally spend a couple of hours in the city before heading on to Nice and the French Riviera on our eighteen-day itinerary.

Now, a number of unusual factors were in play on this particular tour. First, my parents happened to be on the tour. It was their first time on one of my tours and they were having a splendid time. Second, the owner of the tour company, Joran, was also with us. Not for the whole tour, but just for a couple of days to see how things were getting on. Lastly, my Dutch driver, Wesley, had his girlfriend on the tour also. We had quite a few special guests with us on this occasion.

The summer of 2014 was not a pleasant one in Arles; not if you were a Tour Leader or driver. The bus parking lot was well known to have thieves hanging about waiting for groups to go into the town proper. Once the bus was left unattended these thieves would break in and do a quick smash-and-grab of whatever on-board luggage they could take, mostly looking to get cash and valuables. Both Wesley and I knew the potential for trouble.

Arles was an easy place for a Tour Leader to bring passengers. It was a simple matter of walking the group ten minutes from the bus to the coliseum, explain where they could get a bite to eat (there were heaps of little cafes and restaurants around), a quick word on how to find things, point out the direction back to the bus and the time at which we'd be leaving. Generally, two hours was more than enough time. I was just finishing this explanation when I saw a worrying site, Wesley and his missus strolling down the main drag towards the group.

Now, I'm not one to deprive my driver of a chance to see a place, but not at the expense of bus safety. The only thing running through my mind upon seeing Wesley in the middle of town was the knowledge that there wasn't anybody back at the coach park protecting the bus. My spidey-sense was tingling. I had to go back to the bus!

Everything was fine. Having run back to check on things, it seemed my concerns were for naught. Still, someone had to stick around to make sure all remained well, so I was consigned to the role of guard for a while. Bus thieves won't break in if there's anyone around. All was well though, but my sentry duty would continue until Wesley returned.

Drivers never stay away from their buses for long. Wesley was back within a half-hour and opened the front door. Immediately, he knew something was wrong. Wesley, like most drivers, always offered drinks for sale out of the on-board refrigerator. Naturally, he kept a cash float nearby. Wesley's cash float was obviously missing.

"You didn't take it, did you, Will?" Wesley's concern was obvious.

"No, sir, I did not. You're sure you left it here?" I was certain thieves had broken in; a driver's cash float doesn't just disappear and Wesley would have known it was there when he locked up.

I took a quick look at my belongings. Everything was there, but I had, for whatever reason, taken my man purse with me when I walked the group into town. I was thankful now that I had. Walking through the bus, it didn't appear anything else had been taken, but who knew? For now, it appeared that only Wesley's cash (about six-hundred Euros) had been taken.

Wesley and I quickly found where the thieves had broken in. The cargo door near the toilet had been forced.

In time, the passenger's started filtering back, and now it was my unpleasant duty to tell them what had happened and to have them look over and inventory their belongings.

After every passenger had done a personal inventory, it was found that only an iPad had been stolen. It belonged to the passenger sitting directly at the rear stairs and had been left in the open. An obvious item for thieves who had come in via the cargo door near the toilet; they couldn't have missed it.

We needed to report the theft to the police before we left town. The good news was that we had time to spare if we needed it. Passengers would have a bit of extra time in Arles and this time Wesley would be staying near the bus.

Joran, our owner, was extremely helpful. There was a nearby supermarché, so his idea was to get a bunch of cheap beer and snacks and hang out in the bus lot with the passengers. Joran was a great entertainer as well, so that end of things would be covered.

That left a short walk down to the police station for Wesley, his girlfriend, our iPad-less passenger, me, and…..my mom!

"Why do I have to go? I didn't get robbed!" she asked. Mom didn't very much like the idea of being dragged down to the local constabulary to deal with the coppers.

"You're coming because you speak fluent French, absolutely flawless. Mine's good, but good isn't good enough in this situation. You're the official translator!" Mom got a bit more excited about things now. She liked the idea of being the *official* translator.

At this point, my dad also figured he should come along.

"Why? You speak fluent French all of a sudden?" I couldn't imagine how he'd be able to help the situation.

"No, but maybe you need some extra muscle! These French can be tricky, you know!"

"I think we'll just manage without you. Why don't you stay here and help with the beer situation?"

"Really? Well, if you think so. Probably a good idea. Joran probably doesn't want to drink alone."

"I was thinking more along the lines of helping carry it from the supermarché, but, yeah, I suppose the drinking bit too." So dad and Joran had the beer situation under control. With that, we were off with our translator to file a police report.

Not that we needed her actually. The local police were beyond useless! We ended up waiting for an hour and a half with no one in that office giving a rat's behind that we had been robbed and definitely not in the mood to draw up a police report. Mom eventually lost it on them and cursed them out in French. Thankfully, she didn't get booked, though even that would have required the police to do a bit of work, which they were clearly loathe to do.

While we were at the police station, Joran and the other passengers were having an interesting time, too. The thieves actually had the nerve to return in their car and taunt everyone! Joran phoned to inform me of the situation. There wasn't much they could do about it except take the numberplate and snap a quick photo.

After some time, it dawned on me that there was a gendarme station directly beside the police office. They weren't the people we needed, but in this case, I thought they might be able to help. The gendarme in France are always a bit more clued in than the local coppers.

The conversation that mom had with them was brief, but fruitful. It was true that the gendarme couldn't get us a police report. What they did tell us though, and I only learned it in that moment was that a police report didn't have to be filed in the locale where the crime was committed. It could be filed at any police station anywhere in France.

"No point in hanging out here then! Let's get the hell outta here and down to Nice!" I said, making the decision that I get paid the big bucks to make. Everyone agreed with me on this point. Even though we were done, it didn't stop mom from quickly opening the door to the police station and telling them off one last time before we left, which, if you ever need to tell a French person off, "foutre-toi" is the phrase to use.

The plan now was to go to the police station in Nice the next morning after breakfast. Given that it was a free morning, we would have plenty of time to get our business done before heading out for an evening in Monaco later that afternoon. Since Nice is a large and popular city with tourists, I was hopeful that the police would be much better to deal with than they had been in Arles.

So, at nine AM, we gathered ourselves up and headed out to try to get a police report. Wesley, our iPad-less Australian, our *official* translator, and I all in a taxi to the Nice police station.

For as useless as the Arles police were, that's how helpful the Nice police turned out to be. Within two minutes of arriving, we were talking to the head constable on duty who spoke perfect English. Hell, he spoke better English than any of us did! And in a very elegant French accent to boot! Not that our official translator wanted to be out of a job. She insisted on continuing in French. The constable was very apologetic for what we had been through and wanted desperately to make things right. I think he was also well impressed that this tiny Canadian pensioner was just as good at speaking French as he was at English.

"Oui, you have had ze unpleasantness, n'est-ce pas? Alors, we do very quickly, for you, the written report. Please, while you wait, you take the café et un petit croissant! Very nice!" said the constable. I've always loved and admired the French ability to go from speaking English to French, then back to English all in the space of one sentence.

He was true to his word. He made his staff drop all their other work to ensure that we were done as quickly as possible. In his words, "La plage n'attend pas! The beach does not wait! Very important to enjoy your time here! We must do this work quickly. Vite, vite!"

The police reports that we needed were finished in less than thirty minutes. During this time, the constable was quite keen as to why we were reporting a crime that occurred in Arles at the Nice police station. Our official translator told him the whole story. He was dumbstruck by what she told him.

"Alors, these French lawmen ignored you? They did not help you? C'est une sacrilege! It is their job to help! Did they not have this poster in the station?" The constable pointed to the large poster that was posted in the main atrium. The poster quite clearly states all of the rights that all people have in France, one of which is the right to be assisted by the police in a fast and professional manner. We had been in the Arles station long enough to know that that poster was not on display. I had spent the entire time there reading every notice posted on the walls of the waiting area. I knew plenty about all the missing people of the Arles area, but the rights-of-all-people poster had been absent.

"No, it wasn't. Just a bunch of missing persons posters and a sign-up sheet for the bi-monthly police intra-squad football match," I responded. A person couldn't have missed a poster that size.

"This is a big problem then. I will deal with these people! These gangsters! These, as you English say, this scum! They are worse than the criminals!" With that, the constable was on the phone.

"Who are you calling?" my mom asked.

"Just to the national office in Paris. I am an important man; they will listen to me. I will have these police in Arles, how do you English say? Fired? I will have them fired! This gang of bandits! How dare they do this to an Australian! And a Canadian! Even an American would not deserve this!"

The constable remained on the phone for a good bit of time, having quite the heated discussion with whoever it was in Paris he was talking to. By the time he was finished, our reports were ready.

"Et bien! Your reports are ready. Now, it is time to return to the beach, n'est-ce pas?"

"Merci bien! You've been very helpful to us. We are incredibly grateful," I think it was the first English my mom had spoken to the constable all morning.

We asked the constable if it would be possible for him to arrange a taxi back to the hotel. He wouldn't hear of it!

"No, the taxi is expensive! Less money for wine! For our guests, we drive you back ourselves. Please come with me! We go faster in my car! It makes up for the trouble in Arles!"

"Oh sweet! That's brilliant! Can we do blues and twos on the way back!" I asked. I was like a kid on his birthday. We were going to ride in a real police car! Without having been arrested beforehand!

"What is this blues and twos? Is this a special game you play?" The constable had never heard this particular English idiom.

"No, it just means can we turn on the lights and siren?" It would make my day if we could.

"Sadly, no, but we can drive on the tram lines instead. If we see the criminals, then we turn on the lights! Maybe we get the luck! I must remember this 'blues and twos' phrase, you English with your crazy language!" the constable responded. I was really liking the constable at this point. I was keen to spend the rest of the day with him, but he had actual police work to do after dropping us off and I would have to content myself with the consolation of going to a nude beach instead.

Several weeks later I was in the office in London when the operations manager handed me a letter from the mayor's office in Arles. The letter was emphatic in its tone of apology, informing us that a number of officers had been relieved of their duties and that extra attention was now being given to the safety of tourist buses at the city's bus park. It also begged our company to not abandon the city or to take it off our itineraries. So, in the end, some good did come of our misadventure in Arles. They never did catch the thieves who robbed our bus, but if you ever get into a scrape in southern France and need police help, there's a very powerful and helpful English-speaking constable in Nice who'll be happy to help you!

I Hope We Made Things Not So Difficult for You!

(How to make friends with the Italian Mafia)

Strange and unusual situations, as you've no doubt gathered by now, can happen to Tour Leaders at any time and any place. Usually, it's a situation that you have to solve in the moment and you realize straight away that there's a problem. There are rarer situations, though, that only present a problem after the fact. Being ripped off by the Italian Mafia was one of those situations.

Tour Leaders do not work or associate with the Italian Mafia. The mob are far more concerned with their high-value, white-collar financial racketeering, but on one occasion even I became a victim of one of their swindles.

It's an odd thing about Italy that groups quickly catch on to. Every single city, town, and village in Italy makes every single bus pay a tax upon entering the city. Sometimes this can be done online ahead of time, but all too often a bus has to take the time, upon arriving, to visit the local bus tax office. It never takes long; you simply give them your bus registration number and a bunch of money and they give you a single sheet of A4 paper that you tape up in your bus's front window that lets the police know that you've paid the tax. In larger cities like Florence, Rome, or Venice, this tax can be several hundred Euros per day. It can actually be a helpful diversion to go to the tax office as there are always toilets there for the passengers which saves us the hassle of finding toilets for fifty people in the city center.

Now, you may be wondering, with all these buses paying all this tax, what happens with the money? I was told by numerous sources in Italy that it goes to pay for a lot of infrastructure and anything that needs to be built for the tourists, road maintenance is a common example. The only problem with this explanation, especially in the smaller and less well-known towns, is that the roads are often in terrible condition. I once asked about this of our hotelier in a place called Montecatini Terme, a larger town halfway between Florence and Pisa. He was happy to inform me that a good portion of the tax money, in fact, eventually gets into the hands of the local mafia or, at the very least, crooked politicians.

Montecatini Terme was always a fun place to stay for a night. The hotel we usually stayed in was one of those grand Italian hotels built in the old style. Every room was a bit different; the lift was quite tiny, the towels were made out of the same material as the tablecloths, and the keys to the rooms were actual keys attached to the largest keychains in the free world. I really liked the place; it was like going on a school excursion back to 1956.

Upon entering Montecatini Terme, we'd always have to pay the bus tax. It wasn't so much, only thirty-two Euros, cash only! It actually worked a treat because for your thirty-two Euros you got to park in a designated and guarded bus lot. The town had mostly small, narrow streets unsuitable for large buses. You'd have to unload two blocks away from the hotel, so we'd always have passengers just bring an overnight bag with them instead of their large luggage. The one really strange bit of staying in Montecatini Terme was that you had to be out of the town by no later than 7:30 the next morning. At 7:30 they shut down all large vehicle traffic, apparently so that kids could safely get to school. I always thought the reasoning to be a bit suspect as they continued to enforce this rule on weekends and during the summer holidays. If you weren't out by 7:30, you'd have to wait two hours when buses would once again be allowed to move about town.

On one occasion we arrived at the tax office and I had my thirty-two Euros ready to go. No problem! One minute at the tax office, get our tax paper, a receipt for the expenses, and on to the hotel! Easy-as! Except this time the old man in the tax office didn't want cash. For some odd reason it was credit card only that day.

"Are you sure? I have thirty-two Euros cash. Isn't cash better?" I asked, quite perplexed. Who asks for a card payment when there's cash on offer?

"No, signore, card required today!"

I'd dealt with this old Italian (he was old enough; I thought he might be Leonardo da Vinci's brother) on almost every visit, so I thought nothing of it to just pay with my card. For thirty-two Euros, I wasn't exactly concerned one way or the other. Payment made, we went on to the hotel.

The tour continued without incident for the next few days to Florence, Rome, and Venice. With all the taxes that needed to be paid in Italy, I blew through my cash reserve very quickly. This was not a problem as the accounting department back in London was always good at making sure we had a couple thousand Euros on our company cash cards all the time. I had checked the balance in Switzerland a few days before and that had been the case. So, you can imagine my surprise when I went to pull three-hundred Euros from a cash machine in Venice only to see the dreaded words that all cash-strapped folks have seen at one time or another:

CARD INVALID: INS FUNDS

Now this was curious. I still had plenty of personal cash on hand that I could use, so I wasn't in an immediate crisis, but something was up. After a chat with the accounting department, it was unclear as to why my card would have no cash on it. Not quite piecing things together, the office said they'd put another five-hundred Euros on the account. That would tide me over for the remainder of the tour.

So, nothing to worry about then. I'd simply wait until the next day to get my money. You can imagine my surprise, then, the next day in

Munich, when I went to pull money from a German cash machine and once again saw the dreaded message:

CARD INVALID: INS FUNDS

What the Hell! Now, I knew something very wrong had occurred. Taking a moment away from my compulsory stein of beer at the Hofbräuhaus, it was time for another much more serious chat with the accounting department.

It didn't take long for them to piece together what had happened. Looking at the card transactions online there were two very wrong withdrawal listings for a small place in Lombardy, near Milan, that none of us had ever heard of.

"Will, were you anywhere near this place yesterday or the day before?" Given that it was miles away from where our tours go, it was a rhetorical question.

"No, and even if it was me, I wouldn't have withdrawn ALL the money from the card!" Given that I had a tour to run, it was left to the accounting department to sort things out with Visa.

After speaking with Visa's security team, the accounting department figured out very quickly that my card had somehow been duplicated and anytime it was reloaded, the criminals would immediately drain the account. The only place I had used the card had been at the Montecatini Terme tax office.

"Of course, they always ask for cash! When we were there a few days ago they insisted that I use my card! Obviously, they duplicated it when they put the payment through and they've been eating really expensive steak ever since on our dime!" I said to the head of the accounting department over the phone. I didn't really need to be Colombo to have determined whodunit.

The office was very good about things. Mostly because Visa was forgiving it and refunding the money to the company. I didn't even get a lecture when I got back to London. What I did get the next week was a new cash card and a homework assignment. Visa still needed us to write a report about what had happened and because I was the one who had had the card, the office decided I should be the one to draft the report. Given that I had dodged a potential twenty-five hundred Euro bullet, I thought that was fair.

It just so happened that I was going right back to Montecatini Terme the very next week on a new tour. I was keen to meet up with Da Vinci's brother at the tax office and give him what for! Especially as the report I had to write had only been done that afternoon. Instead of spending my afternoon looking at the beautiful Duomo or window shopping on the Ponte Vecchio during my afternoon in Florence, I was stuck in a café doing my homework assignment, detailing how I'd been robbed!

With my report finished and the group back together, we departed Florence for the short drive to Montecatini Terme. As we pulled into the tax office parking lot, I could see that it was indeed Da Vinci's brother behind the window again. I took my exactly counted thirty-two Euros and the bus registration and marched right up to the window.

"Si, thirty-two Euros," Da Vinci's brother didn't give me a second look as I laid the cash in front of him.

"So sorry, signore, cash no good! Card only!" he said. He was up to his tricks again!

"Oh no, you don't! Cash only! Two weeks ago, I gave you my card and you ripped it off and stole twenty-five hundred Euros! I'm not writing another report for Visa! You'll take cash or you'll get nothing!" I couldn't wait to hear what he had to say for himself now!

What happened next was another one of those situations where if I hadn't been there to witness it, I wouldn't have believed it. Da Vinci's brother took a long and probing look at me and suddenly beamed a big smile as he recognized me.

"Oh, si, yes, it's you again! Yes, we got you already with your card! Si, cash is good! We don't do that to you again! I hope we made things not so difficult for you!" Da Vinci's brother seemed genuinely pleased to see me again and equally pleased to let me know that, yes, indeed, he and the Montecatini Terme tax office had ripped off my card!

It was such a strange turn of events that I had nothing to say to him. In fact, the only two words that came out of my mouth as he handed me the tax certificate and receipt was a very perplexed, "Grazie mille," after which I walked dumbfounded back to the bus.

"So, did you give him a piece of you mind for having ripped off your card last time?" asked the driver as I reboarded the bus.

"Um, no, actually, I ended up saying "thank you" to him somehow." I was still in a bit of a nonplussed state.

"Hold on! The guy rips off your card, you come back and call him out on it, and by the end of the conversation you end up thanking him?" My driver was now a bit confused himself.

"Uh, yeah, I guess that's how it went down. At least he took the cash this time around."

"You know," added the driver, "only in Italy could the mafia be that smooth as to have you thank them for their having stolen twenty-five hundred Euros from you in the first place!"

"Venice Fell on the Tourists"

Tour leading is mostly an enjoyable and fun experience. In my opinion, ninety-eight percent of the time that I was on the job there were no problems and I was able to be in a relaxed state and not have to deal with any problems. It's that other two percent of the time, when things go completely sideways, that Tour Leaders really earn their pay and have to conjure up a solution to a problem in order to avert disaster. Sometimes such problems literally come out of the blue and sneak right up on you, such as one did on a famous visit to Venice.

Venice, of course, is world famous for its canals, gondolas, architecture, and history as a sea-faring city-state of old. Another famous aspect of the city is the aqua-alta, or high water. Depending on circumstances, water levels can suddenly rise up and wash the city out completely. We'd always inform and warn the passengers to be wearing footwear and clothing that could handle such conditions. It was on one visit to Venice in my first season that weather conditions in Venice turned so quickly and with absolutely no warning that it made the aqua-alta look like a small puddle.

It was late September and as we arrived in Venice one could not have dreamed of a nicer day to be visiting the Amsterdam of the South. The sun was out, the temperature warm but not hot, and a very gentle breeze enveloped the lagoon. I remember thinking at the time that the conditions were as perfect as one could hope for. I'd never seen such a lovely day in Venice before! The devilish aqua-alta was no problem either. St. Mark's Square and the small and winding streets of the city were as dry as a bone. The late afternoon conditions were perfect as the passengers enjoyed their time on the gondolas and speedboats and exploring the countless backways and alleyways. The sights and sounds of the city were exactly as one would hope for. Things couldn't be any better. It was just nearing the point in time when I would start my long trek back through the city to get to the bus station and board a public bus back to the hotel on the mainland that a distinct change in conditions began to permeate the idyllic, Venetian late afternoon.

It was almost imperceptible at first, just a slight increase in the wind. You could see the flags in St. Mark's Square unfurl themselves just a bit more. Most of the passengers, many of whom were finished their time in the city and were keen to return to the hotel as well, joined me in the thirty-minute walk back to Piazzale Roma and the bus embarkation point. As we journeyed through the city, the weather conditions progressively worsened. The gentle breeze slowly morphed into a brisk gale, the pleasant temperature dropped to an uncomfortable chill, and the azure blue skies quickly darkened, as if by magic, into a mass of roiling, angry clouds. A storm was about to hit. A storm unlike any I'd ever seen before, and certainly haven't seen since.

We never made it to the bus station. Two-thirds of the way back, the heavens unleashed a fury that is usually reserved for stories from the book of Exodus. It wasn't a pelting rain. It started as such, but quickly became something much worse than that. A hailstorm descended on the city that was unparalleled in anything that even one's imagination could drum up. It was as if Jerry Bruckheimer had been put in charge of the weather.

It started with a few small pebbles, but soon increased to marble-sized balls. These soon gave way to cherry tomato-sized orbs. After a few moments, a few golf ball-sized chunks made their appearance.

It was all I could do to tell the passengers to take cover wherever they could. For their own safety, though, it wasn't as if they needed to be told! Everyone immediately ran into the nearest shop or restaurant that they could find! The owners and proprietors could do little about it. One never expects a hailstorm to last long, a few minutes at the most. They generally move on quickly. This one, though, hung around like a Biblical plague! For the next thirty minutes Venice was under assault from a force of nature so violent, one began to wonder if it was the end times!

Of course, it wasn't. What it was, was the largest hailstorm ever recorded in Italy. By the time it was finished, the streets of Venice were covered in several inches, and in some places, up to a full foot of hail stones.

This is when the real trouble started for the group. With the hailstorm and the drop in temperature, a pleasant twenty-three-degree Celsius late afternoon had transformed, within minutes, to a freezing, ice-ridden, eight-degree, early evening. Neither I nor any of the passengers, were the least bit prepared for such conditions. Few of us had a jacket of any kind. Many of us were wearing shorts and a goodly number of us had no shoes, but sandals.

It may have only been a ten-minute walk to the Piazzale Roma bus station, but it felt like a Siberian death march. Slushing through the melting hail stones, our feet and toes quickly started to freeze. There was to be no respite though; not until all the hail had melted, which seemed as though it would never happen. The only warmth to be had was a quick stop for take-away pizza as we neared the bus station.

We eventually made it to Piazzale Roma. It looked like an evacuation scene in a disaster movie! There were hordes of people waiting for buses, looking to abandon the city as though an alien invasion was taking place. Luckily, the area around the station didn't have as much melting hail as where we had come from, but there was still a lot of it. Some of the passengers were starting to shiver quite worryingly. All I could do was suggest to everyone to huddle for warmth while I looked at the electronic bus departures board.

Buses don't exactly run on an exact schedule in Venice. Even so, I was distressed to see that the next number six bus, the bus to our hotel, wasn't due for nearly a half-hour. I wasn't sure some of my people would make it that long! An immediate and bold decision had to be made.

"OK, crew! Everyone listen up! I know I told you that you need the number six bus to get to the hotel, but there's no number six bus at all, probably not for a while! So, everyone, get on this number three bus! Everyone! It's due to leave imminently!" I had what I thought was a decent plan to get out of our predicament.

"Where are we going, Will? Where does this bus go?" asked the passengers as they crammed onto the bus. At least standing in close confines would help to raise everyone's body temperature.

"It gets us the hell off this frozen ice-box!" I responded before adding, "the number three goes by another hotel that our tours have stayed in before. When we get there, we'll sort out a fleet of taxis to get us back to our hotel. For now, though, we need to get somewhere warm and somewhere dry!"

"Is there a bar at this other hotel?" asked one of the passengers.

"There is, and by god, it had better be open!" I answered. One could immediately see the morale starting to come back in the group.

The drive to the alternate hotel only took ten minutes. By this point no one was violently shivering anymore, but the passengers were still cold and wet. Massimo, the receptionist at the hotel, was on shift. Luckily, Massimo owed me a favor and was happy to oblige our wretched group of the damned. It took a few moments, but he was able to contact a cab driver friend of his who had a large twelve-person taxi van. It was only a ten-minute round trip to our hotel and back, and the passengers were happy to do a three-trip shuttle system using the van, three Euros per person. As far as everyone was concerned, it was the best three Euros they ever spent.

Unlike the lifeboats on the Titanic, things proceeded in an orderly and organized manner. The most desperately cold and wet passengers went first. The second group was composed of passengers who were also cold and wet, but not desperately so. The third group was made up of individuals who were also cold and wet, but who wanted to have a drink at the bar first before going back to the hotel.

We were all able to get back to the hotel no worse for the wear. Once it was clear that there were no medical concerns within our group, the absurdity of the situation became the main topic of discussion and humor. The passengers, myself included, simply could not believe the turn of events that had occurred. In the end, it made for a great shared experience.

The next day, as we drove through the mountains of Northern Italy heading towards Austria, Bob, a passenger from the British Midlands, came to the front of the bus.

"Will, have you got a minute free?" asked Bob.

"Absolutely, mate. For you, I've got two minutes free!"

"Great! Look, after the events of last night, I still can't believe what happened! I don't think any of us have ever seen anything like it!" Bob said, as though we had just lived though some sort of supernatural event usually reserved for a Tolkien novel.

"I know I haven't Bob. How could one ever forget something like that!" The events of the previous day were still very fresh in everyone's mind.

"Absolutely. The thing about it, Will, is that, well, I've written a song about it," said Bob.

"You did what?" I asked. I wasn't sure what was more surprising; the storm, or the fact that someone wrote a song about it, overnight! Bob was suddenly reminding me of Gordon Lightfoot.

"Yeah, I got a bit inspired so I wrote a song about the whole thing. Do you think I could have a minute on the mike to sing it to everyone?" asked Bob.

"Yeah, sure, go for it, Bob!" I responded as I handed him the microphone, keen to hear the musical composition in commemoration of our tale of survival.

The song was written in the tune of "Good King Wenceslas," but Bob titled it "Venice Fell on the Tourists" and, in his Midlands tenor voice, sang it as follows:

Tour boss Will, he took us out
On the bus to Venice
Some went sailing out on boats
While others hunted bargains
Then the blue skies turned to black
And the rain came pouring
Worse than that, the hail smashed down
Venice with white carpets

Hiding in all shops nearby
Or freezing, getting pelted

There seemed no way to get us home
We shivered, saturated
Forced march next through hail and rain
Searching for our pizza
Ate it all, then off again
Slush and hailstones melting

Finally bus and taxi rides
Gets us to the hotel
All of us still dripping wet
Grabbing for a towel
But at last we're safe and dry
And the hail has melted
We're ready for the next day out
Or perhaps we're all demented?

Once finished, Bob deservedly received a huge round of applause from the entire bus as though he were Mick Jagger belting out the final words to "Satisfaction." I was impressed that he wrote three verses!

* * *

It was the next spring when I received an unexpected invitation from Bob to come and stay with him and his wife at their home near Stratford-upon-Avon. Naturally, we had a long talk about our Venetian adventure. It wasn't until one night with Bob that I realized what an impact the storm had had. We were at Bob's local pub having a restorative beverage amongst a large group of the locals. After finding out that I was the Tour Leader that had taken Bob to Venice the previous September one of his mates took me aside. He had a serious demeanor and a serious question for me.

"Every time Bob comes in all he talks about is this bloody hailstorm that he claims almost killed the lot of you! It's not really true that the hail was a full foot deep. He's having a laugh, isn't he?" asked Bob's mate.

"Well, actually, I've got a couple of pictures here on my phone...."

This Restaurant Has No Food Today

I always found working in Eastern Europe to be a bit more fun than Western Europe. Places like France, Italy, and Germany do have their appeal, but the countries of the old Soviet Bloc presented a unique and interesting twist. You never knew what odd sort of things you'd see or experience on a daily basis. This was especially true in Poland. Something strange always seemed to happen in Poland!

One particular incident illustrated the oddball nature of this country more than any other. We were on our way from Budapest to Krakow. It's actually an exceptionally beautiful drive between the two cities and you go through some very nice parts of Slovakia on the way. It's a very leisurely drive as well; there was never a rush to get to Krakow. One stop that was a must on this day was at the Polish border. Poland still uses their own currency, the Zloty; and since both Poland and Slovakia are in the Schengen Zone there are no border guards. You drive through without being stopped. The border crossings into Poland are still busy places. There's always a number of small currency exchange huts that offer an excellent rate on Polish Zloty with little commission, so stopping there with a busload of fifty tourists was always a must. The Polish border stop we were using also had a petrol station and a little restaurant and motel. Everything we needed was in one spot, so I decided we might as well make it our lunch stop for the day as well. One hour would be ample time to get a money exchange done and a bite as well.

I've never been one for a big meal on the road. The group had an included dinner that night in Krakow. I love a good hot dog though, and petrol stations in Poland always have a really good hot dog counter. It was always good for the passengers, too. If they wanted just a quick snack or a hot dog from the petrol station, no problem. If they wanted a proper meal, then the restaurant was there, too. The group quickly dispersed to their tasks and I went off for a hot dog.

Ten minutes later, hot dog in hand, is when the absurdity started. Roughly half the passengers suddenly entered the petrol station. These passengers had been the ones who had gone to the restaurant upon arrival. It seemed odd to me that they'd all be in the petrol station now. A couple of them came to me with an interesting story to tell.

The entire group of passengers had entered the restaurant as you do and the waitress showed them to their tables and gave them menus. After a few minutes, she had returned to the table to take their order. Anytime I would take a group to Poland, I'd always recommend the pierogi, a type of meat-filled dumpling. They're always excellent in Poland, but so are the soups and pork dishes as well. Polish cuisine is really quite underrated, but I digress. The group made their order, but every time they ordered a dish the waitress would simply say that they didn't have it. The group tried ordering about a half dozen different dishes, all to no avail. It finally got to the point where frustration set in and they all left, hoping that the petrol station still had some hot dogs left. I was a bit perplexed by the story.

"So, what you're saying is that the restaurant didn't have any food?" I asked. It seemed more than a little odd to me. I reckoned that they had hit on a language barrier issue instead. I mean, what kind of restaurant doesn't have food? Communism had ended quite some time ago.

"Absolutely, Will. Either that or there was a complete misunderstanding in the communication, but her English was really quite good. It was just weird!" responded one of the passengers. It was strange enough that I decided I'd go and investigate for myself.

I walked straight over to the restaurant and was immediately greeted by the waitress, shown to a table and given a menu. The typical Polish foods were all on offer. The waitress came back very quickly with a notepad and pen in hand, ready to take my order.

"I'll have the pork pierogi, please," I said, a plate of which is always nice.

"Oh, I'm sorry, sir, but we don't have any pierogi today," she responded, and so the craziness began.

"OK, fine. I'll just have the pork chop and potatoes then." Also a fine choice, I thought.

"Oh, I'm sorry sir, but we don't have any pork or potatoes today," she responded again, and so the craziness continued.

"Alright, I'll have goulash then, if you don't mind," I said a bit exasperatedly, thinking that this was starting to get very silly indeed, as Monty Python would say.

"Oh, I'm sorry sir, but there's no goulash today, either," she responded once again, and now it had gotten to ludicrous levels.

"Is there any food here at all?" I figured the question had to be asked.

"No, sir, we have no food here today." The waitress said this as though I were the idiot. Of course, restaurants never have food in them! Still, things would get even more bizarre.

"If there's no food, then why are you here?" I asked. It seemed a perfectly reasonable inquiry.

"Because it's my job," the waitress said without a hint of irony or sarcasm.

"But there's no food!" This game was getting a bit old and I was getting a bit frustrated in trying to get this waitress to see any logic, or lack thereof, in what she was saying. I thought I'd give it one last go.

"Look, do you have a chef?"

"Yes."

"And where is he?"

"He's in the kitchen."

"And what is he doing?"

"Waiting to cook the food," she responded. I thought maybe I was finally getting through.

"But there is no food!"

"I know. He's waiting to cook the food!"

"So, he's just standing there then?"

"Sometimes he sits down." Once again, the waitress was missing the point completely. I thought I'd approach things from a slightly different angle.

"OK, OK, OK! Let's try again. You work in this restaurant?"

"Yes."

"And this restaurant has no food today. Yes?"

"Yes."

"So why don't you and the chef just go home?"

"Because this is our job! We must stay at our job until it's the end of the day! And, this way, we can be here to tell people that there's no food!"

"OK, fine, there's no food. Can you tell me where I can go to get lunch?"

"Sir, there is the petrol station. They have hot dogs and potato chips there. Come tomorrow. Maybe we'll have food then!" With that she took her leave and the Abbott and Costello routine was over. I collected my belongings and what was left of my mind and went back to the petrol station.

Most of the passengers were now milling around. Some had hot dogs and others were waiting for new hot dogs to be made. A few of them saw me approaching from the restaurant and started laughing. They knew exactly what I'd been through.

"Hey, Will, did you have a nice lunch over there?" asked one of the passengers.

"As you well know, I did not! I thought you were joking about them being open without any food, but you're all correct. If this were any other country in Europe I'd be surprised, but since this is Poland, it makes all the sense in the world!"

"What do you mean, Will?" asked another passenger.

"What I mean is that this is Poland. As you will see in the next three days, sometimes things in Poland...just don't work the way they should. There's a reason why there's such a thing as a Polish joke and that restaurant is living proof of it! These people are insane sometimes!"

"Will, why in heaven's name would they open that restaurant if they don't have any food?" asked yet another passenger. Our discussion was quickly turning into a bus-wide inquest.

"Look, here's the thing about Poland you have to understand. Things here are completely backwards sometimes and don't ever say this to a Polish person, but there's nothing wrong with this country that the Germans couldn't fix and put right in a real hurry!" It was a bit cruel of me to say so, but there was some truth to it. You'd never see a foodless restaurant in Germany.

"Why wouldn't a Polish person want to hear that, Will?" asked another passenger. Clearly, he'd not read any history, ever.

"Well, the Germans tried coming in here and fixing certain inadequacies a few decades ago. It didn't go over very well with the Poles. Trying to remember what they called that....had a name....oh yeah, it was World War Two! Yeah, it's safe to say that there are still some lingering tensions over the whole thing. I'll discuss it further on the bus."

There was a bit of silence amongst the passengers for just a moment until one of the Malaysians summed things up quite pithily.

"Still, it's a funny joke! In Singapore they make the same joke about us Malaysians and we Malaysians make the same joke about the Thais, who then make the same joke about the Burmese! Can we make more Polish jokes on the bus?

"Uh, sure, so long as they're funny and just don't repeat them to any of the locals. Or do! Given that they open restaurants without any food in them, they might not understand it anyway." It was another slightly crass joke on my part, but they were coming to mind far too easily now.

The tour continued on for the next three days in Poland. Krakow in particular is one of the most beautiful cities in Europe and the Polish people are some of the friendliest that you'll find anywhere. The passengers on that tour, and their Tour Leader as well, also found out that the best way to hear a good Polish joke is to ask a Polish person! They're keen to poke fun at themselves more than anything! The only word of caution on Poland that I can offer is: don't walk into a restaurant and simply assume that they'll have food. They may only have a very bored waitress!

How Hard is it to Use a Toilet!?

It's not always the Tour Leader and passengers that can find themselves in odd and unique situations. The drivers are just as likely to find themselves encountering strange circumstances as well. Such was the case on one visit to Switzerland for one of my favorite drivers, Kevin.

Kevin was a proper legend! He was a well-experienced driver, and when he got put on as a driver for my company, it was decided that he'd come along as a second driver for training purposes. My old friend, Derek, was listed as the official driver, but Derek and Kevin would share the driving duties. For Kevin it wasn't an issue of knowing how to drive, rather it was a chance for him to learn where drop-off points were, routes through the different cities, and learning the driver protocols that my company wanted him to know. It was the only time in my career as a Tour Leader in which I had two drivers; it was certainly a nice luxury to have.

The tour progressed very nicely. We had a lovely group of passengers who were excited and keen about things. Mercifully, there was not a single difficult passenger of any sort. The weather was gorgeous everywhere we went, which isn't always the case in late April. At no point did the tour face any difficulties or problems. It was almost a holiday for us three lads at the front of the bus as well. The passengers were in good form throughout, and because we had such a large contingent of Australian and New Zealander passengers, Derek, Kevin, and I organized an early morning ANZAC Day ceremony for them in Ljubljana. Yes, there was little doubt; we were cruising very nicely through this tour! Everyone and everything was coming up aces!

Once we got to Switzerland, things continued to look good. The temperamental Swiss weather was in our favor. It was warm and sunny in the Interlaken region and our trip up the Jungfraujoch looked as though it would be a memorable one. So it turned out to be, just not for the reasons I expected!

Drivers don't generally go up the mountain. It's a rare occurrence, even though they are allowed to go up free of charge. What I'd often do, is have the drivers claim their ticket anyway. Drivers would always be given a meal voucher for the canteen at the top of the Jungfrau. This way I could at least get a free lunch instead of having to pay a ridiculous amount for some terrible sandwich.

I was just about to go to the train station and buy the tickets for the group the night before we were to go up when Kevin stopped me with a bit of information.

"Will, are you off to buy the tickets just now?"

"Yeah, Kevin. I won't be long, back in a half hour. We'll grab a beer when I get back!" Kevin and I had become fast friends over the course of the tour.

"Let me go with you to the station. I've just been talking to the manager at the bus company and she wants me to go up the mountain with you and the group tomorrow. She reckons it's better if I know exactly what it's like up there. You know the process for getting the driver's ticket?" asked Kevin.

"Yeah, no worries, Kevin. Just bring your driver's license and the ticket agent will take care of everything! Easy-as!" With that said, we walked down to the ticket office at the train station and sorted out the group for the next day. Having Kevin come along would just make the day even better!

The next day dawned clear and sunny with not a cloud in sight! Late April and May is the best time of the year in Alpine Switzerland. The numerous waterfalls are in full flow, but the mountains still have a maximum snow level on them. It's a photographer's dream! The passengers were in a terrific mood, as was their Tour Leader. It was going to be a great day!

Arriving at the top of the Jungfraujoch, I took only a brief moment to explain to the passengers where everything was in the visitor's complex. Toilets, restaurants, viewing areas, souvenir shops, and of course, the many attractions within the complex as well. Most importantly, I also told the passengers where they needed to meet and at what time so that we could head back down the mountain. We were all on the same group ticket and we were required to all come down together as we had a reserved train car.

Being at the top of the Jungfrau is fun, but it does have a degree of physical demand to it. The altitude at the top of the Jungfraujoch is over eleven-thousand feet. The air is a bit thin and can cause breathing difficulties. I'd always tell passengers to take it slow and to breathe deeply. After twenty or thirty minutes a person would get used to it. We would spend about three hours at the top of the mountain; ample time to see everything, get photos, shop, and have a spot of lunch before meeting up to go back to the hotel. Three hours at over eleven-thousand feet would tire out everyone in the group, the Tour Leader included!

The appointed meeting time arrived and the passengers were all there; no problem! They'd all enjoyed themselves and we were just about to head to the train when it suddenly dawned on me. Where was Kevin? He was nowhere to be seen!

"Has anyone seen Kevin?" I asked the group. I myself hadn't seen him since we had turned the group loose three hours earlier.

A number of the passengers had seen him during our time at the center, but no one had seen him for at least a half hour. With no mobile service at the top of the mountain, it was impossible to call him. We waited as long as we could for him, but eventually we had to make our way to the train. We departed Kevin-less!

It wasn't that I was worried about Kevin. He was a big boy capable of taking care of himself. It was just curious as to where he had disappeared to. The visitor's complex at the top of the Jungfraujoch isn't a massive place. You would need to work at getting lost. The only explanation

I could think of was that he had left on an earlier train, but surely, he would have told someone!

Two and a half hours later we arrived back to Wilderswil train station, and lo and behold, who was on the platform waiting for us? It was Kevin! The hotel was a short walk from the station, so I had plenty of time to talk with him about why he had left ahead of the group.

"Kevin! There you are! We were wondering what you'd got up to! Air was a bit thin for you? Had to come down early?" I asked as I came off the train, pleased to see that Kevin's disappearance was much ado about nothing.

"No, not a problem with that. I got thrown off the mountain! Security made me come back early!" Kevin said this with a degree of pride in his voice.

"You got thrown off the mountain? What in the hell for? What did you do?" I couldn't believe it! It wasn't unheard of to be thrown off the Jungfrau. Some people enjoyed stripping off all their clothes up there and getting nude photos of themselves at the top of the Jungfrau, but Kevin wasn't the kind of guy to do that!

Kevin was very much a straight shooter, and the story he was about to tell was an absolute shocker!

"Look, what happened is, I went to go use the toilet after having gone through the whole complex. I went into the men's room and there were these two Chinese blokes in one of the toilet stalls, both trying to use the toilet at the same time with the door open and they were making a proper awful mess. It wasn't number ones that they were getting up to! So, I started yelling at them to pull their pants up and to use separate stalls and after a minute or two some security guys showed up who didn't much care for the scene that we were causing. I tried to explain to them what they'd been up to, but they weren't interested in anything I had to say. They simply escorted me out of the bathroom and straight to the train! I didn't see any of you guys, so I didn't have a chance to tell you what had happened!"

It was an unbelievable story; I'd never heard anything like it! It did offer up a number of questions in my mind.

"Far out, Kevin! What happened to the Chinese guys? They get tossed, too?"

"Not likely! I think they got taken to the fancy restaurant. They certainly weren't on the train with me!"

"That's insane, Kevin! I can't believe it! That's the most unbelievable thing I've ever heard!" I was really quite shocked at the turn of events, but Kevin wasn't quite done with his story yet.

"Look, Will! I need a favor," said Kevin.

"Yeah, sure. What's up?"

"When they tossed me off the mountain, they looked at my ticket and saw that I was a driver. They phoned my manager at the bus company and told her that I'd been causing trouble up there. I spoke to her an hour ago when I got back here about what actually happened, but if you could ring her and have a word with her, I'd appreciate it."

"Yeah, Kevin, that's fine. I'll be happy to phone her straight away. I have to say, I'm rather impressed. To be thrown off the Jungfraujoch on your very first visit! Not bad! I'd have loved to have seen you in there yelling at them! With a guy with a fuse like you, I'm sure you put on a good show!"

"Oh, it was a wild scene, Will! I absolutely let them have it! I mean, how hard is it to use a toilet!? It's not exactly a group activity, is it?"

A quick phone call to Kevin's manager back in England sorted out any trouble that he might have been in. Truthfully, Kevin's manager thought it was as hilarious as I did. I can't say for certain, but I'm fairly sure that Kevin never bothered to go up the Jungfraujoch again. Much easier and less dramatic for him to stay in town where correct toilet usage is not likely to cause nearly as much of a drama!

How Exactly Do You Expense a Bribe?

As a Tour Leader, I was always keen for new challenges and opportunities. Western Europe is a wonderful place and full of fun, but after some time going to places such as Paris, Rome, and Amsterdam start to become old hat. So, after having run tours strictly in Western Europe, I was pleased to be given the opportunity to be based out of Munich instead of London and start running tours through the Balkans and Central Europe. There was a bit of training and research to do before starting this new assignment, but after a long chat with the operations team and Tour Leaders who had already worked there, I felt confident in my ability to conquer unfamiliar territory.

The most important thing that was made clear to me was that working in the Balkans would be quite different from Western Europe. The operations team wouldn't always be able to sort things out from London, so I'd be expected to fix any issues on my own. Another issue that I would have to contend with were border guards. Many of the countries in the Balkans are not part of the Schengen Zone, Western Europe's free travel zone, so we'd have to get our passports stamped going into and out of each country. In certain countries these guards need a little bit of extra motivation to actually do their jobs. Our operations manager made it quite clear that I would need to be prepared to manage such a situation when it occurred. Basically, be prepared to offer a bribe.

Bosnia and Herzegovina presented the most interesting challenge when dealing with the border guards. We were staying the night in

Sarajevo and would be heading to Belgrade in Serbia the next day. My driver, Stan (which wasn't his real name; his real name had a bunch of z's and v's in it, he told me just to call him Stan) and I had a slight issue with our passenger manifests. At the time Malaysian nationals were not allowed into Serbia and we had several Malaysians who did not have the visa required for entry. Now, this is not a big deal; passengers in this situation would simply leave the tour and take the train or bus directly to Budapest and meet us there two days later. For the driver and me, we would simply take their names off our manifests. It was generally acceptable to simply cross their names off the list and we'd never had problems at any previous border crossing. That was about to change.

Our route that day would see us go from Bosnia, briefly into Croatia, and then into Serbia. We had left our Malaysians in Sarajevo, but they were messaging me throughout the day as to where they were. As we pulled up to the Bosnian border post things looked alright. There were no other vehicles and the guards looked quite bored. Having never been to this border crossing before, I wasn't sure how these guards would be doing things. Sometimes the guards want to see the manifests, sometimes not. Sometimes they want all the passports to be pre-collected and placed in a bag or box, other times they'll collect them individually from the passengers. You never knew quite what the deal was until they started talking to you.

On this day, two border guards came on board and wanted to see our manifests and collect the passports themselves. They looked like a comedy duo. They had their matching border guard uniforms and had remarkably similar mannerisms. I decided I'd call them Tweedle-Dee and Tweedle-Dum, as they reminded me of the characters from the Disney version of Alice in Wonderland. I almost laughed at them straight away, but collected myself as they didn't seem like the types to understand laughter or amusement. After collecting everyone's passports they then retired to the small kiosk beside the bus to get to the business of stamping the passports and forms. Standing outside the bus with Stan, I was soon beckoned over to the passport kiosk by Tweedle-Dee. He apparently had a few questions for me.

"What has happened to these people? Names are not here and no passport for these people. Where are people?" Bosnian border guards never did have particularly good English. I was actually surprised they spoke any English at all.

"Those names? Yes, they are Malaysian people. We are going to Serbia today and they don't have the visa, so they are taking the train to Budapest. We will meet them tomorrow." A simple enough explanation, but Tweedle-Dee persisted.

"On train to Budapest? How we know they are on train? How do we know they not stay in Sarajevo?"

To be fair, there was no way to prove these passengers were on a train going to Budapest. I should have just called them up. Instead, I got a little bit lippy with the guard.

"Who in their right mind would stay in Sarajevo?" The minute these words were out of my mouth I knew I'd made a mistake.

"You not like Sarajevo? You not like Bosnia?" Tweedle-Dee was not appreciative of my insolent tone. He had a quick word with Tweedle-Dum who was stamping the passports and then turned his attention back to me.

"Please now, you come with me. Need to talk to boss." There was a definite air of trouble now. Stupidly, I told the passengers that I'd be gone only for a short moment.

Tweedle-Dee led me into the proper customs office. Though it had actual windows, as opposed to the kiosk, it was as dingy and disgusting as one could ever dare to dream of. In short order I was taken into the office of the head border guard who was sitting around chain-smoking and watching YouTube videos, presumably on the only laptop in Bosnia. As Tweedle-Dee had a chat with him in their native Bosnian, I could see that the head guard, who did not have a comedic Disney caricature look about him, was less than pleased at being disturbed. Tweedle-Dee left straight away and the head guard sat there looking at our passenger manifest in complete silence. After several minutes of this uncomfortable silence, he finally spoke to me. Unfortunately, he spoke in English!

"The guard outside says that you have left undocumented travelers in Sarajevo! Why have you done this?" He was not in the mood for any BS on my part.

I explained to him the same circumstances that led to our leaving passengers in Sarajevo as I had to Tweedle-Dee, leaving out the smart-aleck comments about Sarajevo. The guard nodded at this, but remained unsmiling.

"You must understand; this is a major violation of Bosnian law. There is no record of these people. Big problem!" He then stood up and continued, "Follow me now."

He led me into the next room. The next room happened to be a prison cell that looked quite similar to what I imagined a Siberian Gulag prison camp cell would look like. Just a concrete slab with a toilet that had probably last been cleaned sometime shortly before the Nazis had invaded. Things did not look good.

"This is waiting room for you. We wait for judge to come. He will decide things." The head guard seemed quite keen to get back to his YouTube videos.

"And when will the judge be here?" I asked.

"Today is Sunday, today is day off. Judge will come tomorrow," replied the head guard. Clearly, I was in a good bit of trouble.

Obviously, I couldn't stay in this cell for five minutes, let alone overnight. Luckily, with fifty westerners waiting for me outside, they and Stan would be asking about me before too long. Dammit though! I'm a Tour Leader! I'm the one who's meant to be solving problems, not creating them! If my past experiences with Bosnian border guards had taught me anything, it was that they weren't above having their palms greased. In fact, I was confident that that's what this was all about anyway! It was time to test the waters. If worse came to worst, he could simply add bribery to my rap sheet, after which I would have to offer an even bigger bribe.

"Look! I don't have time to wait for the judge! Is there any way that I can just pay a fine?" This, of course, is code for, "How much of a bribe do I have to give to you?"

"Judge will come and decide the fine. Tomorrow," replied the head guard. This was clearly code for "a lot."

"Look! I'm sure the judge will have better things to do tomorrow than to come and decide things. Couldn't I just give you the money for the fine and then you give it to the judge tomorrow? I'm sure that a man as important as you are, knows how much the fine is. It's much easier, I think." And so the worm was on the hook. I could tell by the look on the head guard's face that I'd be out of the dingy prison cell and out of Bosnia very shortly.

"You come with me, back to office. We discuss things." The head guard's mood had suddenly changed after my appeal to his vanity. Upon our return to his office, he shut his laptop, cracked open a bottle of rakija, and poured a glass for both of us.

"Yes, it is possible to pay the fine today to me. This is no problem. The judge will say OK for this." The guard still spoke like this judge was a real person. I was fairly sure by this point that there was no such person.

"And how much is the fine?" Like a proper American, I just wanted to pay this sleazeball off and be on my way, the head guard wasn't quite in the same rush as I was.

"The fine? Don't worry about the fine. We will determine this after we have more of my mother's fine rakija! How do you enjoy this?" Apparently, the finer points of bribery in the former Yugoslavia required a shot or two of rakija. Though, to be fair, most activities in the former Yugoslavia require a shot or two of rakija.

"Your mother is an inspired distiller! You must be very proud. The blueberry rakija is my favorite!" I figured that continuing to appeal to his vanity and his mother's distillation skills, was probably a wise move. Like all good rakija, the stuff tasted not dissimilar to a high-octane jet fuel.

"If you like, I also have apricot," the guard mentioned and he pulled out a second bottle.

"That's immensely kind of you; very, very kind, but I must be getting my people to Belgrade." As much fun as it was to be getting wrecked with this Bosnian border guard, I did have a timetable to keep to.

"Yes, of course, you Americans are always busy running to somewhere! This is not a problem. The fine today is two-hundred Euros."

I had had the foresight to have several hundred Euros on my person that day, anticipating that there might be this sort of situation. As I went to take the cash out of my pocket, the head guard stopped me.

"No, no, not yet! You wait, just one moment!" The guard got up, went over to the window, and closed the blinds. A bit pointless as the only thing one could see out that particular window was a field of onions.

"Now, please, look at this piece of paper on my desk. I will go and get exit papers for your bus. You put fine on piece of paper and then other piece of paper on top of that," instructed the head guard. Paying this "fine" was turning out to be a very convoluted sort of task.

The guard turned his back for a moment while I did this. After only a couple of seconds he faced me again, looked to make sure the "fine" was there, and then pocketed the lot. I didn't bother asking if the judge was going to get his cut. We both polished off our rakija shots and I was free to go. Well, almost free to go; the head guard had a final parting gift:

"Please, you enjoy the blueberry. You must take the remainder of the bottle! A souvenir of your visit to our border post! Enjoy the rest of your trip!" I hadn't expected a bribery souvenir, but at least I was getting something for my two-hundred Euros!

I high tailed it out of that office as quickly as I could and ran back over to the bus. The head guard came out as well and had a quick chat with Tweedle-Dee and Tweedle-Dumb who had finished stamping all the passports and were now having a competition to see which of them could smoke an entire pack of cigarettes the fastest. It was obvious that we were done and free to go. My driver, Stan, was just finishing a cigarette of his own. It was a proper smoker's club out there! In the thirty minutes I'd been away I'm sure he'd been matching Tweedle-Dee and Tweedle-Dumb puff for puff.

"Everything is OK? We can go now?" asked Stan.

"Yeah, everything's good. Let's get the hell outta here!"

With that, I collected my passport, Stan stomped out his cigarette, and we were gone. Stan knew damn well what had gone on in the office.

"How much did they make you pay? How much was the bribe?"

"Two-hundred Euros. But I got a bottle of blueberry rakija for my trouble."

"Two-hundred Euros! Rates have gone up!"

*   *   *

It was later in the day, after we had arrived in Belgrade, that I took a quick moment to call the operations department in London to tell them about the events at the Bosnian border post.

"That's unbelievable, Will! Crazy times in Bosnia! Count yourself lucky that you at least got a bottle of rakija out of it! Usually, they just punt your ass outta there after they've got your money! You've made a new friend!" said our operations manager.

"Yeah, for sure, lucky me!" I responded.

"It's why we pay you Tour Leaders the big bucks! Anything else you need to discuss?"

"Actually, boss, the whole point of the call isn't to tell you about the bribe."

"Well, Will, what is this call about then?"

"Yeah, I was just wondering; it was a two-hundred Euro bribe. What I'm wondering about is how exactly do you expense a bribe? Because they don't exactly issue a receipt for that sort of thing!"

"Oh right, you'll need to expense that. Just mark it in the accounts as a bribe and then make a note for the accounting department. They'll find a way to square it later. Make it their problem!"

"Righto! Thanks, boss!"

I had to use that border crossing a few more times in my career. Every single time we rocked up, Tweedle-Dee and Tweedle-Dumb were there, but they never did cause me any trouble again after that. I never did see the head guard again, which was actually upsetting because I had hoped to get another bottle of blueberry rakija off him.

And I certainly never did meet the judge!

He's Probably Out Back Having Sex

As you've probably gathered by this point, dealing with border guards can present some very strange situations and one must keep on their toes when dealing with them. Sometimes, though, a Tour Leader is faced with a border situation that is so strange that it stretches the very limits of credulity. Such was the situation on one memorable trip through Croatia where we were dealt a shocking moment both going into and leaving the beautiful Adriatic country.

At the time, our company ran a twenty-two-day tour that took in a couple of the major sites of Croatia. We would take an overnight ferry from Bari, Italy to Dubrovnik, drive up along the stunning coastline into the interior and see the Plitvice Lakes National Park and eventually go into the neighboring country of Slovenia. During this time, we'd also duck into Bosnia and Herzegovina for just for a few hours to see the picturesque town of Mostar and its famous, old bridge. Entering Bosnia, it was well known that the Bosnian border guards required a bribe going into the country. Oddly enough, it wasn't a cash bribe. What you'd need to do is organize a drinks package. In a large carrier bag, you'd have to buy at least a six-pack of a Western European or Czech produced beer. I'd always make sure to have bought them in France the week before. Just to further grease the wheels, I'd also throw in a couple of bottles of Coca-Cola and a couple of bottles of water (this particular border post had no air conditioning and would get quite hot even in the spring and fall). I always found it strange that the guards wouldn't be too fussed about the beer but the minute they saw that there was Coca-Cola their eyes would light up and the passports got stamped even faster. This particular journey didn't produce anything strange with the Bosnians though. It was the Croats who made the far greater impression on this visit!

Coming back into Croatia from Bosnia could be a real headache. The border crossing usually had three of four buses in a queue which meant that you could be waiting for up to a couple of hours for your turn at the Bosnian border post to get stamped out of Bosnia and then another hour while the Croats did the same. All the while, the passengers had to remain on the bus at all times. Only Tour Leaders and drivers were authorized to leave the bus in order to visit the different border offices. Since the Bosnian guards were the same guys that you dealt with in the morning, they were usually quite quick in getting you stamped out. You didn't even need to bribe them a second time! The Croatian side was a bit different though. Both the Tour Leader and driver would need to complete a task. For the driver, the job was easy; just go to the Transport Police office and get the green driver form signed. Those lucky devils! This task usually took about one minute. For the Tour Leaders, though, we'd have to go to the Croatian Passport office, a run-down dump of a tin construction hut, knock on the door, wait for the police officer to open it and take your passports, and then, outside the office in the sweltering heat, wait for them to stamp every single passport. This process could take forever, and if the guard decided to go for a smoke break (or two or three), even longer than that!

On this particular tour my driver was Davey, one of my favorites among the British collection of drivers that we had, and a real pro on this route through Croatia. Davey was every bit the classic British bus driver and loved to have a good time and enjoy the tour just like the passengers. We got on like champions and enjoyed teasing and having a laugh at each other's expense. All in good fun!

Getting to the border post in the afternoon we were both stunned and pleased to see that there were no buses at all in the queue to go back into Croatia! It looked like our luck was in! The Bosnian guards took care of us in short order and were in a good mood, even allowing me to make a comment that the head guard always got frustrated with when I said goodbye to him, which I always did at this crossing:

"Thanks very much, boys. We very much enjoyed our time in Bosnia!" I said to the border guard.

"NONONONONO! It's not Bosnia! It's Bosnia AND Herzegovina! You must also say Herzegovina!" The head guard responded in an accent that sounded very much like Arnold Schwarzenegger's.

"Oh right, sorry! Bosnia AND Herzegovina!"

"Yes, important to say both! You always forget! Please don't forget! Next time remember or else you not come into Bosnia!"

"I thought it was Bosnia AND Herzegovina!? And where is this Herzegovina anyway?" I asked. This guard was always fun to play around with.

"Herzegovina? I don't know where this is! But it's always important for the foreigner to say Bosnia and Herzegovina!" Arnold Schwarzenegger's voice double remained animated!

"OK, fine! Next time I'll say it right! Beer was OK, too? You drank it already?"

"Yes, beer was good for lunchtime! Please next time if you bring German beer, we prefer this!"

"OK, German beer next time for our good friends in Bosnia!"

"NOOO!!! It's Bosnia AND Herzegovina!"

With that, I met Davey back at the bus and we proceeded across the parking lot to the Croatian Transport office where Davey presented his papers and had them stamped in under a minute. He then lorded it over me that his task was over, whilst mine would likely be a while.

"HAHA f&%*er! I'm all done! I guess I'll go and sit in the lovely, air-conditioned bus for the next hour! Have fun standing around like a twat for the next hour waiting for the passports to get stamped!" This was Davey's ever so subtle way of saying "see you later!"

"Haha, indeed! Hope your AC gives out for the next hour and it turns into a greenhouse instead!" I didn't actually hope for this, as it would create a busload of irate passengers, but it was the only response that I had in that moment.

So, on I went, alone, to the Croatian Passport office. Easy enough; knock on the door, officer takes the box of passports, slams the door in my face, and I sit there in the baking sun until he's done. With fifty passengers I reckoned it would be an hour for sure.

Except…nobody answered the door! So, after a minute I knocked again, slightly louder, and this time…nobody answered the door!

I couldn't fathom why nobody was answering me. Generally, there is always someone in these offices. They may be sleeping, but someone is in there. With no other option, I opened the door, walked in, looked up, and could understand why no one was answering the door.

The border guard had a very attractive and very much naked woman on the desk and was in the middle of "stamping her passport" as it were.

"Oh, um, hello!" This was as much of a greeting as I could get out of my mouth. I actually felt bad for having interrupted. That said, he really should have put a sock on the doorknob. Yet, without breaking his stride, the Croat border guard was keen to have a chat with me and didn't seem at all annoyed at the interruption.

"Hello!"

"Yeah, I've got a box of passports that need stamps. Should, I just leave them here…?" I was keen to get my passports done, but I didn't want to disturb this guard's good time. I mean, how long could the guy possibly take with this little side task?

"You are with autobus?" asked the border guard, who was still very much focused on the task at hand.

"Uh, yes, British autobus. With Americans, Australians….others too!" I responded.

"British bus….is OK! You go now! Office is too busy!" responded the guard, and I agreed; this office did indeed appear to be very busy! Much busier than normal.

"OK, but what about the passports? No stamp?"

"No, is OK, no stamp today! Bus is fine! Welcome to Croatia! You go now!" Clearly this guard had no interest in me, the bus, the passports, or in continuing this conversation any further.

"OK, thank you! And good luck with…uh…thank you!" I replied, and with that I was done with the passports and back out the door.

Within seconds I was back on the bus where a surprised Davey awaited me.

"What the hell are you doing back so soon?" asked Davey who was halfway through his midafternoon cigarette.

"Um, well, we can go is the thing. Border guard said to get on with things."

"But you were only gone for three minutes. They didn't stamp the passports," said Davey. There was no fooling him!

"No, but there was a...situation in the passport office. Border guard just told us to go."

"What sort of situation? What was happening?" Davey, by now, was more than mildly interested.

"I'll tell you once we get going, but for now I think it's best if we just get the hell outta here!" I wasn't really in the mood to hang about the border since we were already cleared for entry into Croatia.

Picking up the microphone, it was time for a quick bus announcement, "OK, crew, we are cleared for entry. I'll come down and give your passports back. The good news now is that we're well ahead of schedule and should get to our hotel well and early today!"

Moments later, having given everyone's passports back and answered a few questions, I came back to the front of the bus and sat in the jump seat. Davey was keen to ask a few questions himself.

"Alright, now just what exactly happened at the passport office?"

I related the full incident to Davey, who by the end of the story, pointed out a major concern.

"You realize that we now have a big problem tomorrow?"

"No, we don't," I lied. Of course, I was actually well aware of the new problem we faced.

"Yes, we do. We have a major problem! Nobody got their passport stamped! What happens tomorrow when we leave Croatia and they can't find our entry stamp!?" Davey wasn't pointing out anything I didn't already know.

"Davey, it's not our problem!"

"Well, if it's not our problem, then whose problem is it?"

"Davey, this is a problem that tomorrow Will and tomorrow Davey can deal with. We can't do anything about it right now, so what's the use in worrying about it?" My reasoning seemed solid enough. There wasn't anything I could do about it at that exact moment.

*   *   *

The next morning Davey still harbored concerns about our coming predicament at the Croatian Passport Office that afternoon.

"What are we going to do? Not a single one of the passengers has a Croatian entry stamp! They're going to want to know why!"

"Well, the way I reckon it, there's only one thing to do – tell them exactly what happened," I said. It wasn't the best plan in the world, but it was all I had.

"You can't say that! They'll never believe that one of their colleagues was in the passport office in the middle of the day getting laid! It's a horrible idea!" Davey wasn't at all convinced of my plan.

"Well, it's exactly what happened? What would you have me say?" I was open to suggestions.

"Well, not that! Tell them that we got lost somehow or that the border guards came on board and simply looked at them and left!" Davey's ideas lacked originality and didn't really sound like they'd work, at least, no more than mine.

"No, I think I'll just stick with the sex explanation. At the very least it'll be a lot of fun to tell them!"

"No, Will, I forbid it, you….if you say that I will….well, I don't know what I'll do, but I won't like it and it won't work." Davey's threat was, I reckoned, a hollow one.

"Well, Davey, that's what I'm going to tell them and we'll just let the cards fall where they may. I think it'll be far more fun than you're "we got lost" explanation. And I'm all about the fun!" And what ensued, did indeed, turn out to be quite a bit of fun!

*   *   *

Pulling up to the Croatian/Slovenian border that afternoon we seemed to be in luck again. It was a slow day at the border with no other buses going through at that moment. The Croatian/Slovenian border was also run a lot more professionally than the Croatian/Bosnian one the previous day. No bribes were ever needed and the border guards were generally very quick in processing everyone. It was also slightly different in that the driver and Tour Leader would hop off first and get the paperwork done, which only took a brief moment. Once this was done, all the passengers would come off and form a queue and get their passports stamped individually. The other key difference on this day was that instead of two separate passport offices both countries simply had adjacent desks in a single building with border guards for both countries sitting beside each other. The second the Croatian guard stamped your passport, he'd simply hand it straight over to the Slovenian guard who would do the same.

Davey and I hopped off the bus, walked directly to the Croatian desk only to see...the lights were off and no one was home! No one sitting there at all. The young Slovenian border guard sitting at the Slovenian desk looked like she was having the world's most boring day. She also happened to be quite an attractive border guard, which in my experience is a rare thing. I was pleasantly surprised to find that I'd be explaining things to her and not to an overweight and hungover, middle-aged guy named Zvezda.

"Hello, welcome to Slovenia. Passport please!" The cute Slovene seemed genuinely happy to see us.

Davey and I learned in short order through our only semi-embarrassing flirting that her name was Katja and that she had only been on the job for a few weeks. Davey and I generally always flirted with guides, waitresses, and salesgirls. Being able to chat up a border guard was a new one for both of us. Katja for her part looked through my passport three times before asking the inevitable question:

"Where is your Croatian entry stamp? I see a Bosnian exit stamp dated yesterday, but no Croatian entry stamp?" Katja remained friendly and smiling, but it was clear a proper explanation was going to be needed. I glimpsed briefly at Davey with a look of "here goes nothing." For his part, Davey's expression was one of "I can't believe he's going to actually tell her!"

"Well, the thing about the Croatian entry stamp…"

As I related the events of the previous day the look on Katja's face was a real study in expressions as she continued to pore over my passport. It changed over the course of the story from one of annoyance to one of disbelief to one of doubt and by the end to one of thoughtful acceptance as she stamped my passport and exclaimed, "That sounds about right. Welcome to Slovenia!"

Davey was just as shocked as I was as we had the passengers come off the bus to get their stamps done. Katja did them all in record time, not even bothering to scan them electronically. We were done in less than ten minutes. Since we were now well ahead of schedule for a second day running, I decided there was still time to have a chat with this absolutely charming Slovenian border guard.

"Katja, thank you so much for that! You really saved us! But I have to ask; why did you stamp everyone in so easily? We didn't have the Croatian stamp, You could have really caused us trouble! Most border guards would have."

"Oh, I knew you were telling the truth. You couldn't make up a story like that. Besides, I know a lot of Croat men. They're animals! Your story rang true!" said Katja without an ounce of irony or sarcasm.

"Oh, OK! That's great! And just out of interest; where's the Croatian border guard who's supposed to be here?"

"Him? Oh, he's probably out back having sex. It's not so surprising!" Katja said this again, without a flicker of surprise in her voice, as though it were a simple matter of fact.

"Right, well, thank you again, Katja! I certainly hope to see you again here sometime!" Why all border guards couldn't be like Katja, I'll never figure out!

So it was, we were able to both enter and exit Croatia with fifty tourists without getting a single passport stamp. Although, to be fair, we had entered and exited Croatia on that tour once already, so none of the passengers actually missed out on getting a Croatian passport stamp. I've gone through many border controls as both a Tour Leader and just on my own in my private travels, but I don't think I'll ever have as crazy a time as I did on that occasion going through Croatia!

I Can Just Steal Whatever I Can Shove into My Cargo Shorts?

As time went on in my career as a Tour Leader, I was fortunate to be able to lead tours to more and more exotic and interesting places. I'm often asked what some of the more interesting locations are to take groups to and in which to work. While you can make a case for any location, I always found my tours to the Middle East to be amongst the most interesting and compelling.

Our tours to the Middle East encompassed Israel and Jordan. I didn't much care for Israel the first couple of times I went there, but the country grew on me the more I went. As for Jordan, with its Muslim influence and hospitality, it became a favorite of mine immediately. Working in these two countries became an experience that I most looked forward to and enjoyed.

One problem that I always had with the groups was the fact that many of our passengers would book the tour thinking that it was a religious-based tour. This was not the case. Whilst we would visit many important sites that had a religious significance, it was not a tour that was built, designed, marketed, or conducted with a strictly religious theme. This was at times a bit disappointing for our passengers who were Christians, but I would set the record straight on the very first day in my opening comments.

"For those of you who booked this tour thinking that it will be focused on the different Christian religious sites, I can only say two things. First, you obviously didn't read the tour itinerary. Second, we'll be accompanied in Israel by a local guide who is Jewish, in Jordan by a local guide who is Muslim, all the while being led around by a Tour Leader who is an atheist; so, if you think we'll be doing on board homilies or prayer circles you can think again. That said, we'll fit in as many of the holy sites as time permits. Any questions?"

Once passengers knew what to expect, things went fine and we never once had a passenger who was that upset about the fact that we were running the tour in a secular manner. Our guides in Israel were always well-educated Israeli Jews who really knew their religious history, a mandatory requirement in order to be an Israeli tour guide, and we never had the same guide twice. Our guide in Jordan was the same chap every time; an absolute wild man named Hassan who, like me, would say anything to anyone at any time. He'd been educated in America in the 1990's and fancied himself as an Arab man-about-town. He looked much younger than a person in their mid-forties. Hassan and I got on like blood brothers every time we visited Jordan. Hassan also knew every single person in Jordan, it seemed. Like every good Arab, he was well acquainted with every businessperson in the tourist trade.

Our first stop in Jordan would be in Aqaba, a resort city on the Gulf of Aqaba at the very south of Jordan. We never stayed long in Aqaba, just a quick tour around the quickly evolving and growing city and a spot of lunch before we would head on to the famed Wadi Rum. During the Muslim holidays, during which we always seemed to visit, alcohol could be a real potential problem. Not with Hassan! He always had a friend willing to open up their bottle-o in order to satisfy the liquor needs of us blasphemers!

One of my tours to the Holy Land occurred during the Christmas season. It's actually a great time to visit Israel and Jordan. It's not at all hot and neither the Jews nor the Muslims celebrate Christmas, so everything's open as normal. I had a sizeable group of roughly twenty-five passengers (Middle East tours never had as many bookings as European ones) and an extremely limited budget for Christmas. Ordinarily, our company was always keen to provide a small Christmas present for each passenger, but this year I only had about five Euros per person to work with. Five Euros per person doesn't go far in either Israel or Jordan. I would need to be creative in how I went about spreading the Christmas cheer.

I decided that whatever gift package I got for the passengers, it would need to contain an item or items from both countries. It didn't have to be anything fancy. Things like keychains, magnets, stickers, or pens would easily suffice. The first country I would deal with was Israel. I decided to leave my Christmas shopping for the city of Eilat, the Israeli sister city to Aqaba. Both cities are actually tax-free jurisdictions. A very good place to do all my shopping!

The Israeli side turned out to be easy-as! I happened upon a store called "Shekel Saver," which was an Israeli version of a dollar store. They had everything! Magnets, keychains, stickers, Israeli flags, you name it! And at bargain basement prices! I was able to get all those items, and more for only slightly more than two Euros per person! Indeed, the only thing they didn't have were Christmas cards. They had all sorts of cards for other occasions, but without pictures on the cards, it was quite impossible to tell what the occasion was. Not being literate in Hebrew, I thought I'd inquire as to what the different cards were for. The salesclerk was quite helpful as he picked up my pile of cards and described what each was for.

"Sir, these cards are all for a birthday. It says so right across the front. That's Hebrew for birthday."

"OK! That's fine. It's Jesus's birthday I suppose! Yeah, what about the rest of them?" I had a real assortment of cards; they weren't all the same.

"These next cards are all for a nisuin. That's a Jewish wedding," said the salesclerk.

"A wedding ceremony? All right, close enough. They'll never know. What about the others?"

Left in the pile of cards I'd taken were cards for anniversaries, Bar Mitzvahs, graduations, and even condolence and get-well-soon cards. The salesclerk though, took his time with the last two cards that he'd not identified yet.

"And these two cards are for, well, a different sort of Jewish ceremony. I'll be honest, you may want to switch these two out for something else." He was quite nervous with these final two cards.

"Why? What are they for? It can't be anything that bad if they've made a card for it!" I was now quite keen to know what these last two cards were for.

"Well, it's for a very particular Jewish ceremony called a Brit Milah." It was clear that the salesclerk preferred not to say what the Brit Milah was. It sounded like a teenage girl popstar from England to me.

"Is it similar to a bar mitzvah?" I asked, keen to know what this Brit Milah was.

"Well, it's for the boys …. it's a ritual circumcision ceremony," replied the salesclerk.

"Oh! Right! They make a card for that?" It seemed like a very unusual ceremony to have a card for.

"Well, yes. It just says, "Congratulations on the Brit Milah." Most non-Hebrews just call it a bris," the salesclerk was starting to laugh a bit by now.

"OK, well, I've got two female passengers from Australia with a good sense of humor, so I'll take them as well!"

"As you wish, sir. That will be one-hundred ninety-five Shekels."

As I left the Shekel Saver, I thought to myself that shopping for Jordanian souvenirs the next day couldn't get any stranger than what I'd just gone through with the Israeli ones. Once again, I was wrong.

*   *   *

The next day saw us make the crossing from Eilat in Israel to Aqaba in Jordan. Despite the fact that the two countries have full official relations with each other, it doesn't mean that it's a friendly crossing. Bags get x-rayed and scanned in detail as one goes into Jordan and one never knows what the Jordanians will confiscate. On this day, they decided that binoculars were now prohibited, which had never happened to any of my groups before. I was a bit more concerned that they might confiscate my giant bag of Israeli labelled souvenirs. Luckily, no mention was made of them and once we were all stamped into Jordan, we met up with Hassan.

I mentioned to Hassan that one stop that I needed in Aqaba was a well-supplied souvenir store. It was Christmas Day and I needed my presents to the passengers ready for that evening. Hassan knew just the place to go.

The souvenir store Hassan took the group to was the exact opposite of the Shekel Saver from the day before. The most expensive thing in the Shekel Saver cost a Euro. The cheapest items in this Jordanian souvenir store, keychains, were running close to five Euros apiece. The passengers didn't seem to mind too much. I'd warned them well in advance that Jordan was an expensive country. The problem in my view was that this shop was way too far out of my budget. I only had seventy Euros left. If I bought here then the passengers would have to share keychains and that just wouldn't do at all! I mentioned this difficulty to Hassan who had a chat with the owner while I perused the shop. Moments later, Hassan beckoned me over to where he and the owner were having their discussion.

"Will, this is Mr. Faisal He's in charge here," said Hassan.

"Salaam Alaikum, Mr. Faisal. It is a pleasure to be in your shop!" I said to Mr. Faisal as I shook his hand. In Arab cultures, introductions are vitally important to get right.

"Alaikum Salaam, Mr. Will. Likewise, it is a pleasure to have you in my humble store. I understand that you are in need of gifts for your group, but you have little money to spend?" Mr. Faisal was already striking me as the consummate Arab businessman.

"This is true, Mr. Faisal; my company has left me with few funds with which to buy my guests a Christmas present. Perhaps you may be of assistance?"

"We will discuss the matter over a cup of tea," replied Mr. Faisal, and the three of us went to the back for a spot of tea while the group continued shopping.

Tea is an integral part of the Arab identity and important discussions are often had with a pot of it on hand. Mr. Faisal was very keen to get to business just as soon as we all had a cup of chai in hand.

"Mr. Will, it is a great blessing that Hassan has brought you to my shop! We will find a way, I am sure, to meet your needs. What sort of gifts were you hoping to purchase for your guests?"

"The usual sort of trinkets, as we call them. Small and inexpensive items that can be easily packed. Things such as magnets and keychains. The ones in your shop are of a very good quality, but sadly, out of my price range," I replied. One always has to play up the quality of the goods on offer in the Arab World.

"Ah, do not concern yourself with the prices that you see in the shop! How much have you to spend here?"

"I've only got seventy Euros." Ordinarily when dealing with an Arab vendor, one would understate one's resources, but it was a company budget so I didn't see the point.

At this point Mr. Faisal and Hassan engaged in a long and animated discussion in Arabic. Strangely, during the discussion both of them grabbed and shook the pockets of my cargo pants. After a few moments, they reverted back to English. Seemingly, a solution had been found, as Mr. Faisal outlined.

"Mr. Will, I think we can assist you with your problem. You will require a receipt for your purchase, I presume?"

"Well, I am expensing the whole thing, so yes," I could sense that a bit of a scam was brewing.

"You give us your seventy Euros and we will issue you a receipt for that amount. You can then take any souvenirs you want, as much as will fit into your pockets!" Mr. Faisal seemed most pleased with his and Hassan's plan.

"So, what you're saying is I can just steal whatever I can shove into my cargo shorts?" I replied. This was turning into a great deal for me!

"Oh, but it is not stealing! Your people are spending money here most generously, and between us, our mark-up on these items is … profitable. This is no problem! Please, take what you need!" Mr. Faisal didn't need to tell me twice.

"Shukran, Mr. Faisal! Allah's blessings upon you for your generosity!" I downed my tea; I was ready to load up!

Thanks to Hassan and Mr. Faisal I was able to get Jordanian keychains, magnets, stickers, and a bunch of other items for the whole group. Mr. Faisal's definition of pockets included a plastic bag that he insisted I fill up as well. I was surprised that he didn't send out for a steamer trunk!

By the time Christmas dinner came that evening in the Wadi Rum, I had a huge envelope with gifts bursting out of them for every passenger. Mr. Faisal also made sure that I took a keffiyeh for myself, a traditional Jordanian men's head wrap. It made Hassan and me look like twins for the next two days. The gifts certainly went over well with the passengers. I never told them, but each of them received about twenty Euros worth of gifts instead of the budgeted five.

I wish I could say that my experience with Mr. Faisal was a once-in-a-lifetime sort of thing. In fact, I wasn't surprised one bit. Having spent a good bit of time throughout the Middle East, I've found the people there, and the shopkeepers in particular, to be the most hospitable of individuals. To not be offered tea is highly unusual, but to be handed a plastic carrier bag and be told by the shopkeeper to fill it up with whatever you want and to fill one's pockets as well, now that is highly unusual!

Part 4

A Random Assortment
of the Weird

Some things one sees on tour aren't worthy enough of a full story, but are interesting little items nonetheless. From the absurdity of made-up Finnish sports events to strange hotel properties (why does this patio not have a balcony?), there come moments in every tour where you see, read, or hear something strange enough that you swear you'll include it in a book one day. These are them.

Those Are the House Rules

In my career as a Tour Leader, I've taken groups to a lot of different hotels. Some good, some bad, but each one has its own sort of character. Every now and then you get booked into one that's not quite normal for one reason or another. Here now, are some of the more unusual hotel rules, notices, and quirks that I've ever seen.

One hotel that we would use quite often in Tuscany was nice and comfortable enough, but I'd have to make sure that whoever stayed in rooms 213 and 215 were well acquainted with each other. The reason for this is because if you were standing on the balcony of room 213 you had a direct line of sight into the shower of room 215. Additionally, one room whose number I can't remember had a fine large balcony, but absolutely no railing! Just a straight twenty-five-meter drop into the back-alley's dumpster!

The hotel that we always stayed in during our visits to St. Petersburg had installed a lift many years after the hotel had been built and due to the structure of the building the elevator could only stop on the mid-floor stair landings. So, no matter what, you'd have to carry your luggage up or down a half flight of stairs. Adding to the confusion was the fact that the floor buttons in the elevator were labelled .5, 1.5, 2.5, 3.5, and so on.

The same hotel in St. Petersburg also had a cat living in it. Now, there's nothing so strange about that except for the fact that the cat knew how to use the heating ducts to get into any room it wanted to. Many a time I'd have passengers come to me asking if there was some special reason why a cat was sleeping in their room. It also seemed as though the cat would always be in the room of a passenger who was allergic to it.

From time to time in the Rhine Valley we would have to stay at a hotel in a town called Kamp-Bornhofen which had a very odd drinks menu. Depending on which tour company you were travelling with, there was a different menu. Our group, because we weren't there regularly, had to pay more for our drinks. Naturally, it didn't take long for my groups to figure out that all they had to do was to say they were with the tour group that was entitled to the cheap menu. No one ever checked! Very inefficient and illogical, especially so for the Germans! This hotel also didn't have standardized rooms, which drives Tour Leaders crazy! On one occasion, after I had sorted out all the passengers and got everyone relatively satisfied with their accommodations, I went to my room, only to find that it wasn't even a single! The only thing in the room was a very tiny cot, which if you were any taller than four and a half feet was too small. The bathroom was, likewise, designed for a short and/or small person. I would have to stoop down to use the shower. After dinner that night I had every passenger come by my room to see what I was dealing with. My driver eventually took mercy on me and let me sleep on the bus.

Staying in the Rhine Valley, we also would stay in a town called Lahnstein every so often. The hotel we used there had a very elderly husband and wife ownership team who would not allow me to hand out the room keys to the passengers until they had finished their dinner. The dining room also had a unique characteristic as the owners kept their pet parrot there. I'm not sure how the parrot felt about our usual chicken dinner. A little too close to the mark if you ask me.

The hotel that we stayed in in Nice, France, had nothing unusual about it except for one accidental design feature that we Tour Leaders would selfishly take advantage of. The hotel was located one block from the beach, but the view of the beach was restricted by the building on the other side of the street. All the rooms that is, except for rooms whose numbers ended with 13. Rooms ending in 13 were in line with the perpendicular street outside the hotel and thus had a view of the beach and ocean (not a brilliant view, mind you, but a view nonetheless). I'd always ring the hotel the day before arrival and request the highest available room ending in 13.

One hotel in Moscow had a very strange dining room set-up. We would stay here for three nights on our Russian River Cruising tour. It was apparently the largest hotel in Russia and as such has several dining rooms for both breakfast and dinner service. I didn't know it until certain passengers of mine from Malaysia, Singapore, and the Philippines told me, but there are separate dining halls that are segregated just for the Chinese tour groups. Some of my Asian passengers had been directed to the Asian dining hall and not been allowed into what was apparently the non-Asian dining hall. A quick word with the catering manager set that right, although some of my passengers preferred the Asian dining hall as apparently the food was much better there.

It was a common occurrence in many old-time German, Austrian, and Swiss hotels that the room numbers would make absolutely no sense. Room five could be next to room eighteen which could be across from room thirty-four. Go one floor up and you'd be liable to find room eight and room forty-two. Trying to get fifty passengers to their correct rooms could be a real adventure sometimes.

Speaking of Austria, many hotels in that country would actually have their showers installed outside of the bathroom and placed within open view of the beds. This would create very uncomfortable shower situations especially for single travelers who were sharing a room. My only advice to them was this, "Whichever of you wants to have a shower, the other go downstairs for a drink at the bar for fifteen minutes. After that, switch!" So long as passengers were pre-warned, it wasn't a big deal.

All hotels in Berlin, by law, must have a bar that is open twenty-four hours a day, or, failing that, beer must be available for purchase twenty-four hours a day. We certainly used that to our disadvantage on many a tour! Oh, the hangovers!

Speaking of twenty-four-hour bar service at a hotel, one of our usual hotels in Barcelona, Spain, advertised its bar as being open around the clock. It even had a poster in the elevator advertising the fact. It always seemed as though my favorite driver, Ron, and I would be assigned this hotel on our tours. Since we would be staying for three nights, we'd have a couple of late nights at the bar and invariably end up in a fight with the hotel staff at around two in the morning when they tried to close the bar on us. It wasn't at all unusual to have security show up trying to evict us from the bar. One night Ron had enough and actually dismantled the advertising frame from the lift and brought the advertising poster back into the bar and showed it to security. They reopened the bar.

A hotel near Lucerne, Switzerland, that we'd stay at was owned by a fellow from India and specialized in groups from that country. He was very oddly protective of the curry powder on every table in the hotel dining room. If you were eating at the hotel restaurant and you weren't an Indian, he would not let you use any of the curry powder and would take it away for the duration of your meal and bring you ketchup instead.

Trips to Copenhagen would always be a highlight for me because we would stay at a Park Inn near the airport. It was a fine hotel, but I noticed immediately on my first visit that all of the receptionists were uniformly female, in their mid-twenties, five foot eight inches, blonde, and all wearing very tight form-fitting teal dresses. On the same visit I asked to see the manager in charge of hiring (mainly to congratulate him, and it would've had to have been a man doing the hiring), and upon asking him why it was only supermodels working at reception, he responded by saying, "Don't worry. We hire ugly women, too. They're called chefs." Quite shocking and unexpected to hear that explanation from a citizen of the world's most gender-equal country. One would've thought it was Athens and not Copenhagen.

We used all sorts of hotels in Marghera, the access city for Venice. Sadly, many of these hotels didn't quite have the level of customer service that one would want or expect from a hotel in a major tourist city. Quite a few of them had no air conditioning, very small beds, and tiny showers. One of these hotels in particular didn't always stock enough soap or shampoo in the rooms. When passengers would go downstairs to ask for extra soap or shampoo (or pillows or anything, really) they would be told to go ask the hotel across the street!

Almost every hotel in Finland has saunas installed. Great fun to use those, but one of the hotels we would use in Helsinki had very unclear labels as to which was the men's sauna and which was the women's sauna. Passengers would often get it wrong (me included on my first stay) and end up in the wrong changing room. Luckily, Finns are shockingly comfortable with nudity, so it was usually just our passengers who would be embarrassed about things for a minute or two before making their way to the correct changing room.

Another hotel in Paris that I only stayed at once with a group had stocked condoms in the rooms, but no soap! Which seems about right for a hotel in Paris.

The hotel that we used in Stockholm had an odd effect on some of our passengers. The lift would announce which floor you were getting off at when the doors opened. The Swedish word for floor level is "våning" which sounds very much like "warning" and the Swedish word for six is "sex." So, whenever passengers who were staying on the sixth floor got out of the elevator, they would invariably hear a Swedish woman's voice telling them, "Warning, sex." I've generally found that a warning isn't needed so much as a reminder. Coincidentally, also in the same Stockholm hotel, there was always a fire extinguisher on every floor near the elevator. Swedish fire extinguishers are often labelled with the word "skum," which is the Swedish word for foam.

Hotel Name Withheld
for Legal Reasons

One hotel in Paris took things a little further than just an odd rule, strange quirk, or unusual characteristic. It was actually a member of one of the larger hotel chains in Europe, but the management team had decided to take things a step or two further from the rules and regulations laid down by their head office. I only ever took a group to this particular hotel once, and it was clear from the moment we arrived that this hotel had organizational issues. There were three large groups all waiting to get checked in. After twenty minutes with no service I asked one of the other group's Tour Leaders just what was going on. They explained to me that this was quite normal at this hotel and that if one got their group checked in in less than an hour, that you'd done well. The staff was clearly incompetent and couldn't have organized a piss-up in a brewery. After making a giant nuisance of myself the hotel management finally gave me my group's room keys, but not before I read them the hotel rules. Included below, word for word, are the full rules for this particular Parisian hotel, with my thoughts added in parentheses.

Dear guest, welcome to our hotel.

All the team of the (**Hotel name withheld for legal reasons**) is at your disposal to make your stay a pleasant one and ensure security of our guests within the hotel.

That is why we are asking you to follow the rules below during your stay with us:

- On arrival the tour manager will have to give reception the final rooming list, his room number, as well as the driver's room number and a deposit of an amount fixed upon reservation. (*I had never before and have never since, ever had to give a deposit for a group at a hotel anywhere.*)

- Upon arrival you have one hour to report any defects in the bedrooms. After this time you will be held responsible for any damage caused in your room. (*Obviously, I told my group to break as many things as possible within that first hour.*)

- We ask all our guests to have appropriate behaviour and follow a proper dress code within the hotel. (*What was the dress code? Your guess is as good as mine! We never did find out.*)

- Your room access code is confidential. Please make sure your door is shut before you leave your room or before you go to bed. (*Of course, because I routinely make a habit of leaving my hotel door open throughout the night.*)

- Please always look after your luggage and belongings in public areas of the hotel. (*This, actually makes sense, especially in the area of Paris the hotel was in.*)

- It is forbidden to make noise in the rooms or in the corridors as it does not respect other guests' right to privacy and serenity. (*God forbid, we disturb the serenity!*)

- We only accept a maximum of three people at a time in each bedroom. (*OK, I get it, a ménage à trois is allowed; gang-bangs and orgies are forbidden!*)

- It is forbidden to smoke in public areas of the hotel.

- It is strictly forbidden to bring and use alcoholic drinks or drugs in the hotel. (*This nearly caused a riot within the group, who enjoyed their drinks. I reminded them that backpacks make very good liquor concealment bags. Just bring the empties with you when you leave, lest you lose the deposit*)
- For your comfort, rooms must be kept tidy in order to facilitate cleaning by the chambermaid. (*Basically, don't make a mess, or else the cleaning lady will have to do her job.*)
- Breakfast times for the group will be decided in advance with reception. If the time decided for breakfast is not respected by the group, breakfast may not be served. (*This is actually common in hotels that cater to large tour groups. I just resented the snarky way it was written.*)
- On departure the tour manager will have to review the stay of the group with reception before getting the deposit back.

The hotel manager may ask to keep the deposit given by the tour manager upon arrival in case of failure to follow the above rules whose aim is to ensure a pleasant stay for everyone.

The day manager didn't laugh one bit when I mentioned to him that all the threesomes engaged in by members of my group were done quietly, with strictly three people to a room, without using any outside drugs or alcohol, with the doors securely closed, whilst also respecting the dress code, and without anyone enjoying a cigarette afterwards, and everyone made their own beds afterwards so that the chambermaid wouldn't need to go to any extra effort or exertion to make up the room afterwards. Luckily, I did get the deposit back.

Get Asquinted with the Plan

As a Tour Leader one stays in so many hotels in so many different places that they all do tend to look the same after a while. One thing that I found interesting, and that I would always take a good look at in every hotel, was the emergency escape and fire readiness plan that would be included either on the door of each room or near the lift. I eventually made it a habit to read it in every hotel. Not so much to be ready in case of a fire or emergency, but for the comedy value. Due to a lack of written English fluency, they're usually quite funny. There's at least one proper chuckle-worthy sentence in each one. One of the best I ever found was in a hotel in Croatia, which I include below. Again, I've added my thoughts in parenthesis.

DEAR GUESTS

Here is the plan of evacuation and rescue in case of fire in our hotel. We kindly ask you to follow all the instructions and fire protection measures being carried out.
We please you:

- Get asquinted with the plan (*Didn't really see the need to. The font it was printed in was just fine.*)
- Study the instructions which are on the entrance door of your room (*As opposed to the exit door to the room.*)

- Remember the direction where you should move and leave the hotel (*In an emergency when time is of the essence, you might blank out and forget entirely that you should leave the building. And if you forget, you'll just have to go back and study the instructions again.*)
- Learn how to behave in case of fire (*No tomfoolery allowed! This is a serious situation and your parents should have taught you long ago to be on best behavior during a fire!*)
- Believe that the hotel is equipped with all necessary fire fighting equipment and the hotel staff is trained for every possible (*Possible what? You left us on a cliffhanger ending there! And no need for the hotel and staff to actually be equipped and trained for a fire, so long as you believe that they are. That's good enough!*)

In case of fire your greatest support would be to move quietly and without panic towards the exit according to the instructions for evacuation.

Thank You

The Vegetarian Quarantine Corner

When it comes to strange rules, there was one hotel that stood above all others. In the Bernese-Oberland region of Switzerland there was a hotel that we would stay in on almost every visit to the Jungfrau region, perhaps the most beautiful Alpine location anywhere on Earth. The hotelier Ulrich, who you'll remember from the story about Neil, ran a very tight ship! Being Swiss-German, he was very exacting about the protocols and rules of the house. This is not an unusual sort of thing in Switzerland. Many hotels in Switzerland are an extension of the owner's home. In fact, hoteliers view them as exactly that and demand a certain level of decorum and respect from the guests.

Ulrich's hotel was exactly what you'd want and expect from a Swiss Alpine setting. The interior was all wood, it had a lovely and cozy ground floor relaxation area with a bar and a big TV. Ulrich collected lapel pins and he had several thousand of them pinned up on cork board paneling at the bar. He was also a big-time ski champion in the 1980s so his many ski trophies were on display as well.

The guest rooms were relatively basic, but comfortable. Many of them had balconies where you could look out over the beautiful Swiss Alps. In the summer there was a swimming pool available as well. It was always quite a nice place to stay, but as I mentioned, Ulrich ran a tight ship. During the drive into the village Tour Leaders would need to go over the house rules in detail with the passengers, and they were fully expected to follow them to the letter! What were some of the rules you may ask? In no particular order the big ones were:

1. Guests are required to keep the shower curtain within the confines of the shower at all times. Please do not flood your bathroom.

2. When not looking out of your room window, please ensure that it remains closed and firmly latched at all times.

3. No food or drink of any sort is allowed in the guest rooms at any time. A bottle of water is acceptable, but nothing else.

4. No smoking allowed within the hotel at any time. For guests who want to smoke, a smoker's area is available by using the hotel exit adjacent to the bar. Do not extinguish your cigarette butt on the ground. Ensure that it is deposited in the butt dispenser, clearly visible within the confines of the smoking area.

5. Towels will not be replaced from day to day. It is required that all passengers hang their used towel on the provided towel rack in order for it to dry and then be used again.

6. No children under the age of eighteen may use the lift at any time without parental supervision.

7. When leaving the hotel during the day, deposit your key in the key cabinet so that the cleaners can go in and tidy up. It wasn't enough to just leave your key on the appropriate hook in the cabinet either. It had to be hung up in a very specific way. Every time I took passengers to the train station on the morning of the free day to go up the Jungfraujoch, the last thing I would do before leaving was to rehang all keys in the correct manner.

8. When leaving the hotel in the evening, please take your key with you. Ulrich would close the bar at eleven each evening and lock the hotel's front doors. So, if you were out late and didn't have your key, there was no way to get back inside!

9. No electronic devices are allowed in the dining room. This was in force at all times and was very strictly enforced by Ulrich. This wasn't just mobile phones either! Cameras, tablets, any sort of E-device; all of them banned! It also didn't matter if you had it and weren't using it; just having it in the room was a violation of the rule. I actually really liked the rule, though I never let

Ulrich know that. It forced the passengers to actually speak to each other and made for a much livelier atmosphere at dinner time. It was also great fun when a passenger was caught with their phone. Ulrich would actually take it away, keep it for the duration of the dinner service, and only give it back to them after they had apologized to him at the bar. It was like seeing a child who had knocked over a milk carton having to apologize to their dad. Brilliant and hilarious, and they couldn't say that they hadn't been warned!

10. The craziest rule, and the one that drove certain passengers completely bonkers, was also a dinner time requirement concerning the vegetarians and vegans within the group. All vegetarians and vegans were required to sit together at their own special table away from the rest of the group so that they could all be served together off of the same special platter. The table that they were given was also set apart from the passengers dining off the regular menu and didn't have a window view of the countryside either. I used to call it "The Vegetarian Quarantine Corner." Naturally, this made for some strange arrangements. If there was a married couple on the tour and one of them was a vegetarian or vegan and the other one wasn't, they wouldn't be able to sit with each other for dinner. It simply was not allowed and they couldn't appeal to me because it was Ulrich's house and he makes the rules. It was always explained to the passengers in detail that this would be the situation at dinner time and that they'd just have to muck on and live with it! Truth be told, I actually really respected and liked the rule. Most Tour Leaders will happily admit that catering for people with dietary restrictions is the bane of our existence and a complete pain in the ass! Vegetarians aren't so bad, but cranky vegans were always the worst as nothing was ever good enough for them. Ulrich would always have a decent vegetarian option available, but you could tell that he didn't much care for having to cater to them either. Naturally, Ulrich provided a proper three-course dinner for our groups, but he always knew how

to get under my skin. He found out on one of my first stays with him that I abhor pineapple. I can't stand pineapple. So, the dessert course on every single visit would always be a cup of pineapple.

Now, some of these rules are sensible, and once it was explained to passengers, they quite understood. For example, most passengers couldn't understand the shower curtain rule. Why does it matter so much? The reason for that one was that it was a hotel constructed almost entirely out of wood and had no degree of watertightness. If water got out of the shower and flooded things it would seep into the wood and eventually flood the rooms below. Admittedly, there was a method to the madness.

With all these rules and with fifty passengers, it was inevitable that some of the rules would be broken (the food and drink one was the most likely) during the course of our three-day visit to Switzerland. You may ask yourself, what happened then? Well, it wasn't fun. It was never the passengers who would get into trouble for breaking the rules (except for the phone in the dining room rule). Instead, it was us Tour Leaders who would be reprimanded. If a rule or rules were broken, Ulrich would call you into his office late on the second day and have you sit down while he went over the different infractions, who had committed them, when, and to what degree of severity. It could be a proper long lecture. Invariably, the conversation would be something along these lines:

"Will, did you explain to the guests the rule about the food in the rooms?" Ulrich would ask in his very monotone Swiss-German accent.

"Yeah, Ulrich, I explained it to them. I explained it to them several times! And I showed them the sheet as well!"

"I do not think that you explained it so well to them. We found some food in several rooms. Some of them brought cookies. That is very serious."

"Yeah, no, I get it. No cookies! Because of the mouse thing!"

"Yes, Will, it is possible to have mice if food is in the rooms. The mice may come and that is not good."

"OK, Ulrich. I'll do a better job explaining the food next time. Can I go now?"

"Will, one of the guests also broke the shower curtain rule…"

This would go on and on if several rules had been broken. If I'm to get in trouble, I prefer to be yelled at for one or two minutes, but Ulrich would never raise his voice, ever. You could burn the entire hotel down and he still wouldn't yell at you. He would just give you a proper lecture about the rules, the need for them, and voice his disappointment in you for not having taken the rules seriously. It was like being in trouble with a really sweet school principal who, instead of disciplining you and getting angry, just talks about how they expected better of you and that you've really let them down! In my defense, it's absolutely impossible to control all the actions of all the passengers all of the time. Sometimes I thought that some passengers would break the rules just to see what would happen. Then, from time to time, the Tour Leader or driver would get caught breaking a rule!

On one occasion we stayed at Ulrich's house and my driver was Derek (it was always something else with Derek). Instead of going outside to have a cigarette, Derek stayed in his room, tied a sock around the smoke detector, had his cigarette, opened the window, and then deodorized the room afterwards. The problem, and what got him caught, was that he forgot to take the sock down from the smoke detector when he was done. Ulrich figured it out immediately. Since it was the driver breaking the rule, and since we had already left for Paris by the time the infringement was discovered, Ulrich phoned us on the road and gave a proper lecture to Derek over the phone! To be fair, I thought Derek deserved a proper lecture for no other reason than his laxity in covering up the crime. Most passengers would cover up their crime. Most of them would bring food in, but they were reminded by me to remove all evidence of the food when we checked out. No crumbs in the beds or on the surfaces and no rubbish in the bins. The worst thing was to bring the next group in on the next tour and *start* one's stay with a lecture!

The biggest rule of all at Ulrich's house didn't even concern the passengers. It didn't even involve the Tour Leader. The biggest rule of all was the fence rule, and it was for the drivers. Ulrich's hotel was located on top of a hill with a very steep driveway that had a hairpin turn. At the top of the hill, after the hairpin, there was a metal fence along the embankment. Most of the drivers knew how to negotiate this very tricky bit of driving and they'd always get a loud and deserved applause from the passengers for doing so. From time to time though, if the driver were a bit off their game on the day, or if they got the turn just a fraction off, they'd end up taking out the fence. Ulrich would be livid at this! He kept close track of which drivers had done this and how many times they'd done so. If a driver had done it enough times, then they'd be banned from driving up the driveway. In this case, we'd then have a problem as everyone would be forced to carry or drag their luggage all the way up the steep driveway. Not so much fun for the retirees. There was no worse feeling in the world than speaking to Ulrich just ahead of arrival, telling him who the driver was and then having Ulrich tell you to park at the bottom of the hill. It was like a mark of shame for the drivers to be faced with this injunction!

Ulrich and I ended up getting along just fine after a very lengthy getting-used-to-each-other phase. The lectures became less and less frequent as he knew that I was properly explaining the rules to the passengers and respecting the established protocols. You just had to get used to the way Ulrich ran his hotel. We'd also give each other a wide berth and engage in a bit of quid pro quo as well. I wouldn't complain about the pineapple for dessert and Ulrich wouldn't hammer me so much on minor infractions. Ulrich would allow me to bring contraband hot sauce into the dining room provided that I didn't complain about being stuck in room fifty-nine (Room fifty-nine was a single room with no bathroom. In order to use the toilet or have a shower, one would have to go down the corridor and use the communal ones). We learned to live with each other during our visits and eventually got to be friends (or casual enemies at any rate!).

Is that the Real Eiffel Tower?!

It happens every tour. You'll have a passenger make an odd comment or ask a ridiculous question. Sometimes that passenger is not particularly bright, but from time to time, it's an honest question asked out of ignorance. Sometimes it's actually a smart and clever question disguised as a dumb question. Or you'll see a strange sign in a foreign language or an English sign that's been badly mistranslated. Or it's just something else altogether! Here are some of those signs and mistranslations, questions and statements, and/or an oddity with no apparent explanation.

"Why did they build Windsor Castle so close to Heathrow Airport?" – A question asked by a naïve Australian female passenger as we drove back into London at the end of a tour. My answer of, "That way the Queen doesn't have to be driven all across London to get to the airport!" was accepted without a single further thought on her part.

"What's the second toilet in the bathroom for?" – Question asked of me by a young woman from Canada concerning her and her sister's bathroom in a hotel in Tuscany. She had never heard of nor seen a bidet before and assumed that it was a second toilet. She was a sweet girl, but quite naïve and she actually believed me when I then told her that many Europeans enjoy using the toilet together. That way they can keep their conversation going without needing a toilet break!

"How come we haven't seen any fish yet?" – Question asked by an older Australian passenger as we took the Eurotunnel from England to France. This particular passenger believed me when I joked to them that

the windows on the train would allow them a top view of the marine wildlife in the English Channel.

"I was quite certain Mozart was African!" – Comment from a passenger to our Vienna walking tour guide. The passenger was less than impressed when the guide responded that Mozart was actually from Perth, Australia.

"Isn't thirty-two a bit young for your age?" – A comment from a female passenger who got her wording a bit muddled up as she tried to tell me that I looked younger than my years.

"When are we going to see the Berlin Wall?" – A perfectly reasonable passenger question had we been in Berlin when it was asked. Sadly, we were in Munich at the time.

"Are any of these camps still in operation?" – A very ill-timed question from one of my Malaysian passengers to one of the tour guides at Mauthausen Concentration Camp.

"Is that the real Eiffel Tower?" – Asked by a passenger as we drove by the Eiffel Tower. I responded with, "No, it's one of those crafty Chinese replica Eiffel Towers!"

"You mean Belgium is a real country? I thought it was made up, like Narnia!" – Question from a passenger on the bus as we entered Belgium and I started telling the group a few facts about the country.

"I didn't realize that Switzerland is a mountainous country! Are these the Himalayas?" – Comment and question from a Canadian passenger whose public-school education clearly left them a bit wanting.

"Will you be able to arrange for us to meet the Pope?" – A question from a Filipino passenger who clearly thought that I had more sway with Vatican authorities than I actually did. I laughed at the question at first thinking that it was a joke, but quickly had to change tack as it was made clear that it was an actual request.

"Will we be able to stop and get photos of ourselves on the Autobahn?" – "Only if you want to get vaporized by a Mercedes doing one-hundred and eighty kilometers per hour!" The question from an over-eager American and my response to it as we drove along the famed German motorway.

"Is it true that there are no caterpillars in Italy?" – A mystifying and beguiling question asked by an elderly passenger from New Zealand. There may be no snakes in Ireland, but I'm almost certain that if one looks hard enough, one will eventually find a caterpillar somewhere in Italy.

"Does this bridge go forwards and backwards?" – Another nonsensical question asked by a passenger as we drove over the Storebælt Bridge in Denmark. Even if they meant "Does traffic flow in both directions?" it's quite obvious to anyone who looks out the window that indeed it does.

"Does this Notre Dame have anything to do with Notre Dame University in the States?" – Question from an American passenger during a driving tour of Paris concerning the famed cathedral.

"This place 'Ausfahrt' must be quite a big city; there's signs for it everywhere!" – A common comment heard by every tour leader at some point whilst driving through Germany. In fact, Ausfahrt is the German word for exit. The same also works for *"Einbahnstrasse"* which is German for one-way street, most passengers reckoned that it was simply a common German street name.

"Wow, the scenery here reminds me so much of back home in Kansas" – Another comment by an American passenger that doesn't sound odd until I tell you that we were on the Dalmatian Coast of Croatia when it was said. In fact, you don't get two landscapes any more different than Kansas and Split, Croatia.

"Why do Swedish people have such weird-looking eyes?" – A question from an Australian passenger that I never did understand in any way, shape, or form.

"How are the mountains in Austria different than the mountains in Switzerland?" – I was dumbstruck at this question. It was asked by a very sweet female Malaysian passenger. I wanted to say, "Nothing, except for the fact that the mountains in Switzerland are actually made out of Emmentaler cheese," but I couldn't be that cutting towards such a nice woman.

"Is it true that in Switzerland cows have the right of way on all the roads?" – Asked by an American passenger. This got a laugh from all the other passengers, but in fact, is an actual true fact. Cows do have

the right of way on all Swiss roads, as I once got caught in a cow traffic jam as the farmers brought their herds down from the mountains. An equally astute Indian passenger added that in India cows also have the right of way on all roads.

"When did French people start hating Americans so much?" – Another question from an American passenger. My only response was, "Don't worry. They hate British, Canadian, New Zealand, German, Spanish, and Italian people too! You should have been born an Australian!" In fact, the actual answer is probably sometime during the summer of 1945.

"What is this reindeer burger made of?" – A question from a Filipino passenger in Helsinki, Finland, where reindeer is commonly eaten. I'm not sure he quite realized that he was in fact eating Rudolph. Naturally, a reindeer burger is made out of reindeer.

"Why are Finnish people so weird?" – This is a question I would get from passengers on every single trip to Finland. The passengers caught on quickly; Finnish people are a bit weird. It's a country that has odd sports and events like the World Wife Carrying Championship, the World Sauna Championship, swamp soccer, and ice hockey. They also have an officially recognized Sleepy Head Day every July 27th (last one out of bed gets thrown in the lake), a government department whose job it is to review the future, and created and now celebrated every October 13th as a "National Day of Failure." A country that does all that would necessarily have to be populated by some pretty weird people. Then again, I'm Canadian, and shouldn't really be accusing any other country's citizenry of being weird.

"Is that a statue of Hitler?" – Asked by a wild, yet not so clued-in female South African passenger as I was giving a driving tour in, of all places to ask that question, Warsaw, Poland. VERY highly unlikely you'd see a statue of Hitler anywhere, let alone in Poland! In fact it was actually a statue of Charles de Gaulle. At least she asked the question on the bus. Had we been doing a walking tour and asked the question, any Pole within earshot would likely have throttled her on the spot.

"What's the French word for toilet?" – This sort of question came about often in France. I was always quite forgiving with it. The French

word for toilet is "toilette." The French word for beer is "bière." The French word for hotel is "hôtel." In fact, approximately 30% of all French and English nouns have the same or nearly the same word. Passengers would sometimes get so worried about being treated badly in France because they only spoke English that they'd forget that most French people do speak English and are happy to help. As long as you try speaking French first.

"Do my eyes smell like absinthe?" – Question from a college-aged American male passenger in the morning leaving Prague after a number of us had stayed out late the night before. Suffice it to say, he was rocking a fairly substantial hangover.

Every good Tour Leader will teach the passengers how to say "cheers" in any language they might be dealing with. Every time I took a group through the Baltic countries, they'd get really excited about saying cheers in Estonian, which is *"Terviseks"* and pronounced as Tervee-Sex. Quite a few passengers would end up saying "Terrible Sex" when toasting in Estonia, which always got a laugh, especially from the locals (most especially after a few drinks had already been consumed). One group took things even further and ended up toasting each other with "I hope you get laid!"

"How will we know when the tunnel is over?" – Once asked by a passenger when we were about halfway through the seventeen-kilometer-long Gotthard Road Tunnel in Switzerland. I had absolutely no answer for it, but my driver did when he told her, "There's a group of yodelers at the exit who yodel every time they see a vehicle coming."

Europe, like any other continent, has its share of odd or strange-sounding town names. We would pass by a few of them on the different routes and hope that the bus driver would slow down a bit so that everyone could get a picture of the town sign as we drove past. *Middelfart, Denmark* was one such particular town. I'd always tell the passengers to also be on the lookout for Innerfart and Outerfart. Every time we drove through Basel, Switzerland, we'd see signs for the suburb of *Wankdorf,* which was just far too classic. The best one of all, however, was a little village just north of Salzburg, Austria. We wouldn't actually pass by it on the bus, but one passenger on a visit to the city hired a cab to take him the twenty kilometers to the village of *Fucking*, just to get his picture with the town sign (and possibly try to steal it as well). Glad he was able to do it while he had the chance as the village has now changed its name to *Fugging*, which in some ways is even funnier!

In Poland, auto service stations are called Miejsce Obsługi Podróżnych, which always gets shortened to MOP on the road signs along with the town name. One particular service station that we used was located near a town called Police. Thus, the sign for the service station simply read *Mop Police*. After I pointed this out to the passengers, we'd make the obvious lame jokes about making sure that any cleaning materials on the bus were in order and that they'd probably be checking the water buckets and wringers as well.

Ass Nuggets –Throughout Paris one can find little take-away restaurants that are generally run by Arab immigrants. Obviously their first language is Arabic, but all the restaurant's advertising is in French. What these take-away restaurants do is put a giant, well-lit board up with a picture of each menu item with the name of it at the bottom. Many of these dishes come with fries and a few vegetables as well, which in French is simply called "l'assortiment." But because there's not much space on the board to write l'assortiment these immigrant restauranteurs will simply shorten it to "ass." Therefore, these menu boards will have menu items such as "ass hamburger" or "ass hot dog" or "ass shawarma." My favorite will always remain the "ass nuggets," which are meant to be chicken nuggets, but due to the name, is the most unappetizing food item that I've ever heard of!

Cumbag Café – Staying with badly named items that don't quite work, there was one café in St. Petersburg called the Cumbag Café. I realize that Russian is a vastly different language than English and that even some of the letters in the alphabet are different (In Russian a C is actually an S), but this one absolutely caught me nonplussed the first time I saw it, causing me to do a triple take before having the presence of mind to take a photo of it. It was actually called the twenty-four-hour Cumbag Café, which always made me wonder what sort of things they served at three in the morning…The burgers were actually quite good!

Tom Tits Experiment – Our groups would always see signs for this on the motorway as we drove into Stockholm with no indication as to what it was. Amazingly, after asking a local, I came to find out that it was an educational fun fair and park marketed to children!

Lucerne Blue Balls Festival – I had a group in Lucerne, Switzerland, in late July one year and signs for the Lucerne Blue Balls Festival were everywhere! Naturally, the passengers had quite a few questions about what this festival was all about, as did their Tour Leader. It turns out that it's not a festival for lonely men who are desperate to find a woman, but one of Switzerland's largest music festivals. Most Swiss people speak extremely good English, but clearly nobody explained to them what the term "Blue Balls" means in English.

Remaining in Switzerland, I've spent much time in Interlaken and always found it fun that on the main drag of the town, mixed in with the many souvenir stores and outdoor outfitter shops is a sex toy shop which proudly displays a sign in the front window reminding you that it's the *"Last Sex Shop Before the Jungfrau."* Just in case you left your vibrator or lube at home before your trip up the mountain, you'd still have a chance to get the necessities ahead of the train ride.

Hoe Gaat Het – Is the Dutch phrase for "How are you?" Its pronunciation sounds very much like "Who got head?" and many of the cheekier passengers would notice this. On one occasion in Amsterdam, we had just returned to the hotel after I had done a tour of the Red-Light District. A large group of us were having a drink at the bar and I was sitting beside a wonderful couple from New Zealand. The wife had had a couple of drinks and got quite muddled in her attempt to speak Dutch. She turned to her husband and asked him, "Did you get a blowjob?" The husband was caught completely off-guard by this. So, the wife asked him again, slightly louder. The husband remained as confused as ever and had no idea how to respond. Finally, the wife turned to me and said, "Will, you know all about the blowjob thing! Explain it to my husband!" Now, I was just as confused as the husband and really didn't want to get involved as this seemed very much like a situation from which one can get in a good bit of trouble. The only response I could muster was, "No, I have no idea about the blowjob thing. Not when it concerns your husband anyway! What, in god's name, are you talking about?" The wife finally explained what she meant, "You know, the way the Dutch ask how you're doing? The blowjob phrase! I'm trying to ask my husband that!" She had fouled up "Hoe gaat het" and thought that asking "Did you get a blowjob?" was the Dutch way of asking someone how they're doing. Once the confusion was cleared up everyone in the hotel bar had a great laugh over it and for the remainder of the tour anytime anyone wanted to ask anyone else how they were doing, they would simply ask, "Did you get a blowjob!" With the invariable response being, "Absolutely; best one ever!

"That's where Jesus turned into a white guy" – It's not just the passengers who can say moronic things. This is a quote from me during a tour in Israel. We were on Mt. Precipice in Nazareth which has a stunning view of many important Biblical sites from the Gospels including the Mount of Transfiguration. Now, I'm not a Christian nor by any means a Biblical scholar, but it helps to know a bit about these things when leading a tour in the Holy Land. The only thing I remember from the transfiguration story is that Jesus was transformed after being taken in by a bright, white light, but sadly, my words got away from me a bit there. The passengers all had a chuckle though I certainly didn't come out well when I corrected myself by saying, *"What I mean is that…that's where he started to wear white clothing…like Gandalf! But he wasn't a wizard!"* It's probably a very lucky thing our tour of the Holy Land wasn't marketed strictly to Christians!

The Quiz

Every Tour Leader on a coach tour in Europe does one! Vitally important to keep the passengers entertained and doing a quiz of some sort is always a good way to kill an hour or so. Mine was a thirty-six-question quiz with three levels of difficulty. The questions come in all different areas of study, but I always tried to put more of a travel focus on things. One point for each correct answer! Good luck!

1. Which country owns Greenland?
2. In the Harry Potter book series what House do Harry, Ron, and Hermione belong to?
3. What is the only metal that is a liquid at room temperature?
4. Name the three primary Axis countries from World War II.
5. In the 1980's Michael Jackson was known as the King of Pop. Which songstress was known as the Queen of Pop?
6. What is the only country to have won both the men's and women's FIFA World Cups?
7. What is the fifth largest country in the world by total size?
8. The famous quote "Something is rotten in the state of Denmark" is taken from which Shakespearean play?
9. What is the largest planet in our solar system?
10. Who were the first two men to summit Mount Everest?
11. Which actor famously played the role of both James Bond and the Saint?
12. In which board game do players routinely pick up and read cards off the Community Chest and Chance piles?

13. Which fast food chain has the most outlets worldwide? McDonalds, KFC, Subway, or Burger King

14. From 1901 to 1904 Pablo Picasso painted using almost exclusively which colour?

15. Bananas are chock-full of what mineral?

16. Which world leader was famously sent into exile on the island of St. Helena?

17. In the Beatles' "Abbey Road" album cover, which member of the Beatles is holding a cigarette?

18. If the hooker has been sent to the sin bin, what sport are you watching?

19. What unusual occurrence happens to passengers who fly non-stop from Bangkok, Thailand to Vancouver, Canada?

20. Fitzwilliam Darcy and Elizabeth Bennett are the two primary characters in which novel?

21. If you are diagnosed with heterochromia, what unusual attribute do you have?

22. How many men have walked on the moon?

23. Which of the following actors has never played the role of Batman? George Clooney, Bruce Willis, Christian Bale, Michael Keaton, Ben Affleck, Adam West

24. In Australian football, how many points is a goal worth: Three, Six, or Ten points?

25. What was the capital of West Germany?

26. You have decided to go on holiday to the Republic of Karelia. Which country are you going to?

27. You have just finished drinking a beer at a café and the waiter brings you your bill. It says that your beer costs one hundred birrs. Which country are you in?

    A. Ecuador   B. Ethiopia   C. Myanmar   D. Transnistria

28. When Pangaea was a full landmass in prehistoric times, which of these pairs of locations were connected?

    A. France/Norway   B. Canada/Morocco
    C Brazil/United Kingdom   D. China/Chile

29. Which European city is almost exactly antipodal to Auckland, New Zealand?

    A. Seville   B. Sofia   C. Reykjavik   D. Frankfort

30. Which of these countries is double landlocked?

    A. Bolivia   B. Luxembourg C. Kazakhstan   D. Uzbekistan

31. Which of these countries does not lie on the equator?

    A. Equatorial Guinea   B. Ecuador
    C. São Tomé and Príncipe   D. Uganda

32. How many countries are in Africa?

    A. <50   B. Exactly 50   C. >50

33. What is the official capital of Italy?

    A. Naples   B. Florence   C. Venice   D. Rome

34. What is the closest country to the United States that is not called Mexico or Canada?

    A. Cuba   B. Belize   C. Russia   D. Germany

35. With which country does France share its longest land border?

    A. Germany B. Brazil   C. Tanzania   D. Spain

36. How many bridges cross the Amazon River? No clues, you just have to know!

The Quiz - Answers

1. Denmark
2. Gryffindor
3. Mercury
4. Germany, Italy, Japan
5. Madonna
6. Germany
7. Brazil
8. Hamlet
9. Jupiter
10. Sir Edmund Hillary and Tenzing Norgay
11. Roger Moore
12. Monopoly
13. Subway (Almost all my passengers got this one wrong, but nevertheless, it's true)
14. Blue
15. Potassium
16. Napoleon Bonaparte
17. Paul McCartney (He's also barefoot)
18. Rugby
19. You will arrive in Vancouver before you departed Bangkok due to crossing the international date line.
20. Pride and Prejudice
21. Eyes that are different colours
22. Twelve

23. Bruce Willis
24. Six
25. Bonn
26. Russia (The Republic of Karelia is a large jurisdiction roughly the size of Uruguay that is north of St. Petersburg and shares a border with Finland.)
27. Ethiopia
28. Canada/Morocco (Rocks found in Newfoundland on Canada's east coast are identical to rocks found in Morocco.)
29. Seville (The two locations are less then 100km from being exact antipodes.)
30. Uzbekistan (Liechtenstein is the only other double-landlocked country.)
31. Equatorial Guinea (An oddity based on its name. Strangely enough, Equatorial Guinea has land on both sides of the equator, but at no point does the equator touch Equatorial Guinean soil.)
32. More than 50 (depends on who you ask as to the exact number, but all sources have it at over 50.)
33. Rome (An obvious answer. People used to think it was some sort of trick question, I put it in just to keep everyone on their toes!)
34. Russia (Big Diomede Island belongs to Russia and Little Diomede Island belongs to the United States. The islands are found in the middle of the Bering Strait and are only 3.8 km away from each other.)
35. Brazil (Another proper trick question. France is not just in Europe. The France everyone thinks of is actually called Metropolitan France. France also has many overseas territories that are considered to be part of France. One of those territories is called French Guiana and it has a 730 km long border with Brazil. France's next longest border is their 623 km long border with Spain)
36. Zero (There's not a single bridge that crosses the Amazon anywhere!)

Part 5

To Mother Russia, with Love

For every Tour Leader there are inevitable questions that we are asked all the time by our passengers. Have you ever been arrested? Have you ever had to go to hospital? Have you ever been robbed? What's your least favorite place to go to? I could go on and on with these questions. The one question that we Tour Leaders probably are asked more than any other is, "What is your favorite country to take groups too and work in?" For me there was only one answer: Russia!

After a couple of years working in Western Europe and the Balkans I was moved to the Scandinavian and Russian tours. I wouldn't be going to Paris, Rome, Barcelona, or Switzerland anymore. I was going to be working exclusively on an eighteen-day route starting and finishing in Amsterdam. Every three weeks I'd be visiting Hamburg, Copenhagen, Stockholm, Helsinki, St. Petersburg, Moscow, Tallinn, Riga, Vilnius, Warsaw, and Berlin. All these places were great fun to take groups to, but it was always my times in Russia that proved to be the most memorable and for one primary reason. Things happen there that just aren't supposed to happen!

How to Enter Russia Correctly

The fun would start before we even actually entered the country. When you're a Tour Leader taking a group of fifty tourists into Russia through a land border crossing, you'd have to know the rules of engagement with the Russian immigration officials. Oftentimes, it could be a difficult proposition to get all fifty passengers into the country in an orderly and efficient manner. Our route always took us from Finland into Russia and the border crossing we used was not terribly busy early on a Sunday morning. We'd leave Helsinki at 6:30 in the morning, rocking up to the Russian border at around three hours later.

The Russian border post arrivals hall looked like what you'd expect a Russian border post arrivals hall to look like. It was painted a drab olive green with wooden customs booths and a plain white tile floor. The lights were all blinking fluorescent ones that probably hadn't been changed since Brezhnev was in charge. The whole place had a 1960s Soviet vibe to it and possessed absolutely no personality of any sort. It wasn't a place that would inspire any Tour Leader nor fill one with confidence. It wasn't a happy place; arrivals halls never are, but this Russian one took depression to a whole new level. Through a complicated system of trial and error, I was eventually able to piece together the correct protocol for getting my groups through Russian immigration with as little hassle as possible and in as short an amount of time as could be managed.

1. As a Tour Leader, respect the dress code! Don't wear a company branded polo or T-shirt at the border, wear trousers instead of cargo shorts, and definitely no sandals! Cranky Russian Immigration agents like you to look respectful, so a collared shirt and tie are much better! Failure to wear a shirt and tie may result in Olga, the cranky Russian Immigration woman, taking an hour-long coffee break. (On this note, the individual who actually stamps your passport going into or out of Russia was ALWAYS a woman. Certain jobs in Russia are done by men and certain jobs are done by women. Passport stamping, even in the twenty-first century, is evidently a women's only profession in Russia. These women were always dour, unsmiling, stocky in build, and not in the mood to chat at all. I imagined and assumed that they were all named Olga.

2. Don't speak to the aforementioned "Olga" as she doesn't speak English. Just give her your passport and paperwork and shut up. Trying to say anything or trying to make friends with her may result in Olga taking an hour-long coffee break.

3. While Olga is stamping the passports of the Tour Leader and passengers, the driver will go away and deal with "ill-tempered and possibly hungover Russian Transport guy" who will inspect the bus and make sure the driver's paperwork is in order. Like the Russian Immigration women, apparently inspecting buses is a male-only profession in Russia. While your driver is dealing with ill-tempered and possibly hungover Russian Transport guy and you're dealing with Olga, the passengers have to remain on the bus outside, probably wondering if you're ever coming back, or if you've been sold to a local mafioso.

4. After Olga is satisfied with your Tour Leader paperwork and stamps it, you can then bring the passengers into the arrivals hall to be processed and have their passports stamped. Not easy with 50-passengers as the most important rule has to be followed: NO TALKING! CERTAINLY NOTHING ABOVE A WHISPER! Failure for the passengers to communicate in anything besides hand signals and body language may result

in Olga taking an hour-long coffee break. If the place was any louder than an empty library, you were asking for trouble. Make sure to arrange the passengers in an orderly queue.

5. It wasn't a rule, but I found that it made sense to queue up the passengers in order of nationality, in order of who is most likely to be dragged out back and shot. Actually, it never came to that, but it was highly likely that certain passengers from certain countries would be taken out back and put through an entry interview (and quite possibly shot).

   a. Anyone from the Middle East or any individuals who work in the Middle East (almost a 100% chance of an interview.)

   b. Americans (everyone knows that in Russia an American passport is proof of being a CIA spy.)

   c. British (everyone knows that in Russia a British passport is proof of being an MI-6 spy.)

   d. Africans not from South Africa (probably not spies and thus not likely to be interviewed. Olga just didn't like them and would always take a jeweler's loupe to their passports and visas trying to find a reason to deny them entry.)

   e. Asians (never a problem; Asians in our tours were almost always Filipino and Malaysian. By this point, Olga wouldn't be too worried about the rest of our passengers.)

   f. EU Citizens (one never knew; someone with a German or French passport might be a spy, probably secretly working for the CIA. Nevertheless, they'd never be hassled or interviewed.)

   g. Canadians, Aussies, Kiwis, and other English-speaking countries that aren't the United States (they can't possibly be spies; the CIA does their spying for them. Olga would barely even look at their passports.)

   h. Thais, South Africans, South Americans, and any citizen from any country that didn't need a Russian visa (clearly these people were double-agents and would get a big hug from Olga upon arrival after they handed over their spy-dossier.)

   i. Anyone else not covered in the previous categories. It
       didn't happen often, but once in a while you might have
       a passenger from a place like Mauritius. In this case Olga
       might not even know the place exists and have to actually
       call Moscow to verify that the place is a real country and
       that the person is allowed in.

6. If at any point a Russian bus pulls up, then Olga will tell you to
    f%&-off in Russian and allow the Russian group to cut in line
    ahead of you. This was actually a wished-for outcome as it was
    the only way that a second Olga would come to open another
    passport window and get the queue sped up a bit.

7. No sitting at any time! The arrivals hall had exactly three chairs
    available, but these were reserved for people who were to be
    interviewed. If grandma can't stand anymore, she'll just have
    to sit on the floor. "Surly Interview Kid" would come and haul
    off anyone sitting there.

Interviews would be done in a back room by the aforementioned
"Surly Interview Kid," some local 19-year-old, who I'm sure was the
only person in the nearby village who spoke English. He wasn't even a
government employee, he didn't have a uniform, he'd rock up looking
like a Banditi (which I suspect he was), in a leather jacket, aviator
sunglasses, and blue jeans. After a few tours we got to know each other a
bit. The guy's name was Sergei and he was actually a really nice guy who
didn't really want to hassle us at all. It was simply Russian Immigration
policy to interview certain nationals (Arabs, Americans, and Brits) as
to why they were visiting Russia. As for passengers who worked in the
Middle East, they'd want to know why they were working in the Middle
East. A fairly odd policy, but that's often the way things are in Russia.

What I did find funny about Sergei and his interviews is that he
was, apparently, hard up for a girlfriend. He made it a point, whenever
he was interviewing good looking female passengers, to ask for their
phone number and make a Facebook friend request. Generally, once
they "friended" him and were told how good Sergei's mother's cooking
was, the interview would conclude and the woman was free to leave.

Also, because we'd always be rocking up early on a Sunday morning, more often than not Sergei would be just a little hung over from the night before, so he didn't want to press on with long interviews all that often. On a number of occasions Sergei wouldn't be there at all which was always for the best as then there'd be no interviews at all. Over time, the border process got easier and easier as the Russkies figured out that we were a regular group coming through every few weeks and eventually they stopped doing entry interviews altogether. We even started getting along with the Olgas.

On one occasion my Dutch driver, Wim, and I were just getting our passports stamped by Olga before bringing the group in. Wim, as the driver, would need to bring all of his paperwork in and get certain forms stamped by Olga and certain forms stamped by the Russian Transport Officer. Poor Wim could, at times, be a bit disorganized. While searching for a particular form, he dropped his entire bundle of papers, scattering them all over the floor at the passport booth. In his loud and commanding voice, only two words came to him:

"OH, F#%&!!"

Quickly turning my gaze to Olga, I knew that we were probably in trouble for this breach of decorum, and the passengers weren't even queued up yet! Expecting to see Olga leave to go on an hour-long coffee break, I was shocked, instead, to see just the hint of a smile on her face and the softest chuckle I ever heard; the first ever recorded smile and chuckle to ever come from a Russian Border Guard's mouth, I'm sure!

Wim, not yet bothering to pick up his papers, saw the smile as well, and asked the question that only he could be brazen enough to ask:

"Oh, you know what F#%& means?" he asked Olga.

Olga now broke into a full smile and laugh, nodded yes, stamped his passport, and directed him towards the transport officer. Turning her attention to me, her smile remained as she looked at me and said the only English words I ever heard from an Olga:

"Funny man!" She quickly stamped my passport and passenger manifest. Sadly, by the time I got the passengers queued up, the smile had disappeared and Olga's normal service was resumed.

Anyway, once everyone was stamped through and the bus had been cleared for entry, you'd still have to go through a series of police checkpoints. The police checkpoints were actually a good bit of fun for me and my driver. For some reason, the police checkpoints were always manned by attractive female police cadets who would come on the bus and double-check that everyone's passport had been stamped. They would know a bit of English and they didn't mind an American-sounding Tour Leader chatting them up for a couple of minutes. Once two of these checkpoints were finished, then one would finally be in Russia and ready for the madness that would inevitably follow!

Get in My Van...You'll Like It!

Once we'd get through the Russian border, we would still have a three-hour drive to St. Petersburg. A big order of business was to find a place along the way that could serve lunch to fifty English-speaking tourists. Luckily, I had been told by the Tour Leader for the route from the previous year that there was a petrol station that served hot dogs and other ready-made meals and an adjacent café that served proper Russian dishes seventy kilometers from St. Petersburg. It reminded me a good deal of a certain restaurant I knew in Poland, the difference here being, that this restaurant actually did have food.

It was a good spot to stop for an hour for two big reasons. One, the passengers had time to have a bit of lunch. Second, it also allowed us to meet up with my Russian Mafia contact. Both activities had their challenges.

One of the biggest problems in taking a group to Russia is the language barrier. Most of the passengers were completely illiterate upon arrival. Not only could they not speak the language, but they also couldn't even read it! It's not like German or Spanish or even Polish where one can often guess what the word means. Russian uses a completely different alphabet than English. Most passengers were hopelessly lost and unless they were planning to buy a bag of Doritos and Coca-Cola for lunch, they'd be in a spot of trouble. The good news, though, is that Russian is actually a very simple language to learn to read (the basic words anyway) and certain words are the same in both Russian and English. During the drive to the lunch stop I'd hand out the following chart which showed some very quick and easy translations for the passengers to use:

ENGLISH	RUSSIAN TRANSLATION
Coca-Cola	Coca-Cola
Hot-Dog	Hot-Dog
Teriyaki Wok-Box	Teriyaki Wok-Box
Borscht	Borscht
Pizza	Pizza
Beer	Pivo
One, Two, Three	Adin, Dva, Tree (or hold up fingers)
For all other items in the deli-case, please point, smile, and say Pujol-sta. Please put on a Russian accent when ordering any food items.	

The chart made it quite easy for passengers who went to the petrol station to order what they wanted. The wok-boxes and hot dogs were particularly popular, no language mistranslations there! Passengers were always surprised to see how many food items were actually the same in both English and Russian!

The café across the lot from the petrol station was a bit trickier and presented a far more interesting challenge to the passengers who wanted to eat there. The food at the café was excellent, but the menu was written in indecipherable Russian with no pictures; even Google translate couldn't read it! I would tell the passengers that it was Russian food-roulette. Point and hope for the best and don't whine too much when the waitress brings you a stuffed goat's head! Amazingly, I never once had a single passenger complain about their meal. It was clearly a restaurant where every dish was quite good.

Neither the staff at the café nor the staff at the petrol station spoke any English, not a one of them! They were all middle-aged Russian women who had never learned a single word. They were all very pleasant though, and did their best to help the passengers. The women at the petrol station were particularly helpful. They eventually figured out that our buses were showing up every third Sunday and they made little charts for our passengers to use to make the ordering process a bit easier. Truth be told, I think they looked forward to the novelty of selling hot dogs, wok-boxes, borscht, and stuffed meat roulades to a bunch of English-speaking tourists.

The lunch stop also functioned as the site of one of the most unusual events that ever occurred to me in my career as a Tour Leader. It's where I got tangled up and involved with the Russian Mafia

*   *   *

Many people don't realize it, but Russia gets hot in the summer; plus thirty centigrade is not at all unusual. Plenty of passengers would pack a coat, thinking it'd be likely to snow in St. Petersburg and Moscow! As mentioned in the Russian Immigration rules in the last chapter, it was almost compulsory for me to wear a collared shirt, tie, and trousers when in the arrivals hall at the border. The downside of being all decked out was that on a hot day I'd be roasting by the time we got out of there and back on the road. The petrol station would be the first chance for me to change clothes.

It was on one of my first tours through Russia that this incident occurred. Upon arriving at the petrol station, I turned the group loose for lunch and stayed behind on the bus to quickly change back into my cargo shorts and a t-shirt. I was just in the middle of changing my shirt at the front of the bus when a van pulled up beside the bus. It wasn't a new and beautiful Mercedes van either. In fact, it looked rather like one of those vans that creepy men use to kidnap children. It sported blacked-out windows, a few spots of rust on the bodywork and no discernable markings. The Russian man behind the wheel wanted a quick chat with me.

"Hello! Hello!"

I hadn't really expected company at this exact moment and certainly not from a creepy Russian, but one had to be polite. "Uh, hello," I replied.

"He-he, yes, hello. Are you tsar of bus?" The guy had a certain way of talking. He would always say he-he in the course of nearly every sentence, as though he wanted you to know that he was up to something.

"Am I the tsar of the bus?" I responded. I had never heard my role of Tour Leader as being described like that. I liked it!

"Da, are you tsar of bus? This is big bus; must have a tsar, Are you tsar of bus, he-he?"

"Well, yes, as a matter of fact, I am the tsar of the bus." I realized immediately that letting him know that I was the tsar of the bus might precipitate his abducting me and holding me for ransom, but it was a bit late to worry about that.

"Good, good, he-he. Yes. Get in my van!" replied the man. It seemed as though I was right. Apparently, he did intend to abduct me.

"What?"

"Yes, get in my van; you'll like it! He-he."

Now, I hadn't been kidnapped yet, but it seemed more than a likely possibility at this point. That said, the guy seemed friendly enough and he hadn't pulled a gun on me yet. Not quite wanting to surrender myself to a life of slavery under the employ of a banditi in the backwoods of the Karelia Oblast, I thought I'd take my chances.

"Um, no. Spasibo. Now go away!"

"Yes, get in my van. he-he. You'll like it!"

Seeing that the guy was insistent, I knew it was necessary to lay down the law, and since he was by himself and still hadn't pulled a weapon, I figured my fate was still in my own hands.

"No, I don't think I want to get in your little abduction van today. Seriously, go away!"

The guy realized my position, but was still undeterred. He changed his tactic instead. "OK, not get in van. You come look at van, You like, he-he!"

It was now clear that the guy wasn't going to go until I looked at the van, and wanting to get to lunch, I reckoned that it wouldn't take more than a minute to humor him, look at his van, and tell him to f%$& off.

"OK, I'll look at your van, but then you can f%@# off! I'm going for lunch."

"Yes, but I think you like it!"

The guy proceeded to get out -- I was most pleased to see that he was a short, wiry guy. I was confident I could take him down if I had to, but his demeanor remained friendly. I walked with him to the back doors of his van, not quite sure how many kidnapped Finnish day-trippers he might have locked up inside. He pulled open the doors and it was immediately clear to me why he wanted the "tsar of bus" to have a look inside. Contained within his van was enough liquor, beer, cigarettes, perfume, and chocolate to stock a moderately sized duty-free store.

"You, tsar of bus, I give good deal. Good cigarettes, Marlboro man! Vodka, beer, cognac. I sell, he-he, good deal!" It certainly made for a quick attitude change on my part; to hell with lunch! There was a mafia fire-sale to get in on!

"Yes, I see. I like your van much better now! How much for Finlandia?" I asked. The guy had massive quantities of one-liter Finlandia vodka in the back of his van. Cases of it.

"Yes, good deal; four Euro, he-he."

"That is a good deal. What about Champagne?" Same story, boxes of Russian champagne right beside the vodka.

"Yes, very good deal. Good Russian champagne; good to celebrate visit to Russia for guests, he-he. Four Euro!"

"I see. Yes, that's a good deal too. And how much for cigarettes?" The dozens of cartons of Marlboros weren't exactly hidden away.

"Yes, he-he, good deal. Four Euros!"

"Is everything just four Euros? Is the van also four Euros?" I asked; though, to be fair, this Russian's pricing system was consistent.

"Yes, yes, good deal. You buy now. Good deal for tsar of bus!"

And so, the great illegal mafia sell-off was engaged. Just then my driver, Wim, turned back up at the bus and was keen to get in on things as well. Knowing that we needed certain provisions and seeing what a good deal could be had, Wim and I took three cases of Finlandia, three cases of champagne, every carton of Marlboros, and two chocolate bars (I was unlikely to get a hot dog at this point, the passengers no doubt having bought them all by then.). Because we were buying in bulk, our new mafia ally was happy to give a healthy discount and even provided money exchange for us at rates far better than any bank or exchange office. Why a Russian banditi would be so keen to acquire hard currency was not a question that took too much time to answer. By the time Wim and I had finished our deal some of the passengers were just returning from lunch and keen to know what was going on.

"It's a mafia alcohol and cigarette sale! Chocolate as well; get in on it!"

By the time the passengers had finished buying their allotment of vodka and champagne (also cognac, whiskey, and any other liquor one can think of), the banditi's van was nearly empty and his wallet full. I can scarcely remember seeing someone so happy with himself. It was getting time to continue to St. Petersburg, but not before our new acquaintance wanted a bit of information.

"Yes, very nice deal, for tsar of bus and for driver tsar too! Very nice he-he. You come to Russia again?" No doubt the banditi was looking for future deals. Good thing that he was because I was keen for that as well.

"Yes, we will come here every three weeks until October. Will you be here?"

"Oh yes! I come, make good deal. My name is Nikita. I give you phone number. Next time you call, we set time for meeting he-he!"

I figured Nikita – good name for a banditi, and he enjoyed referring to himself in the third person – would write his number on a scrap of paper, but instead he handed me a proper A-4 sheet with about a dozen phone numbers on it.

"Nikita, what in the hell is this? There are a dozen numbers or more here! Which one do I call?"

"Oh, it's OK he-he. Any of them, Nikita answers!" With that Nikita unzipped his jacket, and opened it up to reveal his fleet of burner mobile phones. Can't imagine why a banditi would need so many of them....

"Yes, well, fine! I'll call the first number next time and work my way down the list if need be." I said, and with our transaction now completed, I only had one last thing weighing on my mind concerning my new "friend."

"Thanks, Nikita. Just one last thing I need to ask you because I think we're friends now, yes?

"Oh, very good friends, yes. We've made good deal he-he!"

"Yes, good friends, and good friends can tell each other secrets, right?

"Yes, good secrets. Nikita happy to help. I tell you anything!"

"Very good, Nikita. Just tell me this one thing then. Where did you steal all this stuff from?"

With a look of faux outrage that only a guilty-as banditi could muster, Nikita responded with quite possibly the most hilarious answer to a question I'd ever heard. "Nooooo! Nikita not steal!…Friend gives!" You couldn't argue with that. In Nikita's mind, I'm sure he thought that that was exactly what had happened.

"Of course, how silly of me Nikita. Of course a friend "gave" all of it to you. See you next month then! Make sure to bring rubles. I'll have fifty tourists who need a money exchange done. More cigarettes too!"

Nikita would prove to be an excellent purveyor of all items needed to indulge one's vices and we always looked forward to our meetings with him. In time, Nikita came to expand his product line to include souvenir items and specialty liquor items. For twenty Euros one could buy a bottle of fine Armenian Cognac in a bottle shaped like an AK-47. The men on tour loved them and Nikita would always sell out. Another bottle of Cognac, also for twenty Euros, and marketed to women, came in the shape of the male member. The women on tour hated them and Nikita would never sell any of them; though, seeing him try his sales pitch on the ladies was always entertaining and good for a laugh.

*　*　*

Nikita wasn't exactly upper-level mafia. The guy wasn't involved in the heroin trade, nor was he shipping surplus nukes from Kazakhstan, nor was he a big player in some illicit human trafficking set-up. He was simply a guy from Vyborg looking to make good on his side hustle, which every Russian I met seemed to have. Little ladies had a berry and honey stand on the side of the motorway, Nikita had his van full of stolen duty-free store products. Still, he fancied himself a mafioso on the same level as the banditi in Moscow or St. Petersburg. There was no need for me to burst his bubble. Though, on one occasion, Nikita was thirty minutes late to the petrol station. What was holding him up? The fact that a local police car was parked at the café and the officers were having lunch might be the reason.

"Police and Nikita get along, not so well. Better to wait, and then Nikita comes!" This was Nikita's defense for his tardiness. I rather think that the police were well aware of Nikita and his racket and would've been more than willing to bust him big time if he was seen selling to a busload of western tourists.

Nevertheless, Nikita always enjoyed our meetings, as he always made quite good money off of my passengers and was able to convert his rubles into hard currency. I enjoyed it as my driver and I were able to stock up on cheap liquor and cigarettes (always worth a bit more in Amsterdam) and the passengers would get a great deal on their currency exchange, saving us the problem of making an extra stop at an exchange bureau in St. Petersburg. Most of all, Nikita enjoyed the idea that the passengers really thought that he was Russian mafia. Just for one hour every three weeks, he got to properly live out his dream.

Sadly, his dream and ego took a big hit on one particular visit.

Once again, it was a tour that my parents were on, and my mom got right in the thick of things again. Dad had been to the Soviet Union as a young man, but hadn't been back since. He was keen to see the changes. He was also keen to buy cognac in an AK-47 shaped bottle. Mom had never been to Russia at all and assumed that at some point she'd get involved, unwittingly, in one of those human trafficking rings that she'd heard so much about (what TV channels she'd been watching are still a mystery to me). They'd been told all about Nikita and his mobile duty-free service.

Sadly, my mother didn't quite register that Nikita was an illicit man of business who operated very much on the margins of the law. Whilst he and I got along well, it was a stretch to call us friends. Business associates was probably the best description for our relationship.

Nikita had arrived on this visit with his usual van load of wares. Dad had already had his hot dog and was keen to have a look at everything on offer and to make a deal on his AK-47 cognac bottle. My dad was a wily sort; he knew what kind of guy Nikita was and negotiations were kept on a strictly business footing. Things were going along just fine until my mother came over to see what the fuss was about.

"Oh, Will, is this the man you were telling us about? Is this your friend? What was his name? Nikita?" asked Mom in her usual sweet schoolteacher voice, typical of a woman who'd spent her career as an educator in rural Alberta, Canada.

"Uh, yeah, this is Nikita. He sells us our…stuff. Things we need for…later," I responded, not quite sure how to tell Nikita that this woman was my mother.

I needn't have worried about that! For that sentence hadn't even left my mouth when my mother embraced Nikita in a big old hug, as though the two of them were old navy buddies!

"Oh, it's always so nice to meet Will's friends! Oh, aren't you a short person! You're almost as short as me!" My mother, all five-foot and three inches of her not only had Nikita in a hug, but she didn't look as though she was going to let go either!

The look on Nikita's face was one of abject confusion. And he wasn't hugging her back either! He was clearly surprised and annoyed to be seen as being hugged. He looked like a six-year-old boy being embraced by an overly affectionate aunt.

"Will, who is woman hugging Nikita? This not so pleasant!" Nikita asked me in response to this overly friendly embrace.

"Yeah, uh, Nikita, this is my mom actually. I think she's been looking forward to meeting you. Sorry about the hug thing." Mom still had him in a tight embrace.

"Will, Nikita is important businessman. This is difficult place. Is no good for image if Nikita is seen to be in hugs with people buying! I must look like tough man! I not look like tough man right now!" pleaded Nikita.

"Right, Nikita. OK, Mom, if you don't mind, could you please stop hugging the Russian mafia man! He doesn't like it!" With that Mom let go of Nikita, finally. Nikita took a moment to recompose himself.

"Oh, but it's always so nice to meet your friends! And he's an absolute doll! You always have such nice friends!" Mom was still very pleased to have made Nikita's acquaintance. I don't think I could say the same thing about Nikita.

"Mum, Nikita is in THE RUSSIAN MAFIA! You're not supposed to touch or hug mafia members. It's…just not done. He's here on business. Look at the back of his van!"

With that, Mom took a good and proper look at what was in the back of Nikita's van.

"Ohhhh! That's a lot of vodka! Ohhhh and cigarettes too!" said Mom, clearly impressed by what she was seeing.

"That's right. Did you want to buy any? If not, then you'll have to let Dad finish his cognac deal!"

"Oh, no! I'll be OK! I just wanted to say hello to Nikita!"

In the end, Nikita was no worse for wear. Nobody besides the four of us had witnessed the cheeky hug and Nikita got on with things without too much of a drama. In fact, after the initial awkwardness, he quickly made friends with my mother, who was really rather impressed with his liquor and cigarette collection. By the time everyone had made their purchases (Dad got his AK-47 cognac bottle for twenty Euros), Nikita was ready to bring Mom on as an apprentice.

"Will, this matushka of yours is very funny little woman! If she likes, I bring her to all my stops! I think Russian people will enjoy her talking!" said Nikita just as we were preparing to depart.

"Yeah, I think that might be a new career choice for her. She can teach you Russians how to hug as well!"

"No, Will! Still, the hugs are not so good, but her talking is very funny! Russian people like funny Americans! She is like TV comedy person!"

Every time we stopped on tour for lunch at the Russian petrol station and café heading into St. Petersburg after that, Nikita would always be ready and waiting for us. Except, from then on, instead of saying hello to me, his greetings would instead be sent towards my mother. It certainly helps to have mafia friends!

Sometimes Foreigners Must
Learn Russian Ways!

On a normal visit to Russia the group would have three days and three nights in St. Petersburg. It was always great to be the Tour Leader in Russia because once the group arrived at the hotel in St. Petersburg and were checked in, the local Russian guide would take over the tour completely. I didn't have to do anything until it was time to leave for Tallinn, Estonia, three days later. St. Petersburg is one of the most beautiful cities in Europe, perhaps in the entire world, so passengers were always excited to arrive and be keen to explore and taken in by the mysticism of Mother Russia. To the passengers' surprise, however, by the time we'd finished in St. Petersburg, most of them weren't talking about the sights, culture, or architecture; they'd be talking about our St. Petersburg guide, Svetlana!

Svetlana was a legend! A proper Russian legend! She was a short, stoutish, white-haired woman and could have been anywhere from forty to eighty years old. She spoke with a very lilting voice and was one of these people who didn't try to be funny, but somehow everything she said would make you laugh. It would quite often annoy her when we would be talking to each other that I'd be chuckling at some comment she had just made when, in fact, it was meant to be a serious discussion. She just had that way about her.

Driving tours of St. Petersburg would be an absolute riot with her on a microphone and a complete disaster for the driver. Our tours to

Russia always had a Dutch driver assigned to them and most of the time
it was Wim who was at the helm. Wim and I got on very well, but for
him, the St. Petersburg driving tour would be a proper adventure as one
could never quite be sure which way Svetlana wanted him to go. Whilst
her English was excellent, very nearly fully fluent, she sometimes had a
tough time remembering her directions, often muddling up which way
she wanted Wim to go. Quite often the passengers could hear Svetlana
and Wim having, more or less, the following conversation at the front
of the bus:

"We now are coming past the beautiful Smolensk Cathedral with
its wonderful blue and white exterior. Please remember to take beautiful
photos of the lovely Smolensk Cathedral. And we will now go straight
to the left," Svetlana would say. She was also always keen for everyone
to take "beautiful photos."

Wim would, of course, be a bit confused, "Are we going straight,
or to the left?"

"Yes, that's correct, straight. And to the left!" Svetlana would
respond, not at all helping to clear up the confusion.

Naturally, we would often take a few wrong turns during the course
of an afternoon driving tour, and right-hand turns would be even worse
as she would often confuse them with left hand turns.

"At the next street our lovely driver, Mr. Wim, will make a turn to
the left." Wim, then, would start to make the turn only for Svetlana to
get a bit excited. "Oh no, Mr. Wim, that is the wrong turn; other left
please!"

"You mean turn right?" Wim would ask.

"Yes, other left, opposite way. Very nice!" To her credit, Svetlana
would never embarrass Wim or say that he had got things wrong. It
really added a new dimension to the driving tour and passengers would
be struggling to keep from laughing at the confusing directions that
Svetlana would be giving. How we never had an accident or somehow
drive the bus into the Neva River or a canal I'll never know. We always
managed to work our way through St. Petersburg and see all the major
sights that one would want to see. We would also stop at a souvenir
store during the driving tour for passengers to buy magnets, keychains,

and funny Russian bear hats. The souvenir store would also give us as much complimentary vodka as we wanted, no doubt to loosen up the passengers' wallets. It also had the added effect of making Svetlana even funnier to the passengers.

Svetlana was great and, like me, would say ANYTHING on the microphone. On one occasion the driving tour was just about finished and we were on the way back to the hotel during St. Petersburg rush hour. We were just trying to make a turn from a busy street onto a quieter one when disaster struck. Some Russian moron had double-parked his car in the street. The small space available to pass was large enough for a car but nowhere near enough for a fifty-passenger motorcoach. We were in trouble, and would have to reverse back into the busy main boulevard. Not an easy task for any driver. This didn't faze Svetlana one bit. She called an audible that very much took me by surprise.

"Oh dear, Mr. Wim can't get by. Crazy Russian car has blocked the road. Now brave Mr. Will must get out and stop traffic so we can back out."

I'd had about four shots of vodka at the souvenir store and wasn't quite sure if I'd heard her exactly right. Didn't hurt to ask.

"Uh, Svetlana, I'm going to do what now?"

Without missing a beat, Svetlana doubled down. "Yes, Mr. Will become hero of St. Petersburg now and get out and stop traffic so that Mr. Wim can bring bus back into main street."

This, in my view, couldn't have been a worse idea. The image of me getting mowed down by a banditi who's late to his mistress's house flashed through my mind. Painted into a corner, I had no choice but to go and stop traffic on one of the busiest streets in St. Petersburg and hope that any police officers that might be about would decide not to book me, or worse, assign me to a gulag in Kamchatka.

Luckily, Russians are a very patient lot. I suppose all those years queueing up for bread and socks haven't been forgotten. Every driver clearly saw what was going on, stopped their cars, and waited for Wim to back out of the side street and get himself and the bus sorted out. Not a single honk of the horn or impatient bit of shouting came from a single one of them. A couple of the pedestrians even came out to help and after a couple of minutes of maneuvering, Wim was able to get us on our way again, and according to Svetlana, he also became a hero of the Russian Federation on par with Alexander Nevsky or Yuri Gagarin, if Svetlana was to be believed.

*   *   *

The first full day in St. Petersburg would see Svetlana at her absolute best. She would continue to show the passengers the best the city had to offer. By far the biggest highlight of the day would be a visit to the world-renowned State Hermitage Museum. I would actually have the day off, but I would almost always go with the group to the Hermitage, not because I'm a huge fan of museums. No, I would usually go to watch The Svetlana Show instead.

The woman was unbelievable in there. She would walk around the grand halls as though she owned the place. After two years of working with her, I was very much of the belief that she did. Being rather a short woman, Svetlana always walked through the museum carrying an umbrella with a unicorn tied to the top of it. You certainly couldn't have spotted her without it. With the passengers being so engrossed in the beauty of the never-ending masterpieces contained in the Hermitage, you'd often lose people along the way. I would take it upon myself to keep an eye on everyone and keep them from falling too far behind Svetlana. The Hermitage, even on a quiet day, is chock-a-block full of tourists, so this was no easy task. Luckily, the passengers also all had headphones with Svetlana's commentary always on the go, so one could always hear her familiar lilting refrain:

"Please keep up. Remember to take beautiful pictures, and FOLLOW THE PONY! FOLLOW THE PONY!"

Those were the only two things the passengers needed to do during the entire visit to the Hermitage. Take beautiful pictures and always FOLLOW THE PONY!

One definitely needed to play by Svetlana's rules or face some very dire circumstances, which was a lesson I learned on my first ever visit to the Hermitage with her.

As mentioned already, the Hermitage is a busy place. On any given day, tens of thousands of people will be in the various galleries, having a look at what is, in my opinion, the world's greatest collection of art and cultural treasures from around the world. Svetlana was always very clear. Our group will be the very first one into the museum, and as such we'd have to leave the hotel immediately after breakfast. No dawdling about! If you weren't ready, she'd have no problem leaving you behind! I was particularly looking forward to our Hermitage visit as we had a number of VIPs with us on that tour. Both of the company's owners and founders were on board: Joran (who you met already in the Arles theft story) and Pieter, our head of customer services, Janice, and Joran's then boyfriend, Francois. It felt like a proper company outing: we and the passengers were very keen for our visit to the Hermitage.

Svetlana did well that morning. She had us at the very front of the queue for the group entrance, fifteen minutes before opening. The weather was marvelous in that first week of July and our hangovers were only marginal as Joran, Pieter, Francois, and I stood at the back of the group, listening to Svetlana tell everyone about the rules and protocols for the museum. Within minutes, about fifteen other groups had queued up behind us. The museum was going to be a busy old place this day!

We lads were having such a fun time joking around with each other at the back of the group that we didn't even notice when the doors were opened and that our group was entering the museum...without us! We had committed a cardinal sin and dawdled about! Expressly against Svetlana's instructions! Even worse than that, we were now being jostled about by an Italian group and their guide who were also trying to enter the museum. Like a group of swimmers caught in a riptide, we were being pulled away from where we wanted to be. While all this to-do was going on, two Russian police officers were on sentry duty on either side of the entrance, casually smoking cigarettes and looking as if they were in a really good mood (I don't think the four of us were the only ones nursing mild hangovers that morning.). It was only a matter of time before they got involved as proper shoving was breaking out between us lads and the Italian group. I only had one move available to me; I yelled desperately to Svetlana who was well inside the entryway by now along with the rest of our group.

"SVETLANA! SVETLANA! WE'RE STUCK! WE CAN'T GET IN!"

Svetlana immediately saw the problem and sprang right into action. She ran back towards the entrance in order to save us. Rushing towards us with her umbrella and pony, this tiny woman was going to take charge of the situation. Like Mel Gibson's Braveheart, one could hear her Russian war chant as she ran headlong towards the Italian group's guide, who was in the middle of giving me an authoritative shove:

"GET OUT OF WAY OF SPECIAL GUESTS!"

There are very few moments in life when one witnesses something take place and can't quite believe what they're seeing. This was one of them. Svetlana raised up her umbrella and attached pony, lifted it high into the air and brought it crashing down directly over the Italian guide's head!

WHACK! WHACK! WHACK!

Svetlana had the guide down! And she wasn't holding back! I was in shock. Joran and Pieter were in shock. Janice and Francois were in shock. The rest of our group and the Italians were in shock. In fact, the only people who didn't seem the least bit surprised at this turn of events were the two police officers. They stood smoking their cigarettes, puffing happily away without the least bit of interest or concern. I spoke no Russian at the time. Standing directly in front of the two officers while Svetlana thundered whacks down on the now turtle-squatted Italian guide, all I could do was look at them and point at the attack occurring no more than ten feet away from them. Surely this was a situation under their purview? Instead of taking any action, the senior officer simply took another drag on his cigarette, shrugged his shoulders, looked at me and said,

"Da....Bad move!"

Without another thought or care in the world, the police officers continued to ignore Svetlana's rain of whacks as though it was just a couple of kids playing jacks at the playground.

Joran had his own take on the still unfolding events:

"Will, is this the sort of thing that often happens on your tours? You seem to be in the habit of having interesting things occur. It's always something with you, isn't it?"

"Well, yes, that's true, but even for me, this one's more than a little unusual. Reckon we should step in?" I asked.

"No, I think she's got it handled alright. She seems to know what she's doing," Joran responded.

Meanwhile, Svetlana, after a couple of final whacks, finished her business with the Italian guide, adjusted her jacket, put her pony back in place at the top of her umbrella, and motioned to the four of us and said in her lilting Russian voice:

"Please now, Will, you and bosses, follow into museum. Follow the pony. Very important to follow the pony! Much to see!"

Svetlana didn't miss a beat. She was right back into guide mode and the four of us quickly followed her into the Hermitage whilst the Italian group tended to their fallen guide. Rushing in and catching up to Svetlana, I had to ask her about her unique solution to the prior predicament.

"Svetlana, Svetlana! What was that?"

"What, Will? What is problem? You have concern! What is concern?" she asked, seemingly not even aware of what she had been doing just ten seconds previously!

"Oh, nothing serious, I was simply curious. You are aware that you nearly killed that Italian guide back there, right? In front of two cops. Is that sort of thing allowed here?" I wasn't sure which part of my question was the most unusual.

"Oh, Will, this is not so serious! Sometimes foreigners must learn Russian ways! It's OK! Police understand as well. They also know that foreigners to Russia must behave themselves! The Italian guide will get a bandage and be OK, too!" responded Svetlana in a shockingly matter-of-fact tone of voice.

"OK, Svetlana, I guess that's fine. You'll excuse me for a moment." I really didn't know what else to say. As far as Svetlana was concerned, nothing even remotely noteworthy had occurred.

"Yes, Will, but please, you and bosses, pay attention now. Museum is large. Important to keep up and follow the pony!" With that, Svetlana got back on her microphone and started directing our group in how to check their bags and where the toilets were.

For my part, I always carried a little notebook with me so that I could make little memos to myself. Usually, I was writing down little tour hacks as I discovered them. On this occasion, in bold lettering, I made just one important note to write later into the official tour manual.

NOTE TO SELF: NEVER F%*# WITH SVETLANA UNDER ANY CIRCUMSTANCES! (TELL TO EVERY GROUP AND ADD TO TOUR MANUAL AS WELL!).

And I never ever did again!

It's Like Being in the Bourne Identity!

The following day in Russia was always a free day, but we would offer passengers a day trip on the high-speed train down to Moscow. Oddly enough, the Tour Leader wasn't required to go with the group on the Moscow day trip. I always liked the fact that it was my choice, and more often than not, I would stay in St. Petersburg and have a day to myself. For the passengers who did go it was a brutally long day: leave the hotel at five in the morning and not return until nearly midnight. On occasion, however, it would be necessary for me to go to Moscow, usually for strictly business purposes, but it would allow one to see the marvels of Moscow.

The one annoying administrative duty that I would have to perform was paying for the group's optional activities. At some point during the three days in Russia I'd have to pay InTourist, our Russian supplier, by either going to their office in St. Petersburg or meeting my associate in Moscow. Given that I generally had forty to fifty passengers, and that they would spend on average about two hundred fifty Euros on optional Russian activities, a Tour Leader could easily end up with well over ten thousand Euros that would need to be paid to InTourist. The first time that I ever went to Moscow was with the group and it just so happened to be the same tour in which Svetlana had her run-in with the Italian guide at the Hermitage. Joran, Pieter, Janice, and Francois were all heading to Moscow as well, and thus, I decided that I would also go and take in the wonders of the city. Even Tour Leaders need to go places for the first time.

As I was going to Moscow with the group, my InTourist contact, Dasha, phoned and told me how the group payment for all the Russian optionals would be paid. The bill came to nearly eight thousand Euros! I organized it into a neat package of fifty and one hundred Euro notes.

"Yes, Will, when you arrive in Red Square with the group, please call me on my mobile. Please be standing just to the north of St. Basil's Cathedral at two o'clock. I will see you and approach you. Please have the full payment ready in an envelope for me."

"Right, Dasha, but how will you know me?" I asked. At this point I'd never actually met Dasha.

"It's no problem. I know what you look like already. The Russian State Security gave me your photo," Dasha answered. It was good to know that I was known to the Russian State Security. In fact, Dasha had a good sense of humor and had simply spied me out on Facebook. Still, I was very excited to be making a big money payoff on Red Square. It seemed very James Bond-like to me, so, for this reason alone, I was looking very much forward to the journey to Moscow.

Now, Tour Leaders do generally have a good bit of cash with them all the time. It's just part of the job. It's just that we don't generally have in excess of ten thousand Euros on us in mostly fifty- and hundred-Euro notes. It turns out that an eight thousand Euro stack of fifty- and hundred-Euro notes in a manila envelope is really quite thick. So, to say that my pocket was bulging a bit is putting it mildly. One tends to get a bit paranoid and self-conscious about it. After all, it's not every day that a person walks around Red Square with an envelope containing enough money to put a sizeable down-payment on a lakeside dacha. Joran, who tends to notice these sorts of things, didn't miss it.

"Will, is that a giant envelope in your pocket or are you just happy to see me?"

"It's a giant envelope, boss. Can you believe it? I've got eight thousand Euros in there!"

"Why do you have eight-thousand Euros in an envelope here? Are you having the mafia kill the annoying passengers later?" countered Joran.

"No, they want me to pay for the optional activities and they said it would happen at exactly two o'clock just in front of the cathedral," I replied.

"And then they kill you?" Joran asked, always with a warped sense of humor.

"I don't think so. Not if I pay them what I owe them. It's InTourist, not the mafia. It's not a pay-off for a political assassination, at least, I don't think it is!" I replied, though I was, truth be told, feeling a bit nervous about the whole thing.

"Still, that's very cool. It's like being in the Bourne Identity!"

"Yes, hopefully without the guns and chokeholds and poisoned umbrellas!"

Dasha did meet me, at exactly two o'clock, and the exchange turned out to be very un-movie-like. She introduced herself, I introduced myself, I kissed her on both cheeks as one does in Russia, handed over the envelope, and that was that. Where it did turn into an action movie was ten minutes later when Dasha took me, Joran, and Pieter out to lunch at a restaurant that quite clearly catered to wealthy Russian oligarchs, corrupt government officials, and prospective Bond villains. We each had a tuxedoed waiter serving us and a private washroom. It was also quite clear that they'd never seen idiots the likes of the three of us before. Instead of a tuxedo or suit, the three of us were all clad in polo shirts, cargo shorts, and sandals.

"Dasha, aren't the three of us a bit underdressed? I mean, if Putin walks in here, he'll have his goons take us out back and liquidate us! Shouldn't we at least be wearing shoes?" I asked.

"No Will; don't worry about it. You just paid the Russian government eight thousand Euros. You can wear anything you like! You're with me and you're already inside! Besides, everyone in here could spot the three of you as foreigners even if you were wearing suits! If I were you, I'd relax and take in events as they transpire!" Dasha replied as we were led into our private dining room.

So, in the end, not quite like a Jason Bourne or James Bond film, but for a time it did feel like it. The borscht and wine were top-notch!

*   *   *

One thing that always impressed me wherever I went in Russia was the general humor and hospitality that most Russians have for foreigners, especially for foreigners like me who are in charge of fifty tourists. Our groups were always treated extremely well. Maybe it was because I was a foreigner that there was a laxity towards the rules that the Russians would extend to you and a general spirit and respect for pragmatism. We found this out on the train ride back to St. Petersburg.

Our groups were always booked on the high-speed SAPSAN train between Moscow and St. Petersburg. Instead of an eight-hour overnight journey, it was a much more manageable four-hour journey in a comfortable and modern carriage at speeds of up to two hundred and fifty kilometers per hour. After such a long day, the bosses and I were looking forward to a relaxing ride back to St. Petersburg and to indulge in a few restorative beverages en route. Being cost-conscious consumers, we knew full well that beers at the convenience mart at the Leningradskiy Train Station cost fifty rubles (about two Euros) whereas the bar car on the train was charging one hundred rubles (four Euros) a can. We decided to be cheap about things. We bought as many beers at the Leningradskiy Train Station convenience mart as we could fit into our day bags.

Unfortunately, outside alcohol isn't allowed on the train. Not that that is the sort of thing that would stop guys such as us. We presented our tickets to the platform agent, found our seats and cracked our first beers. Within ten minutes the conductress came by to check tickets and found us well into our second beers and she had a few things to say about that.

"Hello, tickets please," she asked. All the SAPSAN employees spoke flawless English.

"Privet, hello," we replied. We made absolutely no secret of our frothies, not even a passing attempt to hide them. We kept right on drinking them as if we owned the place.

"Ticket is good, but you have beer. This is not beer from on the train. Where did you buy this beer?" asked the conductress.

"In the shop. At the station. It's less expensive there."

"Da, but this beer is not allowed here. You are meant to buy beer on the bar car only," the conductress said, in quite a friendly and non-judgmental way.

"Oh, I'm sorry. We didn't know," I lied, quite obviously. I'm sure the conductress knew damn well that I knew the rules.

"You have bought much beer?" She was turning increasingly into a very inquisitive border guard.

"Um, yeah, we filled our bags actually. It's a long ride back to St. Petersburg," I answered, as I showed her the other seven cans I'd bought.

Without missing a beat, she took the half-empty can from me and proceeded to chug the remainder of the can. It was clear that she was well experienced in such matters.

"OK, next time, you buy better beer. This Baltica is not so nice. Next time you buy a proper beer like Carlsberg. This Russian beer is awful! European beer is much better!" she informed us, speaking with a good deal of expertise in the matter.

"Oh, yes, of course. Spasibo! Thank you!" It appeared as though we were off the hook.

"Da, good! And when you are finished the beers in your bag, you may buy more in the bar car. It's three carriages forward. They have good Carlsberg beer there!" With that, she continued on her rounds. She even came back later to make sure everything was OK and to make sure that we knew where the toilets were.

And that's the way it was every time I took a group to Moscow on the train. I'd happily tell all my passengers that the no outside alcohol rule was loosely enforced on the train. Of course, it didn't take long to see that many of the Russians on board were doing the same thing as we were. It actually makes a good deal of sense in a country where vodka riots are an actual thing.

Acknowledgements

Writing a book is no easy task, and I'd be remiss if I didn't put in a word of thanks to the many people who helped to bring my vision to reality.

Mark Anderson, Jamie Mackrill, Stephanie Plascott, Donna Dimaclid-Tabanda, Mia Griffiths, and Jason and Amy Viljoen. You were all there to read over either my earliest writing samples or what ended up being the final product and contributed a great deal to my building confidence in my writing abilities. I was quite unsure of myself in the early days, but your positive comments and constructive suggestions set me up nicely and drove me to continue when it would have been easy to write the whole endeavor off. My deepest thanks!

No book can be properly published without a proper proofreader. For that task it was my own mother, Anne Michaelis, who performed that thankless chore, and during Christmas week as well! Thanks mum!

To the thousands of passengers that I've led across innumerable countries, my thanks go to all of you. A Tour Leader can't have any amazing tales of both woe and wonder without passengers of every conceivable type and personality. So whether you're a legend like a KFC or Captain Ned, or a quiet and shy individual who simply enjoyed their tour without making a big, memorable impact on my memory, you all had an impact on my final literary product. I thank you all!

To the office staff of the company that I worked for from 2014 through to 2020 (and hope to again once wars and pandemics are in the rearview mirror and we can all travel and go on tours freely once again) I must save a word of thanks to all of you as well. You did your jobs well, and thus, I could do mine well also! Thanks to all of you in London and Cape Town!

The many Tour Leaders and Drivers that I was privileged enough to work and make lifelong friendships with deserve a special mention as well. In many cases, we shared our adventures and escapades. There's nothing more satisfying than meeting up with you whenever possible and trade old war stories! Of course, many of them are far too risqué to put into print, and sometimes it's more fun to save our juicier tales of life on the road for ourselves! Regardless, it's been an honor to work alongside all of you! Cheers and see you on the road again soon!

I save my biggest thanks of all to my great friend Ugo Domizioli. The greatest of all the Bagan Boys! Your continued counsel and assistance was the most important with factor in my final product. You kept me in good spirits and humor as I worked my way through the many nights of difficulty that I did have. I dare say, the gin was probably the best spirit of all! Your inspiration and help won't soon be forgotten and I'll encourage everyone to take a look at your first book "Around the World 80 Questions" which served as an inspiration for my own humble effort. I owe you several drinks for sure!

Lastly, to all the people at Xlibris Publishing who guided me through the ins and outs of the publishing process. I thank you as well! I hope this won't be the last book you help me with!